CHASING FEAR

BRANDT LEGG

vinci
BOOKS

By Brandt Legg

Chase Malone Thriller

Chasing Rain
Chasing Fire
Chasing Wind
Chasing Dirt
Chasing Life
Chasing Kill
Chasing Risk
Chasing Mind
Chasing Time
Chasing Lies
Chasing Fear
Chasing Lost

*As always, this book is dedicated to
Teakki and Ro*

Vinci Books

vinci-books.com

Published by Vinci Books Ltd in 2025

1

Copyright © Brandt Legg 2023

The author has asserted their moral right to be identified as the author of this work in accordance with the Copyright, Designs and Patents Act 1988. This work is a work of fiction. Names, characters, places and incidents are the product of the author's imagination or are used fictitiously. Any resemblance to actual persons, living or dead, places and incidents is entirely coincidental.
All rights reserved. No part of this publication may be copied, reproduced, distributed, stored in any retrieval system, or transmitted in any form or by any means, including photocopying, recording, or other electronic or mechanical methods, nor used as a source for any form of machine learning including AI datasets, without the prior written permission of the publisher.
The publisher and the author have made every effort to obtain permissions for any third party material used in this book and to comply with copyright law. Any queries in this respect should be brought to the attention of the publisher and any omissions will be corrected in future editions.
A CIP catalogue record for this book is available from the British Library.
Paperback ISBN: 9781036705305

Chapter One

NEW YORK CITY

Sunday - 5:57 am - Eastern time

Chase and Wen stood on the abandoned antique concrete platform of New York City's first subway station. The wide, arched opening above them read CITY HALL, just as it had on its opening day in October of 1904.

"This is such a bad idea," Wen said, adjusting the straps of her backpack.

The ghostly, yet elegant space they found themselves in had sat unused since it had closed just after the end of World War II.

"Should have brought Terminators," she added. The private army they'd formed to fight in the shadow wars had recently taken on the AI-inspired name.

"We need this guy, and he wouldn't come unless we were alone," Chase said, not happy to be rehashing this debate minutes before their contact was expected to show up. He thought it was a moot point anyway. They both knew half a dozen Terminators were just above them in City Hall Park.

For two years, since the *End Game* had begun, Chase had been trying to get someone on the inside to talk. Finally, someone had agreed, someone high up in the corruption tree: the Deputy Chief of Staff to the Mayor of New York. However, the mayor was more than a city official, he was one of two candidates running for president of the United States with the general election less than ninety days away.

"Back when I was on the wire," Wen said, referring to her time with the MSS, China's equivalent to the CIA, "we called this type of situation *dinner at a slaughterhouse*. The meat might be fresh, but it's going to be your last meal."

Chase laughed. "It must make sense in Mandarin, but I think something got lost in translation."

She glared at him. "Point being, this is a deathtrap."

"No." He pointed up at the vaulted Guastavino tiled ceilings, natural light filtering in through vintage, leaded-glass skylights. "Don't you feel like we've traveled back in time? Imagine the history that came through here."

"I *know* the history!" Wen always researched everything. "The City Hall Station originally served as the southern terminus of the Manhattan Main Line, designed by Heins & LaFarge and built by Interborough Rapid Transit Company. It's been closed since 1945, and thus earned its nickname as 'the ghost station' or 'the lost stop'. Because of the chandeliers, curves, and arches, in its day it was likened to a miniature Grand Central Station." She pointed to the features to which she referred. "Though, after the final Brooklyn Bridge stop, the tracks are still used as a turn-around for the 6 train, but the station itself remains closed, and given its proximity to City Hall, is considered a high-security location. No one gets in without clearance."

"Except us."

"Us and the Deputy Chief of Staff." She checked the tunnels again, then eyed the staircase. The once magnificent setting, decorated with glittering chandeliers and other accruements, was now muted by a thick layer of dust, rust, and water damage. "Why here?"

"Just what you said. No one gets in here. No cameras, no way he gets seen talking to us."

"He's late."

Chase checked his phone. "Three minutes is hardly late." But he knew it was to Wen, who valued precision and professionalism. Many times he had seen her calculating and achieving incredible feats only because she understood how much could be accomplished in each of the sixty-seconds contained in a final minute.

"Here he comes," Wen said. "Or it better be him." She listened to the footsteps and immediately deduced it was only one person, male, between one-hundred eighty and two hundred pounds, tall, probably six-two. Unfortunately she couldn't tell if he was armed, but experience told her he was not. The stride was quick, tense, and civilian.

"Chase?" the man called as he emerged from the arch.

"Yes, and this is Wen."

He nodded to her, but did not make eye contact. She summed him up quickly. She already knew from his profile on the NYC government website that he was fifty-four years old, and a graduate of Columbia Law School. Other online sources revealed the man to be married with three kids.

"I'm not sure I should have agreed to this," he said. "It's just that we're out of time to stop it."

Chase wasn't surprised. The Deputy Chief of Staff had been waffling for months. But he was here, so although nervous, he was still going through with it, in spite of his protests.

"We're fine," Chase said.

The deputy gave him a look that suggested he might be insulted that mere words from Chase could assuage his fears, but the Deputy had also done his research and knew Chase was a brilliant engineer who had become a billionaire from his breakthrough in AI before he'd turned thirty. The man respected both big brains and big money. He nodded. "Did you bring the cash?"

Chase handed him a briefcase.

The Deputy opened it, looked at the stacks of banded hundred-dollar bills, considered counting it, but changed his mind. "You know I'm not doing this for the money."

"I know," Chase said.

"Why are you doing it?" Wen asked, to the chagrin of Chase.

"They're taking over the world. It may already be too late, but at least now we can still pretend it's like it was before. The money is so I can disappear before they realize it was me."

"Thank you," Chase said.

"Everything you need is on this flash drive," he said, holding it up. "What's not on it can be acc—"

A bullet penetrated his head. The flash drive flew from the Deputy's hand as he fell forward.

Chase dropped to the platform. In his peripheral vision, he saw the drive slide over the edge onto the tracks. Bullets struck all around them, ricocheting off the many hard surfaces. Wen, already returning fire, yelled, "Call in the Terminators!"

Chapter Two

Chase jumped down to the tracks, desperate to find the precious flash drive. Wen, firing a Glock 19 pistol, followed, looking for something else—the only decent cover in the station.

Dropping the pack off her back, she quickly unzipped the black, military-grade bag. Among the throwing stars, knives, and other small weapons were a couple of H&K MP7 submachine guns, extra magazines, and another Glock. She whipped out the MP7 as if it was an extension of her own arm—which, after the thousands of times she'd used one in training and real-world gunfights, it practically was. Her first four bullets killed three black-clad fighters.

"I need more light!" Chase shouted, still scavenging for the drive.

"I need more guns!" Wen yelled back. "There are at least fifteen hostiles. Forget the drive."

Just as Chase was about to do just that, the light from his phone passed over a silver glint. He snatched the precious drive and slipped it in his pocket, then grabbed the other machine gun.

"That looks like more than fifteen to me," Chase yelled as he started firing. Scores of rounds came in every second as the death-squad of now nearly twenty men barraged them with machine-gun fire.

"That's because they keep coming!"

The green and gold tiles shattered and chipped in the hail, adding to the clouds of dust and debris already forming from the shot-up ancient concrete.

Chase took three men down, but six more appeared from the stairs. "Where are they all coming from?"

Wen replaced the exhausted magazine in her MP7. "Your Deputy led them to us."

"Not knowingly," Chase yelled. "He was the first to die."

"You know how the Remies work. No witnesses, no exceptions, ever!"

"Let's shoot now and talk later."

"Now you're talking my language." She looked over her shoulder, concerned additional hostiles would funnel in from the subway tunnels. "Keep an eye on that opening. I'll watch this one."

"I'm more focused on the guys in front of us right now," Chase barked, shooting the legs out from under two more advancing men.

With the advantage of their cover, it didn't take long for Chase and Wen to pick off more of the attackers, soon reducing their numbers to six, and, at least for the moment, no more seemed to be coming.

"It's been kind of like a shooting gallery," Chase said. Though the easy targets were gone now, the survivors were sandbagged behind the bodies of their comrades.

"Apparently they expected to kill us on the platform," Wen said, still trying to figure out the play. The standoff grew more dangerous each second they didn't finish it.

"Just got a text," Chase said. "The Terminators are having a hard time reaching us in the tunnels."

"Are they encountering hostiles?" she asked between taking single shots at the men on the platform, hoping to prevent them from charging.

"Not yet."

"Have them blow the skylights."

Chase looked up at the rows of leaded crystal panels and relayed the message. Minutes later, Terminators above in City Hall Park began blasting the skylights, quickly killing several of the now exposed men below. Chunks of glass and debris rained in on the opulent station, but the operatives outnumbered the Terminators and soon began picking them off.

"I'm out of ammo," Chase announced, rummaging through the duffle.

"Glock or the HK?"

"HK," he said.

"Then it's a good time to run," Wen said, knowing their attackers would be distracted with the Terminators above for at least a few more minutes. "On three."

"Okay, but where does this tunnel lead?"

"Two, three!"

Chase took off with the Glock held high while Wen fired a cover burst with the MP7, then followed.

Chase stumbled, the soles of his shoes slipping on the slick tracks. "What about the third rail?" he panted, eyes darting towards the lethal electrical conduit running alongside the tracks as they sprinted down the dark, dank tunnel, their footsteps echoing off the concrete walls.

"Just stay away from that side," she said. "It should be covered."

"Oh, great, then we're relying on the efficiency of city government workers, because the third rail carries a constant electrical current of at least six-hundred volts—*more* than enough to kill a human."

"Don't touch it then!"

"Good advice."

Chase and Wen continued running. The smell of damp concrete, the flickering of the lights in the tunnel, and the sound of the men now coming up fast behind them confused their senses.

"They're gaining on us," Chase said. "Let's find a place to fight."

"We need to outrun them to daylight."

Chase thought his lungs might explode and doubted he'd last that long. There was no light at the end of the tunnel even visible yet, and the men were closing in fast.

The air was thick with the metallic tang of electricity, and the sound of an approaching train filled the tunnels. A red and black hazard sign warned of the exposed third rail ahead. Wen grabbed it, yanking it from its rusted bracket. "Ancient Chinese proverb says it's difficult to catch a black cat in a dark room, especially when it's not there."

"What the hell does that mean?"

"We do not need to help our enemies survive so they can make sure we do not survive."

Chase and Wen rounded a bend in the tunnel and were faced with a section where there was no platform, or "shoe", covering the third rail as it crossed into the open.

"That's going to either kill us, or save us," Chase said, pointing to the rail as the vibrating clatter in the tunnels was suddenly interrupted by the sounds of gunfire and ricocheting bullets.

Chapter Three

The third rail loomed ahead of them, a constant threat as they navigated the dimly lit tunnel, searching for a way out. Chase felt Wen's hand tighten on his as they made their way around another bend. In the distance, the sounds of their pursuers' footsteps drove them on.

"That doesn't look safe," Chase said as they came to a rusted-out platform. Only a narrow portion of it stretched over the electrified third rail.

"It's not remotely safe," Wen agreed. The buzz of currents flowing through the steel meeting the damp air created a low, sinister hiss.

"We have to cross here," Chase said, his voice steady despite the danger.

Wen nodded, eyes fixed on the dilapidated covering as they stepped onto it. Now so close, the serpent-like hissing of the third rail was all they heard, the electrical current crackling and humming as they made their way across. A decayed piece of metal flaked off under Chase's foot and sparked, causing another section to fail as he stepped away.

Just then, a man shouted from behind them. They turned to see one of their pursuers lunging towards them. Chase grabbed Wen and pulled her to the other side. They slammed onto the regular tracks, rolled, and ended bashing up against the concrete wall before finding their footing again, bruised and battered.

The man after them did not have the same luck. He tripped on the crumbling platform. The hand he threw out to break his fall found the third rail. There was a bright flash of light, the disgusting smell of burning flesh filling the air as the man's body convulsed in the grip of the high voltage current.

Chase and Wen stumbled backwards, watching in horror as the man's body slumped to the ground.

"Come on," Chase said, pulling Wen after him. "This won't slow the others."

As they started to run, they heard more people approaching, their footsteps growing louder. One of the gunmen skidded on the damp ground and went hurtling towards the exposed third rail. Chase and Wen turned in time to see the man's body spasm violently, smoke billowing from his fingertips where they had touched the rail, his life taken instantly by the deadly high voltage surge.

Wen fired at the others before they could attack. She and Chase ran backwards until the curving tunnel gave them cover.

"Another one!" Chase yelled as they heard the sickening sound of a third man making contact with the electrified rail.

"That thing is lethal."

"That thing is our friend."

"We have to stay invisible," Wen whispered in warning

before shooting out a row of lights, plunging a long section of the tunnel into total darkness.

They continued sprinting through the black, dingy subway tunnels, feeling like a separate world from the bustling city above, Chase's breathing labored as he tried to keep up with Wen. Frequent bursts of machine gun fire continued behind them as their pursuers took random shots in the dark. Chase and Wen decided not to return fire to maintain their concealment.

"Where's that train?" Chase asked. Their pounding footsteps could barely compete with the approaching roar of a distant subway train.

"Where is an *entrance*?" Wen moaned, her voice now barely audible over the sound of the train.

"Eventually this leads to the surface," Chase replied. "I hope that's coming from another track somewhere."

Before Wen could reply, they heard a chorus of angry shouts and the clanging of metal against metal. "They're right behind us!" Wen whispered, her grip tight on the MP7 as they pushed on into the darkness.

Chase turned and fired several shots. The rumbling of the train grew louder, completely drowning out the men. The tracks vibrated wildly. The entire tunnel suddenly seemed to be moving. "That train is too loud. It must be on our line!"

"Oh no!" Wen yelled as the headlight suddenly hit them. They could also clearly see the silhouettes of four men after them.

"If they don't kill us, the train will!" Chase barked, but Wen could no longer hear him over the subway's roar.

Chapter Four

The blaring of the train drowned out their voices as Chase and Wen ran as fast as they ever had.

"We're trying to outrun a *train!*" Wen said to herself. "And bullets!" She knew they couldn't slow down to aim, firing behind her back without looking.

Chase could barely breathe. His lungs were on fire.

The train thundered toward them, its headlights piercing the darkness, filling the narrow tunnel with a wall of noise.

A thudding, grinding tumult interrupted the drumming din. Chase and Wen simultaneously stole a glance over her shoulder, just in time to see the oncoming train vanquish the four men. In a chilling blur, two were crushed under the tons of rolling steel. The other pair got sandwiched into the walls.

"We're next!" Wen yelled, hardly able to celebrate the deaths of their would-be killers. Given the choice, she'd rather have taken the bullets over being pulverized to death.

Trapped between the approaching train and the narrow concrete walls of the tunnel, they scanned ahead desperately, searching for any opening or escape. Raging closer by the second, the ear-splitting screech of the train stole their ability to think.

Just behind them now, they saw the outline of the train's engine car, the gleam of its metal surfaces, imagining the wicked grin of the conductor as they bore down on them.

Chase and Wen exchanged a terrified look, both thinking that after all their close scrapes, they'd finally lost their ongoing battle with death.

"These trains are supposed to be controlled by computer systems and automated signals," Chase yelled, even though Wen couldn't hear his words. "Whoever is driving it, somehow they figured out how to override the controls!"

"The tunnel is too tight. We can't get to the sides of the train," Wen yelled, her voice strained. "We can't outrun it!"

"Shoot out the windshield," Chase shouted into her ear, his hand going to the gun in his waistband. "We'll jump *into* the train."

Wen's eyes widened even further. "Are you *crazy*? It'll mow us down!"

"Nothing to lose," Chase replied, pointing to her gun. "It's our only chance."

Without slowing, Wen turned and aimed her MP7 at the oncoming train and fired. Chase shot at the same time. The windshield shattered and the driver fell.

For a heart-stopping moment, it seemed the train might come to a quick halt. Instead, it kept moving, unmercifully heading toward them.

"We're going to be crushed!" Wen yelled.

"Jump!"

Chase and Wen leapt towards the train. His foot found purchase on a bumper. The forward thrust of the massive rig hit him with the force equivalent of falling off a roof, his body rolling up the front of the car. He grabbed something, broken glass—*pain*!

Somehow the momentum carried him in, and he dove through the smashed remnants of the windshield into the cabin. He hit the floor hard, gasping for air as Wen came down on top of him.

She slid off and brushed the glass from her body. The ache in his ribs competed for attention with the lacerations on his arms, back, and hands.

For a few moments, they lay there, stunned and breathless, their clothes stained with blood, grime, and sweat. "We made it," Wen gasped. "We're alive."

Chase sat up and looked around, his eyes taking in the chaos of the cab. The driver lay dead next to them, glass everywhere. "For the moment."

Wen checked the driver's pockets and found an ID. "Not a transit employee," she said. "No doubt he's like the rest—hired gun, former non-US military."

"Better check the train," Chase said, pointing to the connected cars. "We don't want any more surprises."

"Can you stop this thing?"

"I'm gonna try."

The few people onboard were screaming and shouting, their faces pale with fear as they realized what had just happened. The train hurtled on through the darkness. Wen stumbled through the cars, dodging panicked passengers. On the third car, she spotted two hostiles working their way to the front. Before they realized it was her, she'd killed them both, quickly taking their weapons.

Chase managed to stop the train at the Canal Street

Station. He and Wen slipped out in the confusion, the two police officers who'd arrived at the scene busy with the dead and injured.

Chapter Five

MIAMI, FLORIDA

Sunday - 6:53 am - Eastern time

Haris Tane stared at a massive monitor dominating the end of the small conference room. His blue eyes were laser-focused on the events playing out on the screen. A visitor might assume the handsome man with the perfect haircut, wearing an expensive hand-tailored dark suit, was watching an action movie. Perhaps he was a Hollywood producer, maybe even one of the film's stars. However, the subterranean machine-gun battle he watched was happening in real time, its bloodshed *very* authentic.

This was not a pretend tycoon. The distinguished, self-assured man happened to be one of the wealthiest people in the world, and arguably the most powerful. Tane was a Remie, a manipulator of events, and at the moment, more than anything, he was *furious*.

"Don't let them escape, do you hear me? If *they* survive this, *you* won't!" He shut off communications with his men in the field and turned to the person standing in front of him. "This is your fault."

The imposing man shook his head, glaring at Tane as few would ever dare. "I am not in that tunnel."

"They're *your* men."

"No," he replied, "I did not recruit or train them. They are *your* men."

Tane, frustrated, stared at the man everyone simply called Khan, a brilliant operative who seemed to thrive on the violent end of his enemies—thus his codename, taken from the ruthless Genghis Khan. Although Tane knew Khan's real name, he would never dream of using it.

He knew a lot about Khan; about his habit of reading ancient texts, specifically classic works of military strategy such as Sun Tzu's *The Art of War* and Julius Caesar's *Commentaries on the Gallic War*. He knew about his collection of rare knives, and that despite his tough exterior, Khan was not without his quirks. He was obsessed with symmetry and order, and could often be found straightening objects or reorganizing equipment to meet his exacting standards.

Perhaps the most surprising thing about the man who headed his secret strike force, known as the Raiders, was that he had no military service whatsoever. In fact, he'd dropped out of high school in the ninth grade. He'd narrowly missed serving time in prison on several occasions, mostly for being involved in violent fights, but all of that was before Tane discovered him. Now Khan maintained his cool, and kept himself out of trouble unless he was paid to initiate it by Tane.

"Then *fix* it," Tane said.

"Budget?"

"All you need," Tane snapped, turning back to the

screen. "But make sure Malone does *not* get away next time."

The muscled Khan stood tall at six-three, but something in his demeanor made him appear even larger. Perhaps it was his brown hair, cropped close to his skull, the neatly trimmed beard, maybe the tattoo of a Nesmuk knife on the underside of his wrist, but most likely it was his gray eyes. They were a killer's eyes; mad, intense, calculating and cold. Very, *very* cold.

Timothy Blanc, checking his Patek Philippe Titanium watch, walked into the room and shivered when he saw Khan. "Sorry, thought we had a meeting."

"We do," Tane said without turning around. "Khan was just leaving."

"Right," the big man said, spinning on his heel. He moved past Blanc and exited the room.

Blanc, a pale, skeletally thin man, felt as if he'd been assaulted, like he'd nearly been knocked over by Khan, even though the operative had never been closer than two feet from him.

"Unpleasant business," Blanc said, sitting next to Tane.

The two titans of finance and industry had, many years ago, formed an alliance that benefited them each in countless ways, but both knew that one day in the future it would end when one of them rose to the top of the metaphorical pyramid, and *to the victor goes the spoils*.

One of the two men would essentially rule the world. The other would most certainly be dead. Yet, for the time being, the two insanely wealthy, ruthless, and greedy men were the best of friends, old chess players who saw global events as a chessboard. Each man moved their own pieces, each seeking checkmate.

"Chase and Wen gave our agents the slip," Tane said.

"Again," Blanc replied, as if he'd expected it. They had been hunting the pair for more than five years. It had been two years since the Chase Malone-led Flash-burn initiative had almost wiped out their fortunes—*almost* being a relative term since, combined, Tane and Blanc controlled assets of 1.5 trillion dollars back then, and were now down to about a third of that. However, they were rebuilding quickly. "They're planning another Flash-burn. This time Malone and his band of merry men, and the Chinese woman, know a lot more, meaning they might be able to do even more damage. They could even finish us off."

"Flash-burn turned out to be a good thing," Tane said. Flash-burn had been the coordinated attack against the loose affiliation of Remies—global elites who controlled the world-economy and regularly created and manipulated events to their advantage. "Malone erased many of our competitors."

"The easy ones. The weak ones," Blanc said. "We would have taken them down ourselves, wound up with their assets anyway. This reshuffling of assets has been annoying. Khan is on board because he's barely a few shades shy of evil, and I'm not so sure of the few shades. A repulsive man."

"A necessary means to an end."

"Only if he finishes this, destroys Chase Malone and everyone he has ever loved, called a friend, or employed, and *removes* their blight from the world."

Chapter Six

NORTHERN CALIFORNIA

Sunday - 3:02 am - Pacific time (6:02 am Eastern)

Weston, an Ivy League college graduate, had enlisted in the Navy rather than take the lucrative offer from Wall Street because ever since he'd been a kid, he'd wanted to be a SEAL. Not for any patriotic sense of duty, but because he loved adventure, danger, and the adrenaline rush that came with it. At six-four, he was built like a linebacker, and had a chiseled face that could have been on a recruiting poster or an action movie ad and gave him the look that he'd been made for the fighting life.

For his mother, he'd gotten a degree. Whip smart, Weston had no trouble doing the diploma thing. He'd hardly cracked a book and aced it all. But his life really began in the SEALs, where he'd excelled until it stopped making sense. Still, he had to feed his adrenaline addiction.

That had eventually led him to Chase. The purpose and mission of the Terminators resonated with him, with the added benefit of feeding his action habit.

The Terminators moved silently around the vast property, having already patched into the elaborate security system. Remie cash may have bought the best surveillance and security technology, but when it came to tech, Chase's people were even better than all that high finance.

A man lived there, in the garish display of wealth, a place too big for a hundred families, and yet only one man, and his third wife, occupied the plush palace. He owned four other homes of equal scale and gild as well. There was also a mega-yacht, where more families could live, but floated empty most of the time. And a penthouse somewhere. And a Paris townhouse. And it went on and on, and none of it mattered because he was here, tonight, in *this* mansion, and he would never go to any of the other ones again.

In the CapWars, this man, a Remie, had been deemed a strategic target.

How many has he killed? Weston wondered. Most Remies had a certain amount of blood on their hands, but the ones who were targeted with preemptive assassination were the worst of the worst. *Chase told me the last one we took down had been directly responsible for tens of thousands of deaths.*

This was according to the AI research, which extrapolated data and found the course and consequences of the decisions these titans made. "Indirectly," Chase had said. "Hundreds of thousands, maybe even millions."

"How?" Weston had asked.

"These guys control food supplies, toxic chemicals, bad pharmaceuticals, weapons . . . All the weapons manufacturers are owned by Remies—the biggest and most evil Remies. To these people, coups and third world revolts are *good* for business, and wars are *great*. They play with the world economy like it's one big Monopoly game."

All of that fell to the bottom of his mind in the quiet darkness of the inner perimeter of the estate. Billionaires had top-level defenders a few rungs higher than what dictators and warlords relied on. A lot of them used Sepio or Vinton, two of the biggest elite security firms. Others relied on private military companies, some even had their own secret armies. The intelligence on this mission said Vintons, an agency known for its aggressive and violent responses.

Weston was cautious, but not worried. This type of property might have twenty Vintons max. Maybe, in the current climate, with increased tensions, there could be thirty. He'd planned for forty. He'd brought three times that number—one hundred twenty Terminators and a couple of Rogues. Mars, Chase's childhood buddy, ran the Rogues, a hand-selected group of ex-cons and criminals who worked the non-violent side of the war. They were here for the tech —manipulating the automated end of the defenses and then, afterwards, for whatever intelligence could be gathered on Remie operations, future targets, connections, anything of value to opposition efforts.

"It should be quick and routine, if one can call killing a few dozen people 'routine,'" Weston had told his front unit a few minutes earlier.

"Definitely going to be bloodshed, then?" Stokes, a twenty-four-year-old roughneck on his first live-fire outing, asked as they advanced through the darkness a few feet beyond where the motion sensitive floodlights would have normally triggered if the Rogues hadn't hacked the system.

"It's a real war," he told Stokes. "These men are getting paid to kill us. We'll die if we don't take them out first. Got it?"

"Hell yeah."

Weston knew damn well not to speak inside the zone,

but he couldn't help himself. The adrenaline-fueled do-or-die atmosphere had gotten to him.

Unfortunately, that decision sealed Stokes' fate. Maybe Stokes would not have been the first to die, but in less than four minutes, ninety-four percent of the one hundred twenty Terminators and both Rogues were dead.

Weston barely escaped with his life. It wasn't until later that he discovered his survival wasn't due to his own quick thinking, or even dumb luck. The Vintons *wanted* him to tell the story, to report on the devastation firsthand, and explain how nothing was ever going to be easy again.

Chapter Seven

NEW YORK CITY

Sunday - 7:07 am - Eastern time

Chase and Wen sat in the spacious hotel suite, the soft glow of the laptop screen casting shadows on their faces. The luxurious furnishings and rich decor were a stark contrast to the perilous situation they were in. As usual, they used evasive tactics to make sure they were not followed, and the room was booked using an iron-clad alias.

"No one knows we're here," Chase said, wanting desperately to relax.

"That means nothing," Wen said, recalling all the times their enemies had located them when no one knew their whereabouts. "No one can hide in the modern world. At least not for very long."

"I know," Chase sighed, sliding the Deputy's flash drive into the computer.

Wen had kept a watchful eye on the door, scanning the peephole, constantly looking out the windows for any signs of trouble while Chase showered and changed. He did the same for her. Afterwards, they'd both reapplied vIDs. The virtual Image Deviation system had been developed by Chase and the Astronaut, a highly skilled math savant who had, for years, been one of Chase and Wen's most trusted accomplices. With so many people after them, including numerous government agencies, they tried to always keep a fresh coating of vIDs on their faces. The ingenious spray-on application dispersed a mask of countless nano microprocessors, each thinner than a human hair. The translucent gold specks were virtually undetectable to the naked eye, yet they successfully confused and defeated the algorithms that powered facial recognition cameras.

With the horrors of the subway behind them, they were about to find out if it had been worth the cost.

"It's all on Snyder's covert operations," Chase said, his voice laced with a sense of urgency as he read the list of the Mayor's illegal activities and scrolled through the incriminating evidence on the flash drive. "Manipulation of voting machines, influence over the media, bribery, blackmail, voter intimidation, smear campaigns, there's even implications of several murders that have advanced his career. This guy is a monster!"

Wen's face was etched with concern as she listened to the details of Mayor Snyder's corrupt activities. "We have to stop him, Chase. If he wins the election, the country is doomed."

Chase leaned back in his chair, rubbing his eyes wearily. "But how? He's got so much power and money, he's practically untouchable. There's even stuff in here about a large staff of fixers who make sure nothing sticks to him."

Wen's eyes gleamed with determination. "We have to expose him. We'll put our own team on getting corroborating evidence. Get it out there before the election so the voters know."

"As if the public has anything to do with choosing presidents anymore," Chase said. "I'm sending a complete copy of this to the Astronaut and to Bull."

Bull liked to say she was the best female hacker in the world, but in reality, she might be the best hacker period. She'd been on Chase's team for years, and lived with his original business partner, Dez, an African American engineer who Chase always said, with a laugh, "Dez is older and smarter than me. Well, at least one of those things is true."

Wen checked the windows again, then scanned images on her tablet. She had small drones doing surveillance above the sidewalks at the front and rear entrances.

"Still clear?" Chase asked.

She nodded. "A Remie in the White House would be worse than a puppet." The Remies, a group of competing billionaires who created and manipulated world events to increase their power and wealth, were at war with each other, but all shared a common enemy—Chase Malone and Wen Sung.

"The Remies have selected and installed presidents for decades," Chase said, telling her what she already knew. "But to have a Remie *as* president . . . " He shuddered. "We have to prevent his victory."

"There are plenty of other Remies who will want to see him lose this election."

"He'll know that. He's smart enough to be forming alliances."

"He can't get them all. That's our best chance to get him."

Chase nodded, his mind racing with possibilities.

"Working with our enemies, hoping they'll help us destroy Snyder before they kill us."

"Something like that."

"I wonder where Tane and Blanc stand on this," Chase said. "They have to know about it." He pointed at the computer screen.

As he spoke, the laptop beeped with an incoming encrypted video call. Wen's hand went to her concealed gun, but Chase motioned for her to stand down. He clicked accept, and the screen split into two, an image of a dark figure in the other half.

"This is front page data that will never see a reader," the Astronaut said, his voice electronically distorted.

Chase breathed a sigh of relief. "Nash, thanks for calling back. We need your help."

The Astronaut's eyes scanned the room, taking in the serious expressions on their faces. "I've already started exploring the DarkNet, seeing what we can come up with on Snyder, and I'm in Heaven." The ultra-classified inner-government secure network was called Heaven because, like the church's Heaven, people believe it was in the cloud, but no one could prove it actually existed. If it *did* exist, then everything one could possibly want could be found there. The problem was that like the other Heaven, the only way to get there was to die.

Chase, Wen, and the Astronaut were three of the few who knew the government's Heaven was real, and they were some of the fewer who knew how to access it.

Chase began to lay out the full extent of Mayor Snyder's plans, his voice filled with intensity. "He's got a whole network of insiders who are manipulating the voting machines in his favor. He's bribing officials and using smear campaigns to discredit his opponents. He's even going so far as to intimidate and extort voters who oppose him."

Wen's eyes widened in shock. "That's insane. He's already got the entire election rigged."

The Astronaut stared at them. "According to this, he has it won, and there looks to be no way to stop it from happening."

Chapter Eight

SOUTHERN CALIFORNIA

Sunday - 5:09 am - Pacific time (8:09 am Eastern)

Mars sat in a shadowy corner of the warehouse, surrounded by stacks of crates and boxes. The only sounds in the cavernous building were the occasional click of a mouse and the hum of laptop fans.

Mars stared intently at his screen, reading the report from Weston. His eyes remained fixed on messages between Weston and Blitz as he spoke to his top lieutenants, Jack and Lila, both wearing black tactical gear. The long-past-its-prime building should have been torn down years earlier, but its seedy appearance and out-of-the-way location near the waterfront port area on the southern California coast meant it was easily overlooked and forgotten, the kind of place Mars liked.

"We just lost two Rogues on a raid at one of the Remies' mansions," he said, his voice tight. "They're onto us."

"They're going to try to exterminate us," Lila said. She leaned in closer to the screen. She had short, curly hair and sharp green eyes that gleamed in the low light. "Who's the most dangerous?" she asked.

They each knew the mission to target the Remies was an insane venture. "A suicide run," Mars said, but they were all in. Not for the money, but because things *had* to change or it was going to get unbearable.

Mars began listing off names, his fingers moving rapidly over his keyboard as he sent digital lists of assets, companies, and other holdings to Lila, Jack, and a few others. "We've got Bill Doorset, Haris Tane, aka the Maestro, Timothy Blanc, Mayor Warren Snyder, Wes Glodam, Maxim Miner, aka the Judge—"

"Wait, Maxim Miner?" Jack interrupted, his voice incredulous. He was a tall, lanky man with a shaved head and a short goatee, his arms covered in tattoos. "That guy's still alive?"

Mars nodded. "Apparently. And there are many others. And although the Remies don't agree on much beyond their shared belief that the rest of the world's population is of little consequence beyond their value as workers, consumers, and soldiers. They appear completely united in a policy to kill Chase and destroy any and all in his orbit. We need to be prepared for everything."

Lila pulled out her own laptop and began scanning through the lists. "Do we have any intel on their most critical holdings?" she asked. "Their 'lynchpin', so to speak."

"Everything we have is there. The Terminators have strikes planned every night for the next ten days—Federal Reserve, defense contractors, corporate locations, other residences, government offices—seeking evidence and shutdowns."

"We're twisting the knife," Jack said.

"Yeah," Mars replied. "But if the mansion raid is any

indication, they're waiting for us . . . and prepared to act with ferocious force."

"Then we need to act quickly," Lila, a former banker who'd been imprisoned for embezzlement, said. "To interrupt the brutal chess game between all these self-entitled competitors."

"The Federal Reserve is the big lynchpin," Mars reasoned. "It's the one organization they all use."

"Their smoke and mirrors *management* of the economy," Lila said. "The public lets these private bankers manipulate and drive for Wall Street, and they pretend it's some sophisticated economic theories for the good of all. They never explain anything, their statements always seem to contradict themselves and add confusion to already complex topics, it's called *Fed speak*. They don't even pretend, I remember when former Fed chair Alan Greenspan testified before Congress, and he responded to an ask for clarification with, 'If I seem unduly clear to you, you must have misunderstood what I said.'"

"The Federal Reserve is the greatest scam in human history," Mars said. "Having the American people understand too much about them is the last thing they want. Same with Central banks all over the world."

"Whoever controls the economy controls the world," Lila said. "Their power is truly limitless."

They continued pouring through the information on their hard drives, constantly streaming in from operatives across the globe who were delving into Remie activities. At the same time, Mars and his team remained on high alert. A couple of Rogues monitored exterior cameras in case the Vintons or Skyggers or any other private army controlled by the Remies showed up.

However, they could not see the boat just offshore that

was monitoring *them*. On board was a man who did not want them to *stop* their anti-Remie activities, rather he wanted them to *continue*, to succeed—at least to a point. Some Remies preferred to be the last Remie standing, and didn't mind risking everything to win the coveted capstone atop the ultimate economic pyramid.

Chapter Nine

MIAMI, FLORIDA

Sunday - 7:12 am - Eastern time

Tane and Blanc moved down the hall from the conference room into a larger, or rather *longer*, room. The narrow space was scarcely wider than a broad hallway, but it ran more than one hundred feet long.

"The nerve center," Blanc said as they entered.

Tane shook his head. He didn't like Blanc's name for the place. He preferred the room number assigned when the building was constructed, 910, or, as he said, "Nine-ten."

"Yes, nine or ten degrees above zero," Blanc muttered. "Why is it always so frigid in here?"

A man known simply as *the Surgeon* strode into view from behind a large rack of servers with his usual air of confidence. "Computers like the cold."

"Yes, well, I don't," Tane said.

The Surgeon, a thin man with an almost gaunt frame, laughed. "Too bad, too bad." He came around and checked several screens close to them. Despite his nerdy appearance, he possessed an almost animal-like grace when he moved, as if he was always on the hunt for his next target.

Tane glanced around the room, taking in the advanced technology, the dozens of technicians working at their stations. The space had an almost science-fiction appearance, filled with the hum of supercomputer equipment, the walls lined with screens displaying various data feeds and algorithms. Tane turned his stare back to the Surgeon and wondered how this caricature of a man could be in charge of such an effort.

Standing at six feet tall, with cobalt blue eyes that seemed as if he were always preparing for a game, and a wild mane of hair that defied all attempts at taming, his physical appearance was striking. He had a calculated yet crazed expression that left many people wondering what strange distortions occurred in his psychedelic mind.

"We need progress," Blanc said, his tone tense. "What have you found?"

"I have located several individuals who are in close proximity to our target, Chase Malone," the Surgeon said, his Eastern European accent making each word sound like a knife cutting through the air. "They are not the man himself, but they will lead us to him."

"How close are you to finding Malone?" Tane asked, his impatience evident.

"I'm getting closer every day," the Surgeon replied. "But this is not a simple matter of tracking down one man. Malone is smart, and he has a network of people who are helping him stay hidden. It's only a matter of time before I succeed."

Despite his cold and dangerous reputation, the Surgeon had a love for classical music, and was known to hum Mozart's *Requiem* when working on particularly challenging cases. He also had a habit of tapping his fingers in a repetitive pattern when deep in thought which drove Blanc crazy.

"Time is something we don't have," Tane said, his voice rising. "We *need* Malone found and eliminated, and we need it done quickly. He is a liability, always pushing to expose our operations, and we can't afford any more delays."

Blanc raised a hand to calm Tane.

The Surgeon fixed Tane with a cold stare. "I understand the urgency of the situation, yet you may recall that you wanted fear inflicted as well. I am in the position to begin those movements."

For the first time, Tane smiled. "Family and friends?"

"Yes, quite so." The surgeon also smiled. "This is not a clumsy man. He cleverly protects those close to him. And yet, they are not as smart. There are always tiny flashes, little signs. I find those castaways and leftovers, and they will be costly for our Mr. Malone."

Chapter Ten

NEW YORK CITY

Sunday - 7:23 am - Eastern time

While standing by one of the hotel suite's floor-to-ceiling windows, Wen checked the outside drone cameras via the tablet again. *I know they're down there,* she thought. *Agents and assassins, shadows, hunting us. Thugs, working for any number of adversaries, with orders to kill us.* She also monitored the news sites, waiting for reports of the subway battle and the dead Deputy Chief of Staff.

"Someone that close to one of the two men who could be the next president being gunned down under City Hall will be a huge story."

Chase nodded. "That's why we have to move fast. We need to find a way to bring down Snyder before he gets to the White House."

The Astronaut's image flickered. "It is unlikely he can be defeated. This scheme is too deep, too broad. He's been preparing to be president for at least fifteen years. Every-

37

thing he has done has been laying the groundwork for this run. He hasn't left anything to chance."

"We have to try," Chase said. "We can get enough evidence and—"

"His significant control over the media makes that highly improbable," the Astronaut interrupted. "The American public has been increasingly propagandized for decades. The majority believe the stories, however thin and unlikely, that are repeated by their favorite news sources."

"Without getting into a political debate," Wen said, "I can think of many instances during the past few election cycles where minor stories were ratcheted up to be major stories, and major stories were buried. It's not journalism anymore."

Chase listened carefully, his mind filled with more angles and questions. "Taking on the Mayor is no easy proposition. He's a powerful Remie with billions of dollars at his disposal and a vast network of loyal supporters, but Remies also have powerful enemies."

"Other Remies," Wen said.

"Exactly. Turn our enemies into allies.

The Astronaut's image flickered again, and he warned them to be careful. "Willingly walking into the middle of the Remies' CapWar is not advisable. There are extraordinary forces at play, none of them under your control. They belong to the Remies. The odds of success are—"

"Can you suggest another way?" Chase asked.

"No. The Mayor has already won."

"So we've got three months to change that," Chase said.

"Actually, the election is eighty-one days away, and if you factor in early voting, absentee, mail-in, and military ballots, there's far less time to make a change. Of course, this all relies on you first finding a way to correct the programming of the voting machines. And there's still the Tane and Blanc front to consider. I believe that other factors—"

"We don't need the odds," Wen interrupted. "Just wish us luck."

"Technically, luck cannot be wished, and it's most definitely not a part of the equation."

"And yet here we are," Chase said. "The odds are we should have been dead at least ten times by now."

"Thirty-seven, and another twelve that could have gone either way," the Astronaut corrected.

"There you have it."

"However, the very nature of statistics and odds means that with each passing day, particularly when doing what you propose, your chance of death greatly increases."

"Okay," Chase said, "this conversation isn't helping. See what corroborating evidence you can turn up, and find a way to get this information to the other Remies."

As the call ended, Chase turned to Wen. "Snyder, Tane, Blanc, and all the other Remies are too powerful. I mean, they actually control the governments and corporations that control the world, including the militaries. Our only chance at bringing them down for good is to pour gasoline on their fight with each other."

"Take their CapWar nuclear," Wen said.

"Scary choice of words, but yeah. Make them destroy each other."

She nodded. "Before they destroy us."

Chapter Eleven

MIAMI, FLORIDA

Sunday - 7:44 am - Eastern time

The Surgeon sat at his station in Nine-ten, tapping his fingers. His eyes were fixed on the screen in front of him, watching as the Senator's staff attempted to access Remie's confidential files.

He leaned back in his chair, a small smile playing at the corners of his mouth. "Not today," he murmured, and his fingers flew over the keyboard. The Senator's team was blocked. They wouldn't be getting access anytime soon, but they didn't know that yet. He began humming Mozart as he implemented his master defense. "What fools they are to think they can get past me. *Me!*"

Tane entered the room, his expression grim. "We've got a problem," he said, and the Surgeon turned to face him. "Senator Wentworth. We've just discovered he's working with secret Grand Juries in several jurisdictions. He's using his powers to . . . We just need to find a way to neutralize him."

"Yes, he's got a team of skilled hackers working for him. They've managed to infiltrate our systems, and they're feeding him information about our operations."

Tane's face darkened. "Stop him!"

"I don't think so."

"*What?*"

"It's much better to let him have a constant stream of information . . . information we *want* him to have."

Tane smiled. "Yes. Very smart."

The Surgeon nodded, his eyes flickering with a fierce intensity.

"Show me everything that they're into."

"Coming your way."

"How big can we get this?"

"I can create an entire void, billions, hundreds of billions of dollars for them to chase, none of it real. All of it will blow up in their faces, make them fools in court, consume their investigative resources."

"Love it. Do it. Give us nightly reports."

"I'll take care of it." His wild mane of hair caught the blue light, giving him the look of something from a horror movie. "And as for the Senator, if you grow impatient, there is always Khan."

"I'm not known for my patience."

New York City
Sunday - 7:44 am - Eastern time

As Chase and Wen prepared to leave the hotel suite, the laptop beeped again with an incoming message. Chase clicked accept, and the screen split into two, with the image of a young woman on the other half.

"Chase, Wen, it's me," Bull said. "I've got some news."

Chase and Wen leaned in, their attention fully focused on the screen. "What is it?" Chase asked.

Bull's face was serious. "I just uncovered a source line of code based on the data off the drive. The Mayor's team is planning something big. They're going to launch a massive smear campaign against his opponent. They want to discredit him so thoroughly that he'll have no chance of winning."

Chase's jaw clenched. "I don't know if we can do anything about that. See what you can uncover on the voting machines. That's his biggest lock."

Bull's image flickered, and she nodded in agreement. "I'll keep you updated if I hear anything else."

Chase closed his laptop, a sense of urgency settling over him. "We've got to get with Grimes and Shelby," he said. The pair, hired guns who had worked unknowingly under Remies for years, were now helping Chase and Wen to blow apart the elite's corrupt empire. "Let's get out of here."

Wen's device pinged. "It's Blitz," she said.

"Chase, Wen, I have Weston on the line," Blitz said in his heavy baritone. "I'm going to patch him through."

Chase could tell instantly by looking at Blitz's face across the video feed that the man in charge of the Terminators was troubled. Then he saw Weston. At first he thought he might have been horribly injured. His bedraggled expression and worn face made him look twenty years older than when Chase had seen him a week earlier. Chase and Wen listened, horrified, to the report from Weston.

"I'm so sorry," Chase said when Weston finally paused

from his rambling tirade of blame, guilt, and nightmarish imagery. "Those were good people we lost."

"How did they know we'd be there?" Blitz said.

"They were so ruthless," Weston said. "Like, if they had time, they put extra bullets in the dead. They kept yelling at us, 'No survivors, no survivors.'"

"Are you okay to go tonight?" Blitz asked.

"He can't go tonight," Wen said.

"I *want* to," he insisted. "You know, I need to taste victory. I *need* to."

Chase and Wen exchanged a glance.

"We'll double the force for tonight," Blitz said.

"Your call on Weston," Chase said.

"We need every good solider we can get, especially one familiar with the Remies current tactics."

"Good luck then," Chase told Weston. "Wen and I are going in hot on the other side of the Fed raid."

"Yeah," Weston said. "Big DC is a fortress, man. Hit 'em hard, Chase, hit 'em hard. God speed to you."

As Chase and Wen walked out the door, the TV still on in the background showed highlights from a stump speech Mayor Snyder had given the day before. "Why isn't the death of the deputy in the news yet?" Wen whispered as they entered the corridor, the door locking behind them.

"They're keeping it quiet to avoid tarnishing Snyder."

"I know they'd like to, but really? All those dead bodies in the subway, all those witnesses on the train, the Terminators blowing out the glass skylights from the park . . . a *public* park. How do they cover that all up?"

Miami, Florida
Sunday - 7:59 am - Eastern time

Tane ended a call as he and Blanc were standing on the roof of the building in Miami, about to board a helicopter. "Wish we could have pinned the subway fiasco on Snyder."

"Too risky right now," Blanc said, looking out over the ocean, shielding his eyes from the rising sun.

"The investigation could have wrecked his campaign."

"You know nothing is going to do that. He's the next president."

"Like it or not."

"Exactly. We'll deal with him after the inauguration."

"Does there really have to be an inauguration?"

"It'll help set the mood for when we have the State funeral."

"I suppose." Tane looked at the helicopter's rotors as they began to spin.

"Meanwhile, our crew is doing cleanup in the subway to keep any trail back to Snyder clean."

"Except *we* have a trail to him, right?"

Blanc huffed. "Of course."

"You'd better be right on this."

"Yes, yes, I should be."

"And the witnesses?" Tane asked.

"Do you want to know? Because I'd rather not."

"No, I suppose not. Snyder helping with the cover stories in the media should make our producers have an easier sell."

"I'll enjoy not seeing anything about any of this on *the news*. Amusing they still refer to it as 'news' when it is most often the absence of any real or useful news."

Chapter Twelve

NEW YORK CITY

Sunday - 8:02 am - Eastern time

Walking through the lobby of the busy hotel, Chase pulled out his cell phone, glanced at the screen, and made a face.

"What is it?" Wen asked as she scanned the area for a second time.

"I just got a text on my burner."

"From?" she asked, knowing the only people who had the number were his business partner, Dez, their adoptive son, Tu, Wen's grandmother, Chase's mother, his brother, his oldest friend, Mars, the Astronaut, Bull, and Blitz, the head of their private army. However, for security, all calls and texts were strictly scheduled. This meant something was wrong, and that in and of itself was no surprise since something was *always* wrong. Still, the timing, so close to the subway incident, left her unsettled.

"I don't know."

"What?" She reached for his phone, but hers vibrated at that same moment. She slipped it out from the back pocket of her black jeans while steering Chase off to the side of the vast lobby. "It's a text from Anonymous," she said, her face filled with concern.

"Does it tell you to go to a package pick up locker on Lexington?"

"Yeah."

"And it has the code?"

"Yeah," she said, checking the room again, more carefully this time, gazing up at the grand staircase, looking out the floor-to-ceiling windows onto the bustling street. Wen could picture the ambush, knew from where the initial attack would come, the second and third waves—*if* they survived that long. "How do they know the code?"

"They can't." The code was a rotating series of alphanumeric sequences that Chase and the Astronaut had created. It required knowledge of not just the changing origination key, but also personal facts few could ever know. Only those on the phone list had it, but this was from none of them. "What do you want to do?"

"Order in some groceries and call Blitz," she said, 'groceries' being a delivery of weapons.

He shook his head. They each had a handgun. Wen probably had a second one in her pack. Even with the high-capacity magazines, it would never be enough to go against a Circuit attack.

"Let's go check it out."

"Crazy," Wen said, now gripping the Glock inside her bag, looking at everyone suspiciously.

"Whoever this is has our private numbers and the code. That means they're safe."

"Or smart enough to penetrate our inner circle."

"There's one other thing. They know where we are."

"How do you know?"

"That pick-up box is at the end of the block."

Less than two minutes later, they were standing in front of the yellow metal box. "Could be a bomb," Wen said.

"It's not."

Wen shook her head.

They stood back as a short, gray-haired woman came and scanned a barcode from her phone screen. A locker opened. The woman withdrew a blue and white bubble wrapped envelope, tore it open, reached in, and pulled out a folded sheet of paper. She turned around to face them. "Chase?"

Chase, surprised, only nodded slightly.

"This is for you." She handed him the letter and walked away.

Another text came in:

I guessed you'd be too cautious to open the locker yourself. Take the letter. Read it somewhere private and safe.

Chase looked at Wen, whose eyes were still glued to the little gray-haired woman, watching her get lost in the crowd. Wen thought of following her, but too many danger signs were flashing. "Exit," she said through gritted teeth.

They split up, walking briskly in opposite directions. Half an hour later, they reunited at a prearranged location, a coffee shop near the Flat Iron building. Dark, dated, and nearly empty, the aroma of strong brew, baked bread, and chocolate saturated the room. They sat in a booth in the back and read the letter.

"Spraggins," Wen said, sipping her tea. "It's a made-up name."

"How do you know?"

She gave him a look. "*Spraggins?* Sounds like a Hobbit."

"We have to meet him."

Wen's eyes went big. "Why?"

"He knows too much—our phones, the code, where we were. No one knew where we were at that moment. *No one.*"

"*He knows too much* is exactly the reason we should *not* go. It's a trap."

"Come on. This Spraggins character could have easily killed us in the hotel lobby, at the package locker . . . wait, there's another text." Chase checked the message, then shoved the phone across the table as if it was a venomous snake that might bite him.

"What?"

"The text is from Spraggins. Read it."

Wen spun the phone so she could read the screen.

Or now, in this coffee shop. I could have easily killed you again.

Chapter Thirteen

SOUTHERN CALIFORNIA

Sunday - 5:17 am - Pacific time (8:17 am Eastern)

Mars left Lila and Jack to continue building profiles on the key Remies while he worked out details with Blitz for the Rogues participation in the next raids.

Lila studied Timothy Blanc's profile. A wiry man, he almost looked like he had albinism, which made his amber eyes seem almost magical; but since she knew his greedy ambitions, the magic leaned demonic. His preference for expensive Patek Philippe Titanium watches and quiet reserve when ordering executions of people he'd deemed problematic to his ambitions were the traits of a cruel dictator, which was apparently how he saw himself. "Better than everyone else," she mumbled while reading through clips on the man.

Known associates: Haris Tane. *That's no surprise. The two rivals are practically joined at the hip,* she thought. *How is that going to end? One of you will cannibalize the other.* Most people thought Tane would prevail because, outwardly, he appeared more forceful, with a tighter rein on his power. *I'd bet on the silent psychopath, Blanc.*

Another one of his close associates had been former Federal Reserve Chairman Alan Greenspan, who'd served under four presidents as Fed Chair and two others in separate roles. *Interesting.* She kept reading and discovered Greenspan had a decades-long friendship with novelist Ayn Rand, whose philosophies had shaped a generation of economists and politicians. Along the way he became part of her inner-circle, and Rand gave Greenspan his nickname, "the undertaker", apparently because of his penchant for dark clothing and reserved demeanor, but she thought there might be another reason.

Greenspan once said, "It is not that humans have become any greedier than in generations past. It's that the avenues to express greed have grown so enormously," perhaps intentionally signaling the paths the Remies had used to increase their domination.

"The Fed is the Remies' greatest tool," she said out loud.

"That's why they're hitting the Fed hard tonight," Jack said.

She'd forgotten Jack was there, but was happy to share another Greenspan quote, to listen to what he said. "'In my more than eighteen years at the Federal Reserve, much has surprised me, but nothing more so than the remarkable ability of our economy to absorb and recover from the shocks of stock market crashes, credit crunches, terrorism, and hurricanes—blows that would have almost certainly precipitated deep recessions in decades past. This resilience, not evident except in retrospect, owes to a remarkable increase in economic flexibility; partly the consequence of deliberate economic policy and partly the consequence of innovations in information technology.' He *admits* to manipulating the economy."

"To 'help' it," Jack argued. "That's their mandate."

"I know, but they do it on both sides. They manipulate us into trouble and raise rates, lower rates, boom and bust, then *they* acquire all the distressed assets at pennies on the dollar. The Fed is a massive wealth transferring machine from the masses to the elite few, and we have plenty of evidence supporting it."

"More after tonight," Jack said.

"Hope so," she said, moving on to Haris Tane. Where Blanc was creepy looking, Tane, with his blue movie star eyes and handsome looks, seemed friendly and trustworthy. *A true wolf in sheep's clothing*, she thought.

According to all their AI analysis of the elites, Tane remained in the best position to win the CapWar among all the surviving Remies. After Flash-burn, he and Tane had taken advantage of the situation and used the crisis as an opportunity to advance and consolidate their power. The End Game wasn't over, it was just beginning. Everything would be swept into the CapWar until a winner emerged, no matter the cost.

Lila built profiles on Mayor Warren Snyder, Bill Doorset, Maxim Miner, aka the Judge, Wes Glodam, and seven more before she needed a coffee break.

"It's not fixed," Jack said as she stood up.

"Really?" she asked, disappointed, thinking he meant the coffee maker. "Then I guess I'm going out. Want something from Grounds?"

"What? No, not the coffee maker," he said, realizing the miscommunication. He pointed to his cup. "Coffee's fine. There's half a pot." He shook his head. "The economy. It's not fixed. Since the Flash-burn meltdown, the Remies patched things up, made it *look* fixed, but it's not."

"I know."

"No, you only think you understand."

She scoffed. "*Okay.*" She wasn't going to debate Jack with his advanced degrees in economics.

"It's simmering under the surface, ready to explode, but a few of these Remies—Tane, Blanc, maybe Doorset, Miner—they want to control *how* it explodes. They'll manage and benefit for themselves in the resulting chaos, but make no mistake, it's *going* to explode. When it does, it'll make the meltdown look like a blip."

"We're all going to be indentured servants to the creepy elites," she said.

"Something like that."

"Better than being slaves to AI-overlords."

"Don't count on it."

Chapter Fourteen

NEW YORK CITY

Sunday - 8:17 am - Eastern time

The coffee shop instantly seemed to transform into something dangerous, as if they were sitting on a sinking ship, in waters burning from the fuel of blown up tankers, as armed mercenaries positioned themselves for the ultimate kill shot. Living too long with a price on their heads, Wen brought out her Glock from under the table and readied for battle.

A man four booths away caught the moving silhouette of a firearm and yelled, "Gun!" A chorus of screams followed. Six other people in the cafe, including the barista, dropped to the floor, terrified, groping for cover.

"It's okay," Chase said, flashing a phony badge "We're federal agents and we're just leaving."

Another text came in as they hit the sidewalk:

Obviously killing you is not my goal. Ask Nash about me, and then show up at the meeting. Don't be late.

"What meeting?" Wen asked.

Chase read the letter the old woman had passed him while they walked briskly down the street. "There's a lot to discuss in this. I think this guy is for real, but the main thing is he wants to meet with us in person later today, in DC, at five."

"Like that's not a trap."

"He mentions the Astronaut."

"It's too weird," Wen said, shaking off the chill running up her spine. "I feel like this creepy Hobbit is inside my head." She checked her phone, looking for another text, half expecting Spraggins to answer her comment, or at least to protest the Hobbit characterization. There was nothing.

"Let's find a place to call Nash," Chase said. "Maybe this Spraggins guy is another Astronaut."

"If he is, he's a scary one," Wen said. "But you're right, he could have killed us five different ways, three different times." She scanned the skyscrapers towering above them, wondering if Spraggins was up there, or a sniper, or something else. "Yeah, let's call Nash."

Soon they were in another sprawling hotel lobby. They'd sent the Astronaut a call request and were waiting for his response.

"So Spraggins obviously knew we were going to Washington already," Chase reasoned.

A hotel employee signaled them. Chase had slipped the man two hundred dollars to let them use a small private conference room for thirty minutes. They followed him down a long hallway and he let them in, pointed to his watch to indicate the agreed upon time limit, and then disappeared.

"Yeah, that couldn't be a coincidence," Wen said. "Maybe we should call off the meeting with Hale."

"No way. We've waited too long. Maybe we should cancel the Fed raids."

"I guess we'll have to decide after we meet this Hobbit."

"Then you think we should take him up on his meeting?"

"Let's see what Nash says." Wen pointed to her tablet, now filled with the face of the Astronaut.

Nash Graham, the silver-haired math savant dubbed an Astronaut by the CIA, who used the term to describe super intelligent people possessing a computer-like mind that could analyze things differently than computers, gave a rare smile at the sight of Wen twice in one morning. Although AI was expected to eventually replace the need for Astronauts, the technology wasn't there yet, and he, and those like him, were currently targets of the world's intelligence agencies.

Most Astronauts were adverse to touch or close contact with people, but Nash had had a crush on Wen since the first moment he'd laid eyes on her years earlier. He *liked* Chase, but he *loved* Wen. The only other person he was close with was Tu, the boy Chase and Wen had rescued from China. However, living as a fugitive from those who sought to control his unique and powerful gift meant he did not see any of them in person very much.

Tu, now a young teen, and the Astronaut had much in common. They both could tell the day of the week on any date for the past two thousand years, and had a magical ability with numbers. The Astronaut knew the number Pi carried out to nearly a million digits by memory. Tu, however, couldn't do that, or answer 'twenty-six to the eighth power,' as the Astronaut had done at his initial meeting with Wen more than five years earlier, just before he'd saved her life for the first time.

"Two hundred eight billion, eight hundred twenty-seven million, sixty-four thousand, five-hundred and seventy-six," he'd said instantly, explaining that his mind was constantly filled with digits and equations, and that they were all different colors—extraordinary colors. His tone had been almost desperate when he'd told Wen that if he didn't continually use the equations, push the mysteries to be solved—problems needed solutions, things wanted to be created—he would go to a place where the numbers stopped making sense. "A dark and random world where I would be lost . . . where I would go mad."

Wen looked at The Astronaut's face on the screen, his thick hair a perfect example of being windblown and disheveled, yet amazingly neat. It framed a distinguished, close-cut mustache and beard, giving him a clean, yet rustic look. He was a series of planned contradictions, others accidental. She knew that although he had extreme difficulty showing emotion, or even being touched, he loved her completely.

"Tell me why we are talking again so soon."

"Do you know a man named Spraggins?" Wen asked.

The Astronaut's normally stony expression contorted to something she'd never seen before. The man who could predict so many things based on patterns and precise logic was clearly stunned.

"A man named Spraggins told us you would vouch for him," Chase said.

"*Spraggins* contacted you?" the Astronaut said. "He's alive?"

"Apparently."

"He disappeared twenty-one years ago, in the winter."

"How do you know him?" Wen asked. "Is he an Astronaut?"

"No. Spraggins is beyond the Astronauts."

"Really?"

"What does he want?"

"He wants to meet us."

"Where?"

"Washington DC, out in the woods," Chase said. "Do you think we should meet with him?"

"I just have one question," the Astronaut said.

"What?"

"Can I go with you?"

Chapter Fifteen

OUTSIDE BALTIMORE, MARYLAND

Sunday - 8:49 am - Eastern time

In the back room of a small aircraft hangar, Khan smiled at the man reporting in from the field via a video call. "I wish I could have been there to see it," he said, absently rubbing the Nesmuk knife tattoo on his wrist, as if he might be able to brandish the inked weapon and throw it at a Terminator. "Those amateurs have no idea what hell looks like. I'm going to show them."

"Yes, sir."

"Not just show them. I want them to know what it smells like, what it tastes like."

"Yes, sir."

"Burn their eyes out with the raging fires of hell."

"Yes, sir."

The call ended. Khan muttered one of the many passages he'd memorized from Sun Tzu's *The Art of War*. "'Attack him where he is unprepared, appear where you are not expected.'" He turned to face a wall of maps, the old-fashioned paper kind. He scribbled notes, drew lines and arrows across sections in various colors. A scheme emerged, something no one other than Khan could understand. To him it made perfect sense, and it meant one thing: *victory*.

A helicopter landed outside. Khan had heard its approach, even if he didn't expect it. He would have had a pretty good guess that it was an Airbus twin-engine H155. They had many choppers in their fleet. Many were military crafts painted to appear as police helicopters. The H155s were fast, armed with infrared cameras, guns, and high-powered spotlights. However, from even up close they resembled normal corporate choppers.

A couple of men soon found him inside the hanger. Both wore black tactical gear. "We're set for tonight," one of them began. "Four defined targets. They might come with—"

"We assume they will," Khan interrupted, "but know they will not, especially after last night. They are cautious, concerned . . . perhaps *apprehensive* is the word."

"Defending full force at all four locations could prove challenging if they do bring it."

"'The battlefield is a scene of constant chaos. The winner will be the one who controls that chaos, both his own and the enemies',"" Khan quoted.

"Yes, sir, from *The Campaigns of Napoleon*, by David G. Chandler. I did read it. Excellent recommendation."

Khan beamed, proud the man had actually taken his advice and read the book. "Then you know what to do."

"Yes, sir. Any opponent who enters the realm will not leave the realm. No one left standing."

"They must regret every thought they had about how to fight us," Khan said, staring for a moment at the other man, who had wisely remained silent. "Now come and see my plans for another slaughter."

New York City
Sunday - 9:26 am - Eastern time.

Wen checked the time. "Shelby and Grimes are meeting us at the Great Kills Marina on Staten Island at ten. We'll barely make it."

"We have everything covered," Chase said. "We're fine. The question is, will their contact show?"

"Grimes says the man is an ex-lieutenant to Belfort," she said, referring to the former head of Tane and Blanc's Circuit soldiers, known as the shadow people. Belfort was now dead. "We're not sure, but he may even have taken Belfort's place. Grimes swears this guy is legit. He's coming alone."

"Grimes is checking everything in advance."

"Yes."

"Let's hope the name *Great Kills Marina* doesn't turn out to be prophetic," Chase said.

As any New Yorker knew, the drive to Staten Island could be long, or it could be short, depending on bridge traffic. Even with thirteen lanes, the double decker Verrazzano-Narrows Bridge, named for the first European explorer to enter New York Harbor in 1524, routinely saw back-ups. The span handled more than two hundred thousand vehicle crossings each day.

"Gorgeous view from up at the midpoint," Chase said as they approached it. "Especially with the top down." The silver Mercedes convertible had been rented from one of those high-end car rental companies. Chase had a weakness for cars and fast driving. This $200,000 AMG SL 63 Roadster had a handcrafted AMG 4.0L V8 biturbo 577 horse power engine, and could do 0–60 in three and half seconds.

Wen didn't like the visibility and exposure of convertibles, didn't appreciate flashy cars that drew attention, but Chase had very few vices, so she only put up a slight argument each time he found a muscle car.

"Company!" Wen said, staring into the sideview mirror. "Hit it!" The one advantage fast cars provided: they made escaping trouble easier, especially with Chase behind the wheel.

"They're here?" Chase replied, his voice tight. "Who are they?" He made the speedometer climb as much as he could in the busy traffic.

Wen pulled an MP7 from her pack. "When the war is with an empire, the battles never end!"

Chapter Sixteen

Chase often muttered, when pushing his foot on the accelerator, "Chase Malone, professional race car driver," but not today. He didn't like being boxed in on the bridge.

"Nowhere to go," he said, stepping on the gas pedal. The Mercedes careened onto the Verrazzano-Narrows Bridge, the wind whipping through their hair as Chase swerved to avoid other cars.

Unbeknownst to them, their pursuers, who they assumed were a team of shadow agents, stayed close behind in a sleek black SUV. The agents had been tailing Chase and Wen for twenty minutes, but they had finally made their move on the bridge, trying to cut off their escape.

"They're getting closer!" Wen shouted, looking in the side-view mirror.

"Hang on!" Chase yelled, slamming on the accelerator. The Mercedes shot forward, the engine roaring as they tried to outrun their pursuers, but the shadow agents were too well-trained, their SUV easily closing the gap.

"We need to get off this bridge!" Chase said, his eyes darting back and forth as he searched for a way out.

Suddenly, the SUV slammed into their rear bumper, jolting them forward. Chase swore, his hands gripping the steering wheel tightly. "They're trying to force us into the side!" he shouted, struggling to keep the Mercedes on the road, the shadow agents relentlessly slamming into them from behind. "Hold on!" he yelled, swerving into the HOV lane, narrowly missing a delivery van. The Mercedes fishtailed wildly, its tires squealing as they navigated the tight opening around a car pulling a boat, and shot back into the next lane.

The dark SUV closed in on them, its engine roaring as it picked up speed. Chase continued swerving from lane to lane, trying to shake their pursuers, but the SUV matched their every move. Suddenly, the shadow agents were alongside them, and one of the men leaned out the window, brandishing a gun.

Chase ducked as the man squeezed the trigger, bullets pinging off the side of their car. Wen returned fire as Chase veered into them. The bigger vehicle took the impact without so much as a stutter, but the shooter jerked against the roof. The man's shot went wide, as Wen sent two rounds into his neck. He folded down over the outer side of the door, and then his lifeless body fell onto the pavement, the rear tire of the SUV bouncing over his corpse.

Traffic was gridlocked, nowhere to go. The SUV and several other pursuing cars pulled up behind them, some only a few vehicles away, their doors opening as the agents stepped out, guns drawn. Chase and Wen jumped out and started to run towards the edge of the bridge.

"Don't jump!" a woman in a nearby car screamed.

Neither Chase nor Wen had any intention of jumping,

but they couldn't stay where they were. Wen swung down off the side and released her grip as an Olympic gymnast would, landing seven feet below the decking on the narrow walkway on the underside of the bridge. Chase, an experienced rock climber, did it differently, shimmying down a support. They were dashing down the catwalk, more than two hundred feet above the water, while their pursuers were still trying to figure out how to get down to them.

"Traffic is moving again," Wen said, pointing to the slow but steady streams of vehicles not affected by the drama playing out on the upper deck.

"Let's get a car," Chase said breathlessly as they ran, dodging the support beams and jumping over gaps in the walkway.

Suddenly, they heard a loud explosion behind them.

"They're serious!" Chase yelled, but Wen couldn't make out his words. Another explosive device detonated in the air, plunging harmlessly into the sea. Enough cars had slowed on the lower lanes that an escape was going to prove much more difficult now. Wen fired up at the agents peering down from above, then saw several men approaching from the other end of their level.

"They think we're trapped," Chase yelled as he caught up with Wen.

"So it seems," she said, noticing a small opening in the concrete pillar nearby. She grabbed Chase's hand, pulling him towards it. They edged carefully through the tight space and found themselves in a narrow, dark crawlspace that ran under the lower decks.

"It's for utilities," Chase panted, pointing at the large sections of conduit they had to squeeze past. The sound of the traffic directly above them was deafening, even as the vehicles moved at a much more reduced speed than normal.

Wen pointed to the other end of the tunnel. Well behind them, a man was crawling in pursuit. She fired, knowing her shots would miss from that distance, but wanting to slow him.

"We can get to the water," Chase yelled right into her ear, pointing to one of the massive concrete columns supporting the bridge.

She shook her head. "In the open, with nothing to hold onto, no place to hide? A sure way to die."

"It's a good day to die."

Chapter Seventeen

ATLANTA, GEORGIA

Sunday - 9:44 am - Eastern time

Tane and Blanc stood in one of the Circuit's private television studios, which could monitor and override every major network. They had fourteen facilities around the world.

"Nothing is real anymore," Tane said, smiling.

This studio was in Atlanta, their second largest after the Las Vegas facility. It was also Tane's favorite. He liked the blonde bombshells who delivered the news, and had slept with three of them, but that wasn't the reason he preferred Atlanta. It was the proximity to his beach house on Jekyll Island, Georgia. His family had maintained a residence there for generations. He had other coastal estates, but he always said they couldn't match the charm of the Island.

Atlanta was state-of-the-art, and the cable network news pumped from the facility was as professional as anything out there. The three principles of the network were: *Authoritative. Factual. Timely.*

Tane chuckled each time he saw them. My *authority, the things I decide are facts, and at the times I desire.*

The Remies had acquired all the major broadcast and print news services decades earlier. When they ran out of things to buy, they started new ones. "There isn't an independent news source with any measurable reach that isn't owned or controlled by Remies," Tane said, partially out of frustration. At times it could be difficult to plant stories in the media when the other Remies didn't agree, although they often did. Favors were traded. However, getting a phony story or message out broadly and swiftly had, in some ways, been easier in the days when real journalism existed and independent organizations with integrity could still be found.

"New York and Washington have increased their staff," Tane said.

"I hope so. With the war and Chase Malone's refusal to die, there will be considerably more items to shade."

Tane couldn't help but be amused by Blanc's unusual choice of words, his odd expressions. "We are creating fictional news stories to cover up—"

"Nothing so unpleasant as that."

Tane laughed. "*Exactly* something that unpleasant."

From behind the glass, the two billionaires watched the feeds and footage from around the world, specifically from the situation in California, where the mansion had been before the leveling. Due to the security, the location, and the relatively few surviving witnesses, it was an easy story to gloss over.

"Remember the developer who gave us trouble in San Francisco? The one that was from this very room?" Blanc asked.

"Of course," Tane replied.

"The exchange of his views certainly required extra efforts. The shopping center was vacated."

"What are you saying? If I didn't know you were immune to prosecution, I'd check you for a wire. We blew up an entire block to kill the developer. Shopping center vacated—what does that even mean? There *was* no shopping center."

"We leave the world a better place," Blanc said. "Did you read the trackings?" he asked, referring to a daily report which kept tabs on events and news stories being covered by alternative news outlets on the Internet.

"Why do you always ask me that? No, I don't read the trackings, I'm *busy*. Do *you* read them?"

"No, I leave it to staff." They employed hundreds of people to handle the trackings, who then passed on the relevant information to others in the organization. Eventually, if violent action was needed, Blanc and Tane would be informed, consulted, and they would make the final call. However, the routine decisions to destroy or remove anyone knowingly or unknowingly countering their agenda was left to others, a middle management of world builders and life destroyers, depending on what was called for. "Their budget is sufficient. I do grow concerned that there are so many stories, and that more and more these conspiracy sites, or so-called alternative news sites, are getting closer to what's really going on."

"You always say that."

"Because it's true."

"There may be more to deal with, but I think it's easier than ever to dictate public opinion."

"Because of the polarization?"

"Absolutely. The fools are all worried about the other side, red or blue." Tane laughed. "Democrat versus Republican. They're kept so busy hating each other that they don't even notice us."

"Some of them are noticing."

"They are dealt with."

Blanc nodded. He knew the price. *So many dead conspiracy theorists . . .*

Chapter Eighteen

Chase and Wen raced across the steel grates as fast as the tight space allowed. "Damn it!" Chase shouted above the traffic buzzing on top of them. "There's no ladder."

"What?"

"It's on the far column."

"We can't get over there!"

"I know." He studied the massive structure. "We have to go down here."

Wen checked behind them. The man was almost in range, and there were more behind him. "We might really be trapped now."

"Let's go!" He dropped down to a ledge circling the top of the column, only a few inches wide. "Come on!"

Wen couldn't climb like Chase, but she was no novice. Without any other viable options, she slung her MP7 across her back and jumped onto the tiny ledge.

Seconds later, the two of them clung onto the concrete column, their fingers white with strain as they dangled over the water. The impossible descent was their only chance of escape, and they had to make it down before the agents gained position to shoot. Below them, the choppy waters churned menacingly, waves loudly slapping the concrete pilings of the bridge.

Wen was the first to make a move, her fingers seeking out footholds in the rough concrete. Chase followed close behind, his eyes scanning the surface of the column for the slightest imperfection to grip onto. They moved slowly, their movements precise as they worked their way down the column.

The wind whipped around them, making their descent even more treacherous. Wen's hair lashed around her face, obscuring her vision, but she pushed through the discomfort. Chase gritted his teeth, muscles straining with the effort of holding onto the column.

Suddenly, a shot rang out, reverberating through the air. Chase and Wen froze. They looked up to see the shadow agents firing down at them from the top of the bridge. The bullets whizzed past, striking the concrete with sharp cracks.

"Keep moving!" Wen shouted, her voice barely audible over the whoosh of the wind.

Chase nodded, his heart pounding in his chest. They continued the descent, their movements growing increasingly frantic as the gunfire intensified. More bullets struck the concrete, sending shards flying in all directions.

They were still almost fifty feet from the bottom of the column when it happened. A bullet struck millimeters from Chase's hand, sending him spiraling out of control. As he tumbled through the air, the men continued shooting until his body slammed into the water below.

Wen watched helplessly as Chase disappeared beneath the surface. She hesitated for only a moment before leaping after him, hitting the water with a splash. The current dragged them both under, pulling them deeper and deeper into the dark depths.

The men on the bridge continued to shoot, bullets raining down, piercing the water, but Chase and Wen were nowhere to be seen. The water churned and roiled, obscuring any sign of their presence.

A few moments passed, and still, they did not surface. The men on the bridge exchanged glances, unsure of what to do next. Had they drowned? Were they still alive somewhere under the waves?

Atlanta, Georgia
Sunday - 9:56 am - Eastern time

A monitor in the control room filled with images of the battle on the Verrazzano-Narrows Bridge. "Is that us?" Blanc asked through a speaker.

"Yes, Mr. Blanc. It seems Chase and Wen are on the bridge, or were."

"Were?" Blanc echoed.

Tane motioned to another man to scrub the footage from all networks. "Clean it, clean it up now."

"I'm communicating with our people as we speak. Chase Malone was just shot off one of the support columns."

"Get me footage," Blanc snapped.

An instant later, a jittery, grainy shot from a distorted angle showed a figure falling from the column, and then another jumping in after.

"Based on those other images, I'll accept that's Chase and Wen," Tane said as more video showed them on the bridge. "However, there's no way to tell if he was actually shot."

"They have not come up for air," the man said.

"How long have they been under?" Blanc asked. "Because these two were created by Marvel or something."

"Excuse me?" the man said.

"*Superheroes*," Blanc barked. "They don't die like normal people."

Chapter Nineteen

Shelby, one of the two people Chase and Wen were on their way to meet, piloting a silver Quest Kodiak 100 seaplane over the bustling New York Harbor, saw the smoke and fires on the bridge and flew in for a closer look. She spotted Chase and Wen bobbing in the water. The Kodiak's powerful engine hummed as she navigated above the choppy waters beneath the towering Verrazzano-Narrows Bridge. An expert pilot, she put it down less than fifteen feet from them and yelled.

Chase and Wen swam to the plane as the men continued shooting from more than two hundred feet above. Chase clambered aboard, then helped Wen up, their bodies slick with salt water. "Thanks for dropping by," Chase said, panting.

"Did the meeting get moved to the bridge?" Shelby asked sarcastically.

"No, still at the marina," Chase said. "Can you get us there on time?"

"Hold on." Shelby took a quick run along the turbulent

sea, then pulled up. Just as they got airborne, two helicopters appeared. "Where did they come from?"

"They're going to try to hem us in," Chase warned.

"No, they're going to shoot us down," Wen said, pointing at the gunmen emerging from the open sides of the fast choppers.

Gunfire strafed the front of the engine compartment and cockpit. The plane jolted violently. Shelby fought to regain control, but the injury to her right arm made it impossible. Blood dripped down her forearm as she struggled to keep the plane aloft. "Help me!" Shelby shouted.

Chase got there first and assisted in getting the Kodiak level. At the same time, two choppers descended on the sides and a fresh barrage of rounds came in from multiple angles. This time, Shelby's luck ran out. She caught two more bullets and collapsed in the seat. The plane plummeted in a spiral toward the sea. Chase was tossed against the side wall and rolled back.

Still soaking wet, Wen dove into the pilot's seat. Taking control of the yoke, she strained to stop the dive and level the plane. Inches from the churning surface, the plane righted, and Wen pulled it back into a climb. "Were you hit?" Wen yelled.

"No, but Shelby . . . "

The amount of blood spattered around the cockpit told Wen of the severity of Shelby's injuries. "I think she's gone."

The wind picked up again. Wen could feel the Kodiak bucking and shaking as she guided the plane back under the bridge, dodging the massive supports.

Chase crawled into the co-pilot's seat. "I think we're good."

"Depends on those choppers."

"Get me next to them," Chase said. "Shelby's got a mini gun back here."

"Love it!" Wen said. "Thank you, Shelby. General Electric's six-barrel Gatling-style rotary gun is one of the most powerful machine guns in the world, firing at a rate of two to six thousand rounds per minute."

"Yeah, whatever, just get me close."

Without a doubt, Wen was the better shot, but Chase would barely be able to fly the plane whereas Wen could do an air-show performance with the Kodiak. She was also confident that Chase could not miss with a mini gun, especially with where she was going to put the plane.

Wen took the Kodiak into an arching climb, did a short sweep down, then abandoned the tight turn at the last second. "Now!"

Chase fired, obliterating the first chopper and slamming himself back onto the floor with the force of the gun. He slid around as Wen piloted another rash descent, doing a partial roll to avoid the second helicopter. Chase pulled himself up in time to see that she was going to ram it from above. "You can't!" he yelled.

But her plan had been for the chopper to drop and spin to avoid the Kodiak's collision. All she had to do was guess which way they'd spin. "Ready with that gun?"

Chase regrouped and wedged himself against a seat and a hold bar.

"We're not going to be as close this time, so start shooting early!"

The plane dropped. She pushed hard, and guessed right.

"Go, go, go!"

Chase went full in. More than a thousand rounds ripped into the helicopter. "Boom!" he yelled as fire and smoke erupted from the chopper, now nothing more than a flying carcass.

It took more fancy flying by Wen to avoid the spiraling wreck from clipping the Kodiak, but they escaped, and Chase cussed a celebration as the smoking heap hit the water. He looked up and saw they were still in line with the massive span. "Can we get away from this damned bridge?" Chase said as Wen swept under the Verrazzano-Narrows one last time.

Just as they cleared the other side, two men jumped onto the plane from above.

Chapter Twenty

ATLANTA, GEORGIA

Sunday - 10:06 am - Eastern time

Blanc and Tane watched the events unfolding around the bridge in disgust. "Can't we get a better view?" Tane growled.

"Sorry, it's all chest cams now that they took out our birds," the aide said, regretting it immediately.

"How did they do that? Those are *military* pilots!" Tane said.

"I told you," Blanc sneered. "They aren't *real* people. They have superpowers."

"Then we need to get some kryptonite."

"Agreed," Blanc said, already convinced that Chase and Wen had escaped yet again. "We have a lead on Wen's grandmother and a boy they've raised as their own. Find them and kill them both, and make sure we have footage of it. I want to show it to Chase personally."

"Yes, Mr. Blanc," the man said. "And are we still to pursue Malone's brother and mother?"

"Of course," Tane said, as if the man were an idiot. "They should already be dead. So should anyone he's ever known. Kill them *all*."

Southern California
Sunday - 7:07 am - Pacific time (10:07 am Eastern)

Jack and Lila sat in the back room, lit mostly by high, partially opaque windows and some old soot-covered skylights. Papers were strewn across the table, along with the remnants of a carry-out breakfast, an empty donut box, and coffee mugs needing to be refilled. Jack rubbed his tired eyes and leaned back in his chair.

They'd been moving through Remie profiles all morning. Now on Snyder, Lila read aloud for a few moments. "Warren Snyder is an American billionaire politician, the owner of a media conglomerate that controls a significant portion of the world's media landscape. He inherited a small media company from his father and transformed it into a global powerhouse through aggressive acquisitions and strategic investments."

"I hate him," Jack said. "Not for his money, but for his politics."

Lila hushed him. "Holdings: Snyder's media empire includes several television networks, hundreds of radio stations, newspapers, and digital media platforms. He also owns a significant stake in several major technology companies, including a social media platform, a streaming service, and a search engine. His combined holdings and power rival that of anyone else in the world."

"Danger with three capital Ds," Jack said, taking a sip of coffee.

"Snyder is known for his shrewd business acumen and his ability to wield his media influence to further his own interests, and he is rumored to have significant political influence in several countries. His media outlets have been accused of biased reporting and promoting his own agenda."

"Well of course!"

"One of the worst," Lila said.

"This Snyder guy is pure evil," he said, shaking his head. "He's got more power than any one person should have."

Lila nodded, her eyes scanning the pages of the dossier. "I know. His media empire alone is staggering. Did you hear all of what he owns?"

"And don't forget about his political influence," Jack said. "He controls politicians throughout the country."

"*That's* what's most terrifying," Lila said. "He can manipulate the news to suit his own interests."

Jack sighed. "I just can't believe someone like this can exist. It's like he's straight out of a thriller novel."

"And he's going to be the next president of the United States." Lila flipped through the pages of the dossier, looking for any evidence they could use against the billionaire. "We have to find something," she said, her eyes scanning the text. "Something we can use to take him down ourselves, because we'll never get the message out."

Jack leaned forward, his eyes focused on the pages in front of him. "What about this?" he said, pointing out a paragraph. "Eight people in his orbit dead over the past eleven years. Two more missing."

"Missing?"

"At least not where anyone can find them."

Lila nodded. "That's a start. We could investigate those ten people, come up with something that connects them."

"Snyder connects them."

"I know, but why did he have them killed?"

"That's almost a death a year. Hazardous job, working for the next president. We need to get into his fricking systems," Jack said, his frustration showing.

Lila chewed her lip, thinking. "He isn't going to have anything digital. We need something more concrete. Something that can't be ignored."

Jack sat back in his chair, thinking. "What about someone close to him? It says that Reid Klamath is Snyder's chief legal counsel. He's a brilliant attorney with experience in both corporate law and criminal defense."

"He's fiercely loyal to Snyder and has helped him navigate numerous legal challenges," Lila said. "He'll never turn on him."

"Keep reading. During our deep dive AI audits of Snyder's operations, we uncovered something. It looks very likely that Klamath has been embezzling funds from Snyder's accounts for years in order to fund his lavish lifestyle."

"Really? I hadn't seen that yet."

"Yeah, I just got to it myself. Klamath has extensive knowledge of Snyder's business affairs and legal vulnerabilities."

Lila's eyes lit up. "That's it. We could use that. We could pressure Klamath to expose his corrupt practices to the public."

Jack grinned. "Yeah, that could work. We just need to show Klamath we have the proof."

Lila nodded. "But Klamath would know about the deaths of the others."

"That's what we're counting on. He can bring him down, send him to prison."

"But wouldn't he be afraid? Wouldn't Klamath rather risk going to jail himself rather than being added to the list of dead Snyder associates?"

"I guess we'll find out."

Chapter Twenty-One

Wen had no chance to compensate for the two former special ops shadow agents hitting the wings of the seaplane.

"What the hell!" Chase yelled.

The sudden weight shift again sent the Kodiak into another deadly spin. Wen fought to regain control as the men forced their way inside and tried to overpower her.

With the plane in a dive, Chase lost the mini gun, which he never could have used inside the plane anyway. Somehow he got his hands on a Glock, but he wasn't going to risk hitting Wen with all the vibration and jostling. No one had footing, or even real orientation, yet Chase found an extinguisher, pulled himself over to the cockpit, and clubbed it over one of the men's heads. The dazed man released Wen, but spun and swung at Chase. Now only a foot from his target, Chase had a clear shot and put a bullet into his chest. The dead man fell onto Chase.

Wen could feel the second man's hot breath on the back of her neck as she fought to keep the plane in the air. She elbowed him in the face, yanked back on the yoke, and brought the wobbling plane back to steady. The pontoon floats kissed the water, then they began to climb.

The second agent recovered and lunged at Wen again. Chase, who'd freed himself from the corpse, grabbed the agent from behind and, without hesitating, snapped his neck in a move he'd learned years earlier from Wen.

"Nice work." She looked over at Shelby. "Check her."

Chase took Shelby's wrist to test her pulse, but he'd seen enough death to know. Shaking his head, sadness washed over him. "She's gone."

"Sorry Shelby," Wen said.

"She saved us."

"It cost her her life," Wen said. "Let's not let her down."

"Yeah," he whispered, looking at Shelby again.

As they put more distance between themselves and the double decker nightmare of the Verrazzano-Narrows Bridge, Wen allowed herself to relax for a moment. "We're going to be late to meet Grimes."

"He's going to be devastated," Chase said. "Grimes always put on that she was just another woman, but he adored her."

"No one else in the whole world ever loved him. It was only Shelby." Wen was silent for a few moments. "Grimes may kill us for this."

"Poor Shelby . . . poor Grimes."

"Oh," Wen said, a faint note of dread in her voice. "We're losing fuel."

"I'm surprised this thing is still able to fly with the amount of bullet holes it has in it."

"The tank, or maybe the line, must have been hit or cracked in the stress," Wen said.

Chase looked back at the bridge. "Still no sign of anything in the air after us."

"I can see the marina," Wen said. "I think we can make it."

"Remember, it's called *Kill Great*, so be careful."

"It's Great Kill."

"Same thing," Chase said. "Although, I guess it depends on which end of the gun you're on."

Seconds ticked by, and the fuel gauge continued to drop. Sweat trickled down Wen's back, and she cursed under her breath. "Come on, come *on*," she muttered, willing the engine to hold out just a little longer.

"We'll make it," Chase said, seeing the marina getting closer.

The hum of the engine suddenly cut out, leaving only the sound of rushing wind. Wen's knuckles whitened, gripping the controls, trying to coax the silver Kodiak into a safe landing as they glided towards the sea, wind stirring up whitecaps below.

Chase checked the air space around them again, worried they were now defenseless against any incoming attacks. "A police helicopter is just arriving at the bridge, but otherwise we're clear."

Wen fought to keep the plane level, but it was no use. The nose of the plane dipped, and they angled sharply toward the water. "We're not going to make it!"

"Damn!" Chase saw the water coming up fast.

The nose of the plane dropped further, and now they were hurtling out of the sky.

"Brace for impact!" Wen shouted over the howl of the wind.

Chase clutched his seatbelt, eyes wide, mouth dry.

The crash was jarring, throwing them both forward and sending a spray of water through the cabin. Wen struggled to keep her head above the surface as the plane began to sink.

"Come on!" she yelled. "We have to get out!"

"The door's jammed!"

They both shouldered into it.

"It's not budging!"

The surprisingly cold water, already waist-deep, pulled at them. They could feel the plane sinking beneath them.

"On three!" Chase yelled. They shoved all their strength against the door, and with that one last desperate push, they forced it open and scrambled out into the frigid water. Seconds later, the Kodiak disappeared below the dark waters, taking Shelby and the two dead shadow agents with it to the depths.

Chapter Twenty-Two

ATLANTA, GEORGIA

Sunday - 10:18 am - Eastern time

A second aide ran into the room with the latest report. "We've got a drone up over the bridge. We couldn't take it too far out of range, but it's high enough to see."

"See what?" Tane asked.

"The plane with Chase and Wen. It just crashed."

"Survivors?" Tane asked.

"We don't know. It just went in the water."

"Oh, they're alive," Blanc said. "No simple plane crash will kill these freaks."

"Get Khan on visual."

After a brief cycling of screens, they found Khan. "I'm on this," he said, his tone short. "I'm on the West coast, but commanding this operation. We're dropping a couple of CoRRaCs into the Bay. If there's anything left of our heroes, they'll be properly rescued."

"What about—" Blanc started.

"Questions come before or after a mission, not during

it," Khan said. "This is my forte. Don't get in my way." He stepped off camera.

"What a prima donna," Tane muttered. "What's a CoRRaC?"

The aide quickly looked it up on his phone. "It's a Combat Rubber Reconnaissance Craft, a specially fabricated rubber inflatable boat often used by the Navy or Marines."

"Impressive he has those on site," Blanc said.

"One thing Khan knows is combat. He's ready for anything," Tane said. "This may be it for Chase and Wen."

"We'll see," Blanc said. "We've been here too many times for me to get excited."

Tane pointed to the images and maps on the screen. "If they survived the plane crash, where are they going to go? Khan's men will be there in minutes."

Waters off Staten Island
Sunday - 10:19 am - Eastern time

Chase and Wen treaded water, getting their bearings for a moment. "I think we can make that swim," Chase said, panting, as they looked toward the shore.

"Maybe," Wen said. "But can we do it before someone comes to investigate the crash?"

Chase turned to her, noticing blood on her face. "Hey, are you okay?"

"Just some cuts and scrapes from when my face hit the side of the cockpit."

"But you can swim?"

"I can always swim."

"Look." Chase pointed.

A speed boat swaying in a wide arc barreled toward them. "I've got no gun," Wen said, thinking it would be a little challenging to get to the throwing stars strapped to her legs, but would be very difficult to throw them while in the water.

"I still have one." Chase felt for the Glock in his waistband. "Whoever it is, they're coming at us with force and purpose." Chase aimed the gun, ready to take out the captain.

"It could just be someone coming to rescue us."

"After this day, you really think—"

"Wait, it's Grimes!"

Chase lowered the gun. "Finally, a break."

"Until he finds out about Shelby," Wen said sadly.

The boat slowed alongside them, listing in the swells. "That's a hell of a landing," Grimes called out.

"Shot up fuel tank," Wen said.

"Where's Shelby?"

"Shelby didn't make it," Chase said.

"What? No!" Grimes cried out. "Where is she?"

Chase looked down into the depths.

"She's down with the *plane*?" Grimes shouted, barely getting the words out before he jumped into the water.

Wen scanned the area for threats as she swam to the boat, then climbed aboard. Chase waited in the water for Grimes to surface.

Grimes broke the waves with a gasp, gulping air. "It's too far. She's down too deep. I can't get her! I can't get Shelby!" He dove back down. This time he didn't last as long. He came up cussing, crying. "I have to get her, man. I *have* to . . ."

Chase swam to him. "She's dead, Grimes! She died before the crash."

"No, if I can reach—"

"I'm sorry, man . . . she's gone." Chase touched his shoulder. "Let's get to the boat. The cops will be here any minute."

Grimes pushed him away and went back under, but only for a few seconds. "Damn it Shelby . . . you left. You *left*. Why'd you *leave*?"

Wen pulled the boat closer, so it was right next to them. "Come on, Grimes." Wen used her softest voice. "Shelby wouldn't want this. People will come. We have to go."

He looked back at the vastness of the water in front of him, then up into the sky.

"Come on Grimes, get in the boat," Chase said. "You don't want to fight them swimming in the water with no weapons."

"Shelby was supposed to be here," he said, climbing onboard. "I don't understand . . . how did she get into your fight? How did you get on the plane?"

"I think her flightpath brought her in line of the bridge heading to the marina, and she must have seen the fire and smoke on the bridge."

"Who killed her?"

Wen steered the boat around and headed to the marina.

"We killed them," Chase said. "Helicopters. Took them out."

"I should have been there to protect Shelby." He pounded a fist against one of the vinyl seats. "I should've been there on that bridge."

"There were a lot of them," Wen said. "Shelby saved our lives."

"She flew in like an action hero," Chase added. "Into a war zone."

"Who killed her?" Grimes demanded. "Who did they work for?"

"Tane and Blanc most likely, but we may never know for sure."

"Remie scum! Damned Remies, all of them!"

"Is our meeting still over there?" Wen asked, looking back at the Marina, hoping they could grab the guy and have a discussion on the boat.

"Are you kidding?" Grimes asked, gazing at the sky. "He took off as soon as the plane came in hot. He was too jittery."

"Not sure we'll get another chance?" Wen said.

"Not likely," Grimes said, cussing, looking back at the water. "Let me drive."

"Why don't you just relax," Wen offered. "I've got it."

"That boat over there is coming in a little too fast," Chase said, pointing it out. "I'm betting they're not out fishing."

"Fishing *us*," Wen said,

"We need to get out of here," Chase urged. "They'll get back on top of us again and we don't have any advantages here."

"Oh, I've got advantages," Grimes said, opening a panel in the deck, revealing a cache of weapons. "Bring those bastards to me."

"Trade," Wen said, grabbing a submachine gun. "You're a better driver."

"And you're a better shot." Chase hit the throttle and the boat lurched forward, the engine roaring as they tore through the waves.

Wen checked her weapon, her eyes fixed on the incoming boat. "There's a second one."

Chapter Twenty-Three

WATERS OFF STATEN ISLAND

Sunday - 10:28 am - Eastern time

Chase captained the boat as they sped through the choppy waters of the Lower Bay, just off Staten Island, pursued by a group of armed men in smaller vessels. He could feel the bouncing and jolting as the attackers fired their weapons. Bullets beginning to hit the boat told him they were too close.

"Lose them!" Wen shouted, gripping the sidewall tightly. She only fired occasional bursts to keep the shadow agents from lining up their aim. "Those are CoRRaCs."

"What?" Chase shouted.

"Rubber boats," Grimes answered before Wen could. "Meaning we can shoot them out of the water. Sink them."

"But it'll take more than a few holes," Wen added. "CoRRaCs are made with isolated hulls. They may even have bullet proofing."

"I want every man dead," Grimes snarled.

"Then that's the plan," Chase said. "Looks like six shooters on each raft."

"The real advantages CoRRaCs have is their maneuverability."

"Oh yeah," Chase said. "We'll test that!" He gripped the steering wheel tightly as the speedboat flew across the open waters. He swerved to avoid the incoming fire as the craft jolted and rocked in the waves.

"Let them get closer," Wen yelled.

"Risky." Chase could see the New York City skyline in the distance and knew that meant they needed to end this quick. Too much attention and they'd be caught by authorities even if they did escape these shadows. He glanced over his shoulder and saw Grimes and Wen crouched behind him, firing at the attackers.

"That second boat is gaining!" Grimes shouted. "Get ready!"

Chase gunned the engine and steered them towards a container ship, feeling the wind in his hair and the spray of the water on his face. The operatives were only seconds behind him, but he didn't slow.

"Let them close in," Wen barked.

Chase swerved to avoid the incoming fire, feeling the boat jolt and rock in the waves.

"What are you *doing*?"

Wen and Grimes exchanged a glance, figuring out his plan at the same time, then nodded in agreement.

As they approached the ship, Chase hit the throttle and raced towards its massive hull. The smaller boat pursued them, firing their weapons as they closed in. Just as they reached the ship, Chase hit reverse and spun the boat around, causing it to skim along the side of the ship like a skipping stone. The attackers tried to follow, but their boat hadn't slowed in time, and they crashed into the metal side of the ship's hull.

Wen and Grimes pumped hundreds of rounds into the shadow agents and the CoRRaC, which started sinking, its full crew already dead.

Chase gunned the engine again and raced away from the container ship, leaving half their troubles behind.

"Here comes round two!" Wen yelled.

"Enough of this!" Grimes smirked. "We've got explosives. Let's give them a little surprise."

He opened a different panel and pulled out a grenade launcher, aiming it at the incoming boats. At such close range, the explosion was thunderous, sending men and the CoRRaC flying into the air. The Shadow agents were thrown into the water, their screams drowned out by the echoing of the blast.

Grimes dropped the launcher and picked up his machine-gun again. "This is for Shelby!" He filled the water with enough bullets to make sure they didn't resurface. "No survivors."

Atlanta, Georgia
Sunday - 10:44 am - Eastern time

Tane poured himself a club soda, squeezed a lime into the glass, and wished it was something much stronger.

"I don't like to say I told you so," Blanc said to Khan after he reported the loss, "but we have some questions now."

"Fine."

"Where are they?"

"Unknown. We're working on getting recon up and using all assets to track."

"But *presumably* they're still on their intact boat?"

"The Lower Bay off Staten Island is an expansive body of water, covering approximately fifty square miles. Depending on the speed and direction of their craft, they could potentially have already traveled a significant distance," Khan said evenly.

"Yes, but we must be able to find them," Tane said. "They were *right there*!" He pointed to the map.

"We are getting aircraft up, but they have a head start. It may not seem significant, but the Lower Bay is connected to several other bodies of water, including the Ambrose Channel, which is the main shipping lane connecting the Bay to the Atlantic Ocean, the Narrows, which connects the Lower Bay to the Upper New York Bay—"

"We do recall the *little* bridge which spans that section, where we had some trouble earlier."

"Right. Then there is the Raritan Bay, another large body located to the southwest of Staten Island. Arthur Kill and Kill Van Kull are nearby tidal straits, then—"

"We get the idea."

"These are not typical targets," Khan said. "You have been stymied by them for years. That is why you brought me in. I will get them. However, by now they could be almost *anywhere*. Look at that area, the density of marinas, inlets, and private docks. They could already be in a vehicle. Do you know how many vehicles are in that area? Millions."

Tane contemplated suggesting they create a crisis that would allow them to close all the roads, but it was a fleeting thought that was interrupted by Blanc's much better idea.

"We *will* find them," Blanc said. "Chase and Wen will come to us as soon as we kill their family."

Chapter Twenty-Four

WATERS OFF STATEN ISLAND

Sunday - 10:47 am - Eastern time

Wen took over driving after making a quick call to the Astronaut. "Nash has arranged to have groceries and a chartered plane waiting at Newark," she told Chase and Grimes. She had wanted to call Tu, she always liked to touch base with their adopted son after a surviving a traumatic event, but it was too risky to make contact. She knew he was safe with her grandmother, and protected by the best security money could buy.

"Great," Chase said, desperately wanting dry clothes, which would be in the *groceries* delivered by a company started by some ex-CIA guys, who, for a high price, would deliver weapons, cash in the local currency, fresh clothes of any size and style, fake passports, anything needed—even actual groceries—in an incredibly timely and extremely confidential manner.

"I'll drop you on the shore," Grimes said as Wen steered the boat toward Newark.

"You should come with us," Chase said.

"What, to DC? No. I'm going to put together a dive team, get Shelby out of the cold."

"Yeah, okay."

Wen hugged him. "Remember, the Circuit is still looking for you. Don't let them find you alone and sad."

"Oh, I welcome them," Grimes said. "We have to take out every last Remie."

"We're going after them," Chase said.

Grimes laughed. "You're not going after them, you're trying to take them to court."

"We've had success."

"That's a joke, too. It's been more than two years since the Flash-burn. They've prosecuted, what, fifteen or twenty of these guys? They've all gotten off. They escape through loopholes, make deals, their witnesses turn up dead and the evidence vanishes. I've never seen anything like it."

"It's a process."

"A *process*? Listen to this guy. These Remies are magicians."

"You can't just go all vigilante anymore."

"Like hell I can't."

"Listen Grimes," Chase tried to reason, "we will eventually get them. We've shut down a few, and you know we're going hard at targeting their business assets and financial interests. We will never let up."

"The only way to stop them is to kill every single one of them. If we don't, whoever is left just fills the vacuum."

"What, we're supposed to be judge, jury, and executioner?" Chase asked.

"Hell yes! That's exactly what I'm saying. In fact, you can be the judge and the jury, I'll happily be the executioner."

Chase looked at Wen for help. "We can't just start killing everyone who disagrees with us."

Wen, still piloting the boat, remained quiet.

"It's the only way," Grimes said, checking the sky. "Nothing else has worked. Two years ago, we cut into them, made them bleed, but now it's like that never happened."

"It made a difference."

"Not enough of one," Grimes insisted. "You have no idea how big they're getting under the surface. Remies are like a horrible virus. They just keep adapting, growing stronger, no matter what we throw at them. They mutate into something more, something worse, something lethal."

"We're going at them in so many—"

"For a hundred years or more, they've been using every bit of knowledge and power to get more and more power, to increase their footprint. You can't go anywhere for help. They own the government, the media, the military—it's *all* them." He checked the sky again. "The only way to stop a virus like the Remies is with a bullet to the brain of every last one of these parasites. We'll be like a super antibiotic, wipe them off the face of the earth."

"But our way—"

"Your way isn't *working*," Grimes snarled. "It's *never* going to work."

"It just takes patience, man," Chase insisted. "I know you're upset about Shelby, but if we sink to their level and become like them, they'll win."

"*Wake up*, man! They *are* winning!"

"Our plan will succeed. There *is* progress, it's just—"

"Go ask Shelby how she feels about your plan."

"That's not fair."

"Fair? Remies don't *know* fair. They have to be eradicated. You built a damn army, now use it."

"We *are* using it. The Terminators are raiding Remie facilities, gathering evidence."

Grimes glared back at him. "You're playing right into their hands. Time is on their side. Get the Terminators to start taking the Remie pigs out one by one."

"Straight assassination? How do you think that will play out in the Remie media? How do you think they'll twist and use that to convince the masses? They'll be martyrs. Does that sound like a good strategy?"

"You think if we'd had a chance in World War II to assassinate Hitler that it wouldn't have changed things? Do you think the Allies weren't trying to off that evil piece of—"

"Sure, but—"

"They sure as hell were trying, because everyone knew it would've made all the difference in the world!"

"He was too protected," Chase said. "And the Remies are even more protected."

"It's a different era. With all the surveillance, all the tools, the AI you've got, you can find their weaknesses. Tear their hearts out. I mean it, man. Tell me where they are. Give me a time, an address . . . one by one, I'll waste every one of the filthy maggots."

Chase stared at him. "A little more time. Dominoes will start falling, empires will crumble. I will still have the rule of law on our side to rebuild a fair, equitable, free society for everyone instead of this monstrosity the Remies have created masquerading as a good world when it's all actually putrid corruption."

"Good for them, though." Grimes looked at Wen. "You know I'm right, Wen. Nothing will work except ending these dirtbags."

"I do agree with you, but Chase deserves a little more time to do it his way."

"*See?*" Grimes yelled. "And what about Shelby? What does she deserve?"

"Not what she got," Wen said as she pulled the boat to a private dock within sight of the Newark Airport grounds.

Chase, not surprised Wen agreed with Grimes, now faced them both, imploring them, "This is a big week. Give us *this* week. Then, if they don't start falling, I'll give you all the location information we have, and you can do whatever you want with it."

"I'll win this damned Remie CapWar is what I'll do with it," Grimes vowed.

Chapter Twenty-Five

SOUTHERN CALIFORNIA

Sunday - 7:30 am - Pacific time (10:30 am Eastern)

Lila and Jack, along with seven other Rogues, continued working in the warehouse by the docks. "It's all here," Lila said to Jack. "They are Remies not because they are super wealthy, but because of how they view the world, as if it's their own game."

"And they each want the power. But like junkies, it's never enough. More, more, more. These guys really do want to rule the world."

"They all have massive equity positions in Banks and financial institutions, pharmaceutical firms, defense contractors, major holdings in Agrochemical, AI tech, Media and social platform stocks." She pointed to the charts she'd been building. "Their power seems divided between those six pillars. Through them they manipulate and profit."

"It's a cruel and brutal circle with cold attitude toward the masses, like farm animals."

She nodded. "The elites censor and control opposition through divisiveness."

"Tane and Blanc's Circuit has never faced any real opposition, but are they more worried about Chase's fifteen hundred Terminators and the Killtron advanced AI fighters, or the other Remies? Snyder, Doorset, Miner, they each seem to have their own front organization, like the Circuit, mostly formed as foundations—the Phoenix Foundation being one of the most powerful."

"Something big is coming," Lila said. "Look."

"Oh my god," Jack breathed, staring in disbelief. "We may have cracked it."

"We've got to get all this to Chase so they can process it and isolate the event." Lila packaged the data and wrote a quick summary of their findings, then uploaded it to Chase's secure cloud server. She hit send, then started working on something else, another profile, when suddenly the whole work area and all nine Rogues researching there were ravaged, shredded by constant high velocity machinegun fire. Lila dove to the floor half on purpose and half because six or seven 30mm rounds had all but destroyed her left leg. She tried to lay still as her body writhed in agony and blood pumped from the bullet holes. The room above her, computers, monitors, lights, desks, papers, crates, *everything* turned to confetti. The air filled with dust, filtering in the streaming sunlight.

To Lila, it seemed as if the entire world had been ruptured in a slow-motion explosion, that all the physical and material parts of the building had been put in a blender, that hours had passed. In reality, seventy-nine seconds had elapsed between Khan's men bursting in and when the shooting finally stopped.

Khan walked deliberately through the disaster scene

while a crew of three stripped hard drives from computers. The broken parts of furnishings and equipment, the remnants of the coffee maker, and a mug crunched under Khan's heavy boots as he marched in, checking the results, making sure no one was left to tell the tale. He heard a moan and paused, looking at a man in a fetal position on the other side of a desk. Khan put a bullet in his head as if it was the most natural thing in the world. Lila could not hold back a short scream.

Khan turned, ready to let another bullet go, but something made him stop. "Oh, honey, are you okay?" He scooped her up off the floor before she could respond. Clearing a desk with one arm, he laid her down on the hard surface a bit too roughly. "Let me look at this."

Khan gripped her leg, squeezing and probing while she screamed at the unbearable pain he inflicted. He released her just before she would have passed out. "Yeah, that leg's going to have to come off. No chance of saving it. Too bad. You're a pretty thing."

"Screw you!"

He laughed. "No thanks, you'll be dead before I can get undressed." He gave her leg another squeeze, his hand soaked with her blood.

This time she gritted her teeth and managed to hold back most of the scream.

"Want to tell me about the work you were doing here?" Khan asked, sounding almost sweet. "We might be able to get you some help with that leg."

She shook her head.

"Okay then. When I kill your boss, that convict called Mars, I'll let him know you did the right thing. Might even put in a good word for you when I watch Chase Malone die." He smiled, impressed with himself. "Have you ever met him?"

She shook her head, the pain, the fear taking hold, stealing the fight from her.

"He's a self-righteous piece of trash, and he got you killed today. Did you know that? Chase Malone is the only reason you won't see tomorrow."

"No," she said, the word as if taking a knife in her gut. "It's because of you! You are an evil man."

He laughed. "It looks that way because you can't see straight, but I'm a necessary force in the world."

She shook her head, wondering why she had to endure this horrible creature, but couldn't concentrate long enough to have the thought. "How do you sleep?"

"You met the devil and wasted your final question with that cliche? Too bad, but I'll tell you this. I'll have forgotten your pretty face by morning. You might not believe that, but you cannot *begin* to fathom the amount of death I've seen. How many people like you I've killed. So, so many." He put a pistol between her eyes, then smiled. "A nice surprise you are. Most people would close their eyes, a few would cry or beg. You staring at me that way, it makes me feel special."

He pulled the trigger.

Chapter Twenty-Six

WASHINGTON, DC

Sunday - 2:42 pm - Eastern time

The hot, sticky August air hung so thick it could almost be seen. It was the kind of humid heat only Washington DC could produce. Wen wore a tank top and shorts to combat the tropic-like weather. Chase opted for a short-sleeved linen shirt and jeans. "Never too hot for jeans," he said when she gave him a look.

"It's a strange place to meet," Wen said as they stood on a high hill inside Rock Creek Park. The three-square mile refuge, created by an Act of Congress in 1890, was only the third National Park in the country.

"Spraggins is probably with the CIA or NSA, or some other federal agency, and can't stray too far from work."

"So? Plenty of decent restaurants, hotel lobbies, or bars around here." The scent of blooming lilies and fresh cut grass wafted around them.

"Look around. This whole area is heavily wooded, and likely has little or no surveillance, especially in these primitive sections," Chase said, picking his way through the narrow side trail as they tried to get a better view of the site.

"Says here that Fort DeRussy dates back to 1861," Wen read from her phone, research being one of her required talents from her MSS days.

"American Civil War."

"Yes," she agreed.

"A lot of people don't know that Washington was surrounded by enemy territory. The Confederates were always threatening an attack on the capital city."

"And they did attack," Wen said, impressed with Chase's knowledge. "The Union Army had built more than sixty fortresses to protect Washington DC, and in July of 1864, the rebels tested the defenses."

"Battle of Fort Stevens."

"How do you know this stuff?" she said, looking back at her phone.

"I like history. And even though the battle was not significant to the overall outcome of the war, it was important in that it was the only battle in US history when a sitting president was in combat and fired upon. Abraham Lincoln was there."

"At Fort DeRussy?"

"No, but he was at the battle. And Fort DeRussy was located nearby to Fort Stevens and helped defend it during what turned out to be the only attack on Washington DC. But this was only four miles from the White House!"

"Apparently a Union surgeon standing next to Lincoln on the Fort Stevens parapet *did* get shot. That's when Lincoln finally took cover."

"Could you imagine if he'd been killed that day?" Chase said. "Wow!"

He and Wen rejoined the main dirt path and crossed an old, dry moat.

"There isn't much left," Wen said, on guard herself, feeling as the Union soldiers must have, knowing the rebels were on the prowl. "But if we imagine most of these trees weren't here back then to obscure the views, this hilltop would have been an extremely strategic vantage point."

Satisfied there was no ambush in the making, they moved on, passing remains of magazine storage areas, old trenches, mounds, earth walls, and the well-preserved parapet.

"Where is he?" Wen asked, tense in the unknown area.

"He's still got five minutes," Chase replied, checking the time. "Remember, we got here extra early to get the lay of the land."

"We're just a bit exposed."

"We're in an old military fort, in the woods, in the middle of Washington, surrounded by thousands of trees. We've got the high ground and trenches. I feel a lot less exposed here than in the subway, on the bridge, or in that plane," he said, suddenly thinking of Shelby.

"Maybe," Wen said, pausing when a couple of twigs snapped. She held up a hand to quiet Chase and pointed her Glock toward the sound.

A full minute passed before she looked away.

"Could have been a squirrel," Chase said.

"It's never a squirrel."

Chase nodded. "General Early, who commanded the Confederate raid, told one of his officers after the battle, 'Major, we didn't take Washington, but we scared Abe Lincoln like hell.' The General probably said that before they lost the war."

"Any idea what that cabin is over there?" Wen asked, ignoring his history lesson.

Through the woods, on the other side of a thin creek, Chase could just make out what she was pointing at; a small log cabin, which appeared as if it had grown there with the large chestnut oaks, American beech, and a scattering of holly trees.

Wen looked it up on her phone. "It was once owned by Joaquin Miller, a 19th-century poet."

This time, it was three twigs snapping. Wen moved behind a large oak tree and drew her MP7.

Chapter Twenty-Seven

A man with disheveled gray hair, a thick white beard, and a matching mustache that made him look like he'd just stepped out of an old west saloon stood with his hands up. "Don't shoot. I am Spraggins, and I am armed only with information."

Wen held her gun pointed at him, scanning the area.

"I assure you, Wen, it's only me, and we have much to discuss, so if you'll be so kind as to point your weapon somewhere else, preferably at the ground, we can get on with it."

Wen made no effort to move her gun.

"How do we know it's you?" Chase asked.

"Please, who else would I be? I called you here, and we have already established I could have killed you at the coffee shop, the hotel, last week when you were in Youngstown, Ohio, two weeks earlier, Santa Barbara . . . Need I go on? This is a little frustrating, and I have only seven or eight seconds of patience left."

"Then what?" Wen asked, still pointing the gun.

"Then I leave, and you never hear from me again. You two have too many people trying to kill you. I may be the only one who can save you. Time's up." He slowly turned and began walking back into the woods.

"Wait," Chase yelled, signaling Wen to put the gun down.

"So let's talk about an event you have never heard of that is very close to occurring," Spraggins said, walking back toward them. The subtle pinstripes in his wrinkled suit pants indicated a long-lost matching jacket. The white collared shirt, crisp and clean, pressed cotton, seemed out of place, as did the old navy-blue canvas sneakers.

"What's that?" Chase asked, expecting a bomb threat, maybe more of Snyder's planned corruption, possibly a plot to take out a small government somewhere, probably something to do with the Remies.

"The Overwhelm," Spraggins said, now close enough that they could see his hazel eyes, weary and wise, taking turns staring at them intently, as if expecting a long series of follow-up questions. His mind, having worked on the issue for so many years, had difficulty realizing what others did or did not know about it.

When they just looked at him, waiting for more, he continued, motioning for them to follow him. "Ah, yes, let me explain. Since the beginning of human history—and I'm not going to debate the starting point on that, because that is an entirely different subject and clearly archaeologists have missed on their theories—but as I said, that would be another topic, and yet it could easily be applied into the process to which we reach the Overwhelm. Obviously everything can to a *certain* extent—"

"You were saying about the beginning of human history?" Chase said.

Wen, her hand still gripping the MP7 inside her light duffle, noticed they seemed to be heading toward the old poet's cabin she'd seen earlier.

"Ah, yes. The Overwhelm is a story about fear, and fear is a power like no other. Every animal, including humans, has a fear level that fluctuates. And going back to, say, the time of primitive humans, commonly referred to as cavemen—however, that is a gross generalization, which does not take into account the various lines, Neanderthals, and—"

"You were saying about fear levels?" Chase prompted him again.

"Ah, yes, human fear levels have remained relatively constant throughout history. It would have been high during the primitive times when it was fight or flight, so you might imagine, elevated compared to later eras because they could die at any minute and limited, inconsistent food supplies, the lack of availability of medical aid, even adequate clothing—you get the point."

"We're going to the cabin?" Wen asked suspiciously. They were less than fifty yards from the structure now.

"Yes. It's fascinating, really.

Spraggins stopped and pointed to the front of the cabin. "Do you know of the poet—"

"Joaquin Miller," Wen said.

"Yes, that's right," Spraggins said, obviously pleasantly surprised. "You've read his work, then?"

"No," Chase said. "Wen looked it up. She researches everything."

"Well, this Miller was quite a character—a rebel sympathizer. He was a long way round to becoming a poet. He was also a pony express rider, a gold miner—although some say he was only a mining camp cook, who gave *himself* scurvy from only eating what he cooked—he was a lawyer and judge, a frontiersman, some say a liar, probably at least a grand embellisher. He married a Native American woman, and there's a long and wildly interesting story about their relationship and a kidnapping, but there isn't time for that right now."

Wen said a silent thank you for that.

"Miller was also a horse thief. He actually got caught and arrested for it. Some years later, he came to Washington to be a politician." He paused, as if deciding whether to delve deeper, maybe say something more, then continued. "Can you imagine a horse thief as a politician?"

"Yes, I can," Chase said.

Spraggins allowed a quick chuckle. "Anyway, while pursuing politics, he built this cabin."

"In 1883," Wen said, trying to move the story along, wondering if this had anything to do with *why* they were meeting him, wondering just *why* they had met with Spraggins at all.

"Yes, in another part of the city," he said, "for a retreat to find rustic peace and inspiration. Kind of need those things in this great city." Another little laugh. "Miller stayed here until 1885, when he returned to California. A couple years later, he sold the cabin for $5,100 in 1887."

Chase raised his eyebrows. "That's a lot of money back then."

Spraggins nodded. "Indeed. But that is not the end of the story."

Wen rolled her eyes.

"In 1911, the area surrounding the cabin was being developed, so it was going to be torn down."

"No suspense left, since we're standing in front of it," Chase said.

"No," Wen said, forcing a smile. "Some senators, the state of California, and the Columbia Historical Society all intervened to save the structure from demolition and relocated it to Rock Creek Park." She pointed at the pretty structure.

Chase surveyed the cabin, taking in its rustic charm. "It's amazing to think that such an old cabin still exists in the heart of the city."

Spraggins nodded. "It's more amazing than you can imagine." He fumbled with a fob and pushed a series of numeric buttons. "Let's go inside."

Chapter Twenty-Eight

Inside, the rustic cabin looked as it might have a hundred years earlier—sparsely furnished with a handmade wooden table and chairs, a few antique children's toys scattered about, and a cast iron cooktop woodstove, iron kettles and skillets and an old teapot stacked on the black surface as if someone had just left to tend to outdoor chores.

Spraggins waltzed in like he owned the place, his sneakers landing softly on the worn, rough-hewn wood planks.

Chase gazed around, wondering what they were doing standing inside this nothing little exhibit to a forgotten poet. He certainly wasn't amazed by anything inside the musty cabin. Wen did a quick visual scan for bombs or other devices or methods that would result in their deaths.

"Fear, fear, fear . . . where was I? As civilization became more advanced and more *civilized*, traditional fear levels went lower. This resulted in stability. For most of the last ten thousand years, the fear index, which quantified the degrees of fear that people felt continually, reduced little by little. Of course, there were spikes along the way."

"Can we get to the amazing part?" Chase asked, sensing Wen's growing impatience.

"Obvious spikes were the World Wars, Sputnik, JFK's assassination," Spraggins said, ignoring Chase. "Less obvious would be the ones caused by the 1969 Moon Landing, the US Ice Hockey team beating the Soviets in the 1980 Olympics—the measurements are precise, and it can be fascinating to see what drives the index up and down."

"Exactly how do you measure it?" Chase asked, still trying to see anything remotely amazing.

"However, in the last thirty years or so, the spikes have grown more frequent, and they have resulted in a pronounced upward trend line. There have been no significant corrections, and this is not rising little by little, as it had decreased. These are more like jumps."

"No surprise," Wen said. "The world has grown more complex and more divided. The twenty-four-hour news cycle makes sure we don't miss a single piece of bad news. So is this a big deal?"

"*Very*," Spraggins said gravely. "If the index rises too far, and based on the movements, I should really say *when* it gets too high, there will be dangerous side effects which will cause even more fear, and if we get to eight point two-nine, then we've reached the tipping point."

"What happens then?" Chase asked, almost bored.

"Once we reach the tipping point, it's just all out-of-control. Fear results in total chaos, a complete breakdown of our society. Dystopian or worse."

"Worse?"

"Apocalyptic."

Wen scoffed. "All from fear?"

"You say *fear* as if it were merely a word, some casual letters arranged in a harmless little way, behaving nicely, but fear is not that at all. It is an energy, an urgent and powerful force. There is nothing that cannot be bulldozed and wrecked by its presence. Fear can destroy *everything*."

"I understand what you're saying."

"No, you don't," Spraggins said, holding up his arm, clearly insulted. "Fear *kills*, period, and that fact scales exponentially. If the Fear index reaches a level above eight point two-nine, even by a fraction, we reach the Overwhelm, and fear will run away like a freight train. It will become unstoppable. We will die, many of us, and those that don't will wish they had."

"And you can prove this?" Wen asked.

"Of course I can. But the greater question is, why are you so calm in the face of such a catastrophic prognostication? Is it that you don't believe it? Because that seems the most likely answer, and if that is the case, then I have wasted my time."

Wen shook her head. "No, it is because I *do* believe you, and this is how I address a crisis, a threat, or death. I do not allow fear to have any control of my thoughts or my emotions. Even when fear exists at its most dangerous, when the situation is thick with it, I act free from fear."

Spraggins smiled. "I chose wisely." He pushed another few digits on the fob and the wood planks beneath the old stove began to lift. The stove remained fixed to the portion of the floorboards that opened like a hatch, resting on its side now, revealing a narrow opening. "We are ready to begin." Spraggins pointed down.

"Begin what?" Chase asked.

"The race."

"Against the fear?"

"No, against those who make it."

Chapter Twenty-Nine

ATLANTA, GEORGIA

Sunday - 2:44 pm - Eastern time

Tane and Blanc sat in the control room, fuming and knowing that the video call on the screen would do nothing to improve their moods. However, these men were experts at compartmentalization as well as linking events.

The Surgeon appeared on the screen, his expressionless face giving away nothing.

"The failures in apprehending Chase and Wen in New York are interestingly connected to the situation we need to discuss." Blanc leaned forward, his hands clasped together in front of him. "We need to deal with Mayor Snyder. The election is less than three months away, and we cannot afford to let him win."

The Surgeon's fingers tapped rhythmically on the keyboard. "I've been working on it," he said. "But your influence is not as strong as it used to be. Since the Flashburn event, we have lost—"

"We are *painfully* aware of what we've lost since

Malone's war with us began," Blanc barked. "This is not the issue. Our power is still formidable, and exceeds Snyder's."

"Snyder has a significant lead in the polls," the Surgeon said, deciding not to correct Blanc that Snyder technically held more power, and would soon shoot past them as he rose to the presidency.

Tane scowled. "We need to do something drastic. We can't let Snyder become president. It would be beyond disastrous for our operations."

The Surgeon looked up at them, his cold cobalt eyes meeting theirs through the screen. "I have a plan," he said, his voice low and measured. "It's risky, but it could work."

Blanc glared at the screen, his face tense, tired of the Surgeon's theatrics. "What is it?"

The Surgeon hesitated for a moment. "My plan is complex, involving a series of coordinated cyber-attacks on Snyder's campaign infrastructure, coupled with a targeted disinformation campaign aimed at discrediting him in the eyes of the public. It will take time, effort, and resources, but if executed correctly, it could swing the election in favor of our candidate." He pressed a key. "I've just sent you the details."

"We've tried all this before," Tane said, irritable.

"This is *more*, different . . . extreme," the Surgeon said. "Read it."

"Interesting," Blanc said, already starting to peruse the outline.

"It also involves another, bolder initiative," the Surgeon explained, "targeting Snyder's most influential supporters and discrediting them. I can make it seem like they're involved in scandals or illegal activity, and the trails will all lead back to Snyder."

"How exactly are you going to do that?" Blanc asked skeptically, an eyebrow raised.

"I have access to sensitive information and resources that can be used to manufacture false evidence against them," the Surgeon replied, a slight smile creeping onto his face. "It won't be easy, but it is doable."

Tane nodded in agreement.

"Make it happen," Blanc said firmly.

As the Surgeon began to type away at his computer, Tane and Blanc exchanged a worried look. They knew that the Surgeon's methods were a long shot. Snyder was smart and connected, but most of all, he had an organization that exceeded their own.

The Surgeon's fingers flew over the keyboard again as he began to set his plan into motion. As he worked, his wild hair seemed to take on a life of its own, swirling around his face like a storm cloud. Tane and Blanc watched in silence for several minutes. They knew what Chase had learned two years earlier, that the only way to beat a Remie was by controlling information. Despite the Surgeon's quirks and oddities, there was no denying that he was a genius at what he did, and in a world where information equaled power and power topped everything, genius was the ultimate weapon.

Chapter Thirty

WASHINGTON, DC

Sunday - 2:58 pm - Eastern time

Staring down into the opening, lit by the glow of several small monitors and dozens of tiny LED indicators, Chase realized Spraggins had created something very sophisticated, but didn't know exactly *what*. "This equipment here . . . appears custom."

"Yes." He smiled benevolently, as if Chase had just told him his child looks just like him.

"What is it?"

Spraggins' face shifted. "The Fear Meter, of course."

"You're *actually* measuring it?"

"In real time," Spraggins confirmed.

"From right here?" Wen asked, scanning the room again, checking the view from the windows.

"I have these in most major cities."

"In the country?"

"In the world."

"What constitutes a major city?"

"For my purposes, any city or metropolitan area with a population near or above one million people."

"But there must be hundreds," Chase said, trying to imagine how he'd built and installed so many machines.

"Seven hundred and ninety-one," Spraggins said. "However, several cities—Tokyo, Delhi, Shanghai, São Paulo, Karachi, etcetera—have multiple devices installed."

"How did you . . . " Chase began. "Or, more importantly, *why* did you?"

"It's the only way I can track it."

"The fear?"

"Yes."

"But then what?" Chase asked. "So everyone is afraid . . . and what are they afraid *of*, anyway? I mean, losing their jobs, getting in an accident, house burning down, eaten by a shark, what?"

"All those factor in," Spraggins replied. "Some people are actually afraid of vending machines. Did you know two to three people die every year in vending machine accidents?"

"What?"

"However, what *really* moves the needle are the major stories that grip the public, or at least the larger population centers. The wars, pandemics, murders—this would include super advanced weapons, AI taking over, the surveillance state—*that's* a significant issue in China, and it's been growing since Covid, so now government monitoring and privacy concerns are also registering high in the US, Canada, Australia, and across Europe."

"And it shows up in *that*?" Wen pointed down, nervous to be in such and odd place with such an odd man.

"Yes." He smiled proudly. "Another one impacting the reading lately is China collecting DNA to alter and shape human existence. Even things you might not expect such as social credit scores, 5G mind control, terrorism, controlling the weather, depleting earth's soils, UFOs, distrust of the media is spiking, then there's—"

"Okay, we get the idea," Wen said.

"*Do* you?" Spraggins said, almost angrily. "Because there's so much, so fast . . . the fear ratio is rising closer to the Overwhelm. We are down to *days*, but anything could shift that to hours, even minutes. *That's* how dangerous the current state is."

"I'm sorry," Chase said. "Did you say 'overwhelm'?"

"*The* Overwhelm. That's when we've reached the tipping point."

"Meaning?"

"Once we get into the Overwhelm, there will be no recovery from it."

"But what *is* that? What does it *look* like?"

His face went pale, as if he might vomit. "Haven't we covered this? The Overwhelm is the *end*. All order is gone. The Overwhelm is us losing control of *everything*. Instead of all the things we are afraid of—nuclear war, asteroids, global warming, a real pandemic, AI destroying humanity—something *worse* takes over. All those extinction events are merely inflictions. The whispers and rumors, the threats of all that, are what *lead* to the Overwhelm."

Wen shook her head. "So?"

"The Overwhelm is the truly invisible threat to humanity, or at least organized civilization. Once we get to a certain point, and once we pass eight point two-nine on the Fear Meter, it's over."

"What is?"

"*Our civilization*," he said, exasperated. "Pass eight-two-nine, and there's no turning back. Civilization is going to either spiral into a horrible dystopian nightmare, or simply end itself by nuclear war or some other fear-induced reaction."

"The Overwhelm," Chase said.

"The Overwhelm," Spraggins repeated. "The media seeds the initial fears, then word-of-mouth takes over, then the human brain's logic center takes over, because it sees so many other problems with whatever that initial fear was before it can even come up with a potential solution—if there even *is* a solution—then fear is introduced, and the next one, and the next, and so on, until that part of the brain cannot focus on solving one crisis. These are all tremendous disasters, horrible occurrences that could potentially be handled one at a time. If separated, these could be addressed and solved. But imagine trying to land a man on the moon at the same time as you are fighting World War II, while category five hurricanes hit the southeast, major earthquakes decimate California, and 9/11 happens. Collectively, with more trouble coming every day like machine-gun fire, suddenly you can see the Overwhelm, where we are consumed by our own fears."

Chapter Thirty-One

ATLANTA, GEORGIA

Sunday - 3:12 pm - Eastern time

"I have a team working on Snyder, but there is a more pressing matter," the Surgeon said across the encrypted video stream. His wild hair and oddly frantic face filled the six-foot monitor in the DC executive control room.

"I can't stand seeing him that big," Blanc said under his breath.

"A man who goes by a single name, Mars, is one of Malone's oldest friends," the Surgeon continued. "This Mars has become a top lieutenant to Malone. However, he works on the non-violence side of the war. He is essentially my counterpart, however not nearly as good."

"Of course not," Tane said, unable to conceal his sarcasm.

"So Mars has enlisted hundreds of ex-convicts, mostly nonviolent criminals, who are so-called *experts* in the dark web, and apparently highly intelligent hackers and schemers. These misfits are operating under the codename 'Rogues.'"

"Criminals?"

"Let's just say . . . yes. Full stop."

"Violent?"

"These Rogues have taken various transgressions against the system, so, for years, without realizing it, they have been fighting the Remies."

"Fighting us."

"Here is a direct quote from Mister Mars. 'Remies control the corrupt world. We can use that corruption against them.' That does sound like a threat, wouldn't you agree?"

"Absolutely. Can you give us his whereabouts so Khan can pay a visit and take out this piece of garbage?"

"Not yet. But Khan has just taken out a Rogue cell in California."

"But Mars wasn't there?"

"It seems Mars has been the architect in the system that has kept Chase and Wen invisible all these years. It's a specialty of all the Chase Malone people—running, hiding, being cowards."

"Close the noose," Tane said. "Next time I hear about Mars, I want us to be talking about Elon Musk building a house on that planet. Understand?"

"We'll set a digital trap for these trolls."

"Make sure it's a death trap."

Chicago, Illinois
Sunday - 2:16 pm - Central time (3:16 pm Eastern)

Mars walked through Chicago's O'Hare international airport to initiate their latest attack on the financial system, which had mostly recovered from a major collapse induced by Flash-burn two years earlier. However, the Remies' hold had proven stronger than anticipated, and their house of cards was more resilient than Chase and Wen had hoped.

"The Remies have manipulated the system for more than a century," Chase had said at the time. "It's going to take more than a few years to bring it down."

Mars loved airports. After so many years confined in prisons, the constant movement at airports and the freedom to be anywhere in the world in a matter of hours was intoxicating. He glanced at the crowd though, leery of the potential for trouble. Instead, he spotted Laura, one of his Rogues.

Laura, whose real name remained unknown since all of his Rogues used aliases, was a short haired African American woman who had been involved in criminal enterprises since her teens. After serving time in various prisons on and off for twenty years, and now in her forties, she'd finally found and taken the real job she had always been looking for. Laura liked getting paid full-time by Mars, although she knew it wasn't his cash, and had no idea that Chase bankrolled the Rogues. It was a steady paycheck. Even though technically she was still breaking the law, it was as close to a legitimate career as she had ever had.

Laura smiled when she noticed Mars through the streams of travelers. He motioned for her to join him at a small dining area.

"Dangerous times," she said, repeating one of their typical greetings.

"For them," Mars said.

"Soon."

"We won't know when the system starts to fall," Mars said. "All we can do is keep going after it." He gave her a small envelope with all the details of their recent moves and data gains. Whenever possible, they preferred paper. "These days a paper trail is safer than a digital one," Chase often warned them. Laura would destroy the papers when she landed in New York City.

Two more Rogues joined them. Mars gave them each their assignments.

Steve's envelope sent him to Miami, and Paul would be going to Seattle. Mars was catching a flight to Dallas, but that was just a connection. He never took direct flights. "Direct means death," he'd told Chase once.

Laura, Paul, and Steve did not know how, but each assignment connected to a greater plan codenamed *Bastille*, which quite simply meant the complete annihilation of the Remies, the ruling elites, and the corrupt leaders throughout the world.

Paul, who had done work for the Mafia over the years, was the best at picking out surveillance. When he brushed Mars's arm and mumbled the word *shadows*, Mars took it seriously, and quickly texted the person providing security for the Rogues from a distance. Rogues could fight, but their focus needed to remain on their expertise—the financial "white-collar" aspects of the fight. The Terminators were the grunts in this war.

I see them, the Terminator replied.

Mars was annoyed that the Terminator hadn't seen the shadows *before* Paul noticed them. "Why do we need to do this Terminator's job for him?" Mars muttered, wanting to say the same thing to the Terminator, but he refrained.

Mars had learned in prison that you never did anything that might annoy someone who you were counting on to save your life.

Chapter Thirty-Two

CHICAGO, ILLINOIS

Sunday - 2:27 pm - Central time (3:27 pm Eastern)

Determining that they hadn't actually been spotted, that the Remies just had agents stationed at the main airports looking for Chase and Wen, Mars made the decision to carry on with their assignments. Mars had also learned in prison that to panic was the quickest way to die.

"We don't have much time," he told his crew. "As always, make sure you're not followed onto the flight, and if you are, shake them on the other end. Be one hundred percent certain, or call it in and abort."

They continued scanning the area as they walked toward the gates. Mars provided details that were not contained in their information packets, which contained the least amount of information necessary.

"No trace," he reminded them.

As Mars arrived at the main terminal, where they would split up and head to their final gate destinations, he checked in with the Terminator again. This time, he got no response.

Paul immediately scanned every face, trying to pick out killers in the crowd. "Looks clear."

Standing next to Mars, Laura fumbled with her packet. "Should we call it off?"

Months of planning had gone into this attack. He was convinced they were still actively concealed, meaning the Remies didn't know what was coming.

As far as Mars knew, none of the others were on the Remies' watchlist, at least not in connection with Chase.

"Feds?" Mars asked.

"It wasn't the FBI," Paul said. "And the FBI didn't take out Watchtower," he said referring to the Terminator. "These were from the Remies' armies, but which one?"

Mars had been briefed on them, but there were way too many to keep track of. Every surviving Remie, and another fifteen or so aspiring Remies, had various levels of security forces, from corporate police to full armies. Certain ones also controlled state agencies and actual national militaries. Some Remies could tap into special ops when needed, and it went on and on. Most of them were untraceable. "There are too damned many," Mars said. "Ultimately, it doesn't matter who's shooting at you." He agreed with Chase that the only way to make them stop was to imprison every Remie. He also agreed with Grimes that if that didn't work, Remies should be killed.

"What are we doing then?" Steve asked.

Mars looked at Paul, who shook his head, not seeing anything.

Mars thought of calling Chase to see if the Astronaut could get in on any of the cameras, but the first flight was going to board in seven minutes. He decided to chance it.

"We're a go," he said. "Make your gates. Look sharp. Safe travels."

It was a decision he would regret within hours, but even later, he wasn't sure he would have done it differently.

Laura and Steve never made their flights. Only he and Paul got clear.

Paul was killed inside the airport at his destination.

Atlanta, Georgia
Sunday - 3:47 pm - Eastern time

Images from the airport killings filled the screens. "Nice work at O'Hare today," Tane said.

"Would have been better if we'd taken out all four."

"We did get three of them, and that Terminator," Tane said, like a kid talking about getting a high score on a video game. "Even better, we got a new news story. *The Airport Killer.* I like that. All in a good days' work."

"Have Khan's people kill a housewife getting on a plane in Omaha."

"Why?"

"Just to keep the story going. And maybe take out a flight attendant in Indianapolis." He paused as if he were a mad scientist who might have been reconsidering such an evil plan. "We just need to space the murders geographically far enough apart so the *'killer'* will have time to travel from airport to airport." Another pause. "We'll wait a few days before the copycat killings begin at other airports around the country."

"Panic will ensue," Tane said. "People will stop traveling."

"I've already shorted airline stocks." He smiled. "It'll get worse once a few real crazies jump on the bandwagon."

"New calls for gun control."

"Yes, even though the horrible Airport Killer uses plastic hunting knives exclusively. Actually, a high-grade polymer resin."

"Violence is always blamed on guns."

"We see to that, though, don't we?" Another smile. "Have them run some stories on how guns and gun culture inspires violence of all kinds."

"It also increases ratings for our news networks."

"And ratings increase control. A neat, tidy, vicious little circle."

"Not so little."

Chapter Thirty-Three

GEORGETOWN UNIVERSITY, WASHINGTON, DC

Sunday - 2:58 pm - Eastern time

Spraggins insisted on bringing Chase and Wen to Georgetown University, where they walked across the grounds as they continued their discussion.

"How can you be so sure about the Overwhelm?" Chase pressed.

"Don't you realize? I can see the future. The past, the present, it holds all the clues, all the data points, every predictive subset of data we need to become soothsayers."

Chase and Wen exchanged a glance, both thinking about his greatest secret, SEER. The Search Entire Existence Result program Chase had developed employed advanced photonic quantum information processors and utilized deep learning, AI, quantum algorithms, and virtually every data point in digital existence to predict the future with stunning accuracy.

"By quantifying fear and relating it to the past outcomes?" Chase asked.

"Once AI came into the picture, I was able to verify all my theories and test the accuracy of the Fear Meter and its predictions."

"I have a program," Chase said. "It does what—"

"Yes, SEER, I know."

Chase looked back at him for a long, shocked moment, then shook his head slowly. "No one knows."

Spraggins laughed. "There is nothing no one knows. Give me enough time—and I'm talking minutes or hours, not days or weeks—and I can tell you what you had for dinner last night, even give an accurate prediction as to what you will eat tonight. You think a program like SEER can be kept secret? Maybe from the broad and dim percentages in the sunlight, but not those of us who toil in the shadows, who know the music of equations."

"So the Remies know about SEER?"

"Enough of them do, which begs the question."

"What's that?"

"How are you still alive?"

Chase shrugged. "You tell me."

"I have a number of theories, but it may be as simple as this: You are extremely smart, you are young enough to not realize the limitations of your situation, and Wen is frighteningly lethal. It's a good combination."

"But is it enough?"

"So far." Spraggins stared at him for a moment. "You have also been helped by the battlefield. Your wars—*all* wars—now involve your area of expertise: AI and far advanced technologies. You are a master in that universe."

"It's moving too fast for me to remain that for very long."

"True."

"So my time is limited."

"Very," Spraggins said. "Sorry, that's just what the data says now. Ask SEER if you want more details."

Chase shook his head again.

"It can change," Wen said.

"True enough," Spraggins agreed. "There is another variable that both helps and hurts your chances for survival."

Chase stared back at him, waiting for the answer.

Spraggins sighed. "I thought you'd guess, but that is a rather challenging moat to cross."

"What is it?"

"Tess Federgreen."

"You *do* know a lot about us."

"I know everything about you."

"It doesn't mean you know *us*," Wen said.

"Yes," Spraggins said, his face all business. "Yes, it does."

He led them through a doorway. Soon they were in a long, dark tunnel. "I went to school here. That's when I stumbled on the fear quotient. I was doing my thesis on the Cuban Missile Crisis and what the fear of a world ending event did to the population. In comparing it to other times when society was on the brink, I came up with a Fear Index. Back then, I did everything manually. Now, forty-five years later, I have precise predictive measurements, and twenty-some years ago I automated by inventing the Fear Meter."

"Where are we?" Wen asked, impatient and concerned. The damp, musty air pressed down on them, and the only light came from the flashlight Spraggins carried until Wen took out one of her own. Chase shivered involuntarily, feeling a sense of unease that he couldn't explain, not excited about being in their second tunnel of the day.

"These tunnels have a long and storied history," Spraggins said, his voice resonating in the hard, tight space. "Some say they were used as part of the underground railroad during the Civil War."

"Is that true?" Chase asked, wishing he could bring Tu to see these tunnels. Tu was fascinated with mazes, and secrets of history. *One day,* Chase thought, *when everything calms down I'll come back to Washington with Tu and show him.* But he wondered if that day would ever really come.

"Washington was one of the southernmost places where slavery was illegal. It seems logical the underground railroad would come through here. Many of these tunnels are very old. The university was founded in 1789, the same year George Washington was inaugurated as the nation's first president. Several of the campus buildings were used as a hospital during the civil war—for both sides."

"Is that why Georgetown University's colors are blue and gray?"

"The tunnels are a guarded secret," Spraggins continued, ignoring the question. "Those that know of them believe they end within a block or two of University grounds, but they go much further. They are part of the secret escape route for politicians during a national emergency. There are rumors that several presidents have traveled these corridors."

"Really?" Wen said.

"It's like a maze down here. Different branches lead into DC, and then off to different parts of the city."

"But why are *we* down here?"

"I want to show you one of my repositories, in case . . ."

"In case what?" Chase asked.

"Fear is a powerful thing," Spraggins said, ignoring

Chase. "It's a basic human emotion, but more than any other, it can control us in ways we never imagined."

"What do you mean?" Chase asked as they walked deeper into the tunnels.

"Studies have shown that fear can actually shut down our rational thinking processes. It activates the amygdala in our brains, which triggers our fight or flight response. This can cause us to make impulsive decisions and act irrationally."

"That's why it's such an attractive tool to those in power," Wen chimed in.

Spraggins nodded. "Explains why the media is constantly bombarding us with stories of violence, crime, and tragedy. It's not to inform us, it's to scare us. And when scared, we're more likely to support certain policies, politicians, or even products."

"They use fear to sell products, too," Chase said. "Think about all the commercials that show the worst-case scenario if you don't buy their product. It's all about playing on our fears."

"True, but fear in the hands of the government is most dangerous of all because people trust and count on authority," Spraggins explained. "After 9/11, people were terrified of another terrorist attack. So the government implemented the Patriot Act, taking away many of our traditional rights and our privacy. The TSA and other security measures were implemented. People were willing to give up their privacy and personal freedoms for a sense of safety."

They rounded a corner.

"Back in the early 2000s, I developed the Fear Meter. It saved me a tremendous amount of time from the prior manual equations."

"We're down here in case *what*?" Chase tried again.

"This is all I have ever done," Spraggins continued, still ignoring him.

They arrived at a small door no taller than five feet high with no visible knobs. He manipulated something behind a steam pipe and it opened. A large, sealed aluminum box about the size of a standard refrigerator stood inside a tiny room not much bigger than the box. They stepped inside. There was just enough area to walk around the box. Spraggins closed the door. A faint purple light illuminated the space.

"The Fear Meter is at seven-point-eight, six, three, two, two, one," he said. "It won't be all the scary stuff—nukes, AI, asteroids, whatever—that do us in, it will be the sum of all our fears. Franklin Roosevelt had it right. 'The only thing we have to fear, is fear itself.'"

Chase nodded somberly.

Spraggins touched the box as if it were a religious relic. "We're almost certainly down to that last seventy-two hours of life as we know it."

Chapter Thirty-Four

WASHINGTON, DC

Sunday - 4:57 pm - Eastern time

A typically muggy August afternoon, and the US National Arboretum was alive with the colors and scents of summer. Chase and Wen made their way down a winding path lined with a sea of flowers.

"Beautiful place," Chase said, happy to be away from the dark tunnels under Georgetown and away from the dark prophecies of Spraggins.

"Established by an act of Congress in 1927," Wen said. "It's grown to four hundred forty-six acres."

"I like coming to a city like Washington and spending our time in Rock Creek Park and the Arboretum," Chase said. "It's like not really being in the city at all."

"They also house an herbarium with more than eight hundred thousand specimens of wild and cultivated plants!"

"Where are we meeting him?"

"Over there." She pointed.

"The Capitol Columns," Chase said. He already knew

about the twenty-two Corinthian columns that had once been part of the East Portico of the United States Capitol building from 1828 to 1958, but were now parked at the Arboretum. "It's like something out of mythology."

"A good place to meet a senator."

"What's harder to find in Washington in August than a senator still in town?"

Wen gave him an impatient look.

"A cool breeze." He laughed.

She groaned.

"Chase, Wen, good to see you both," the senator said, greeting them with a nod. "Let's walk and talk. I've got twenty minutes."

As they strolled the gardens, the senator began to share his concerns about the Remies' power and their ability to influence those in Washington.

"It's worse than we thought. Everywhere I turn, everyone I think I can trust, turns out to be a Remie connection."

"We're about to blow their world apart," Chase said.

"They have too much control," the senator said, his voice low. "Their greedy fingers are in *everything*."

Chase and Wen nodded in agreement, their eyes scanning the foliage and flowers around them. They knew that Vintons or other Remie agents could be anywhere. They were wearing vIDs, but the senator could easily be a target if any of the Remies had figured out Wentworth was on a crusade against them.

"We need your help," Chase said firmly. "We can't do this without you. Stay with us. We need the classified documents."

The senator nodded slowly. "I'll do what I can, but we need to be careful. They're watching us, and they won't hesitate to . . . These people will murder my family, your family, anyone in the way."

They continued to walk, their conversation intense and focused. The senator shared what information he could about the Remies and their network while Chase and Wen listened intently.

"We need you to get the bill passed. It's already passed the house," Chase said, referring to legislation that subjected the Federal Reserve to an immediate audit, and regular ones thereafter.

"The president will never sign it."

"Let us worry about that."

The senator raised an eyebrow, but didn't want to know the details. "The vote is Friday."

"Is there a chance?" Chase asked. "Can you twist enough arms, horse trade the right deals, work the angles?"

"I'm going to stop you before you mention smoke-filled back rooms," the senator said. "I'll do what I can. It's not wholly impossible."

Chase knew the senator was too honest, so he did not mention that Mars had a couple people working on *legal bribes* of some senators through lobbying and campaign contributions to get their votes—even one straight out illegal bribe of a big enough number that it couldn't be ignored.

"I don't know how much longer we can keep this up," the senator said, his face tense with worry. "Tane and Blanc, Doorset, Miner, Snyder . . . these men seem to have only gotten stronger since Flash-burn. It's as if we pruned the garden and ended up just giving these weeds more room to grow."

Chase and Wen exchanged a look, both understanding the gravity of the situation. They had been working for two years to take down the corrupt billionaires, but progress had been slow.

"We have an ongoing push that is targeting their assets," Chase said, his eyes scanning the area for any potential eavesdroppers.

"And there are things in process that it's best you don't know about," Wen added, her gaze fixed on a bed of bright pink azaleas.

The senator nodded in agreement. "We also need to clean up the corruption at the DOJ, White House, and other agencies. It's beyond frustrating. Every tool we would use is already compromised."

They passed a cluster of vibrant red roses and a bed of purple and pink coneflowers. The colors and scents were a stark contrast to the tension in the air.

"I know this won't be easy," the senator continued, his voice barely above a whisper, "but we can't let these corrupt swine destroy our democracy."

As they walked by a bed of tall pink flowers called Joe-Pye weed, Chase spoke up. "The Terminators, my private army, took a big hit last night from the Remies."

The senator looked at Chase skeptically. "I'm sorry to hear that, but I've warned you about doing anything too visible. We don't want to attract unwanted attention."

"Have you seen anything on the news?" Chase asked. "No, because the Remies are more interested than us in keeping this war hidden."

Wen's eyes flashed over to a bed of delicate white lilies. "We need to finish this before they turn the US Military against us."

The senator mulled it over for a moment. "They'll brand you and your organization domestic terrorist and then all bets are off."

"That could come at any time," Chase said. "You're on the Intelligence Committee. You have to find someone we can trust who can stop that from happening."

"We need to be strategic and calculated in our approach. We can't rush into this blindly, or they'll see me coming."

As they neared the exit, the senator turned to them.

"I appreciate your dedication to this cause. I believe this is the right strategy. There are many good, honorable people in the intelligence community and in the military. I'll find them."

"Thanks Lowell," Chase said. "Find them before the others find us."

Chapter Thirty-Five

WASHINGTON, DC

Sunday - 6:44 pm - Eastern time

Spraggins, Chase, and Wen were the only three people in the museum as they walked through the gallery, continuing their earlier discussion about the power of fear.

"This is a closed section of the Smithsonian," Spraggins whispered. "It's used only for academics."

"And they study fear?" Chase asked, surprised.

"Fear is the most important force in human existence," Spraggins said. "However, they don't study it. I do. I, and a few others."

The exhibition halls, made to be filled with visitors admiring priceless artifacts, were now empty. Wen found the place creepy, and kept alert to hidden threats.

"From ancient times, fear has always been used as a tool to control the masses," Spraggins said, his eyes scanning the priceless sculptures on display. "It's one of the oldest and most effective ways to keep people in line."

Wen nodded. "The threat of punishment, whether

physical or psychological, has been a common theme throughout history. It's been used by governments, religious institutions, and even businesses." She thought of her homeland. "The Chinese Communist Party has made an artform out of using fear to control nearly 1.5 billion people."

"They are showing the rest of the world elites how it is done," Spraggins said. "Technology and surveillance have given oppressors unprecedented tools to control the masses." Spraggins pointed to a statue of a fierce-looking god. "In ancient Greece, the idea of fear was personified in the form of deities such as Phobos, the god of fear. The Greeks believed that fear was a natural part of the human condition, and that it could be harnessed to create order in society."

"I'm not sure it's ever good," Chase said. "But at the very least, fear can be a double-edged sword. As you've shown, too much fear can lead to chaos or worse. What is the difference between what the Remies are doing now and what the Nazi regime did with fear and propaganda?"

Spraggins nodded. "Hitler and his followers used fear to control the masses, creating a climate of fear and mistrust. They portrayed themselves as saviors who could protect the German people from imagined enemies, such as the Jews, homosexuals, and other so-called undesirables."

Chase shook his head. "And the end result was the Holocaust, the worst genocide ever, along with the most destructive war in human history. Tens of millions of lives lost, countless others shattered."

Spraggins sighed. "That's how catastrophic things get when fear runs out of control. The fools think it can be an effective means of control, but it takes on a life of its own."

Wen looked at him skeptically. "I think the Remies know

exactly what they are doing. They believe their wealth and power can insulate them from anything."

Spraggins stared at an eight-foot by ten-foot photo of the *Unknown Protestor*, sometimes called *Tank Man*. He had stood in front of a column of tanks in Tiananmen Square during the 1989 student protests. "There's a man with no fear."

"Whatever happened to him?" Chase asked, turning to Wen.

"No one knows." She looked sad. "Some believe he escaped, that his identity was never known. Others say he was executed. I like to think he got away."

"Resisting the fear like Tank Man did is not easy," Spraggins said. "Most of us would crack under that kind of pressure, with the things that are coming. There is good fear, such as the kind that prevents us from breaking laws and the like. It is true we need just enough fear to keep society in line, but not so much that it stifles our spirits. The Remies have pushed it to the extreme. As the French philosopher Michel de Montaigne once wrote, 'The thing I fear most is fear.'"

Chase took a deep breath. "Maybe truth is the best remedy for fear."

"Yes," Spraggins said. "As a scholar, I've spent most of my life studying it, trying to understand it. There is an elusive line where prudent use ends and dangerous oppression begins. Once crossed, fear ultimately grows out of control, and becomes its own indecent force. That's when society descends into uncontrolled chaos."

"Eight point two nine," Wen said.

He nodded. "As Chase says, we must regain the order of truth, break the Remies' lock on the media so the real story can get out."

As they walked through the silent museum, Spraggins explained how he'd analyzed the role of fear in politics, religion, and culture.

"There is but one way to save us. To stop the Remies and reverse the Fear Meter. Truth."

Chapter Thirty-Six

WASHINGTON, DC

Sunday - 7:00 pm - Eastern time

Spraggins pressed the up button next to the elevator. A second later, the silver doors slipped open.

"Do you know this guy?" Spraggins asked as a man stepped off.

Nash Graham, with thick white hair and a confused look, stood there for a moment until Wen threw her arms around him.

"I thought you were in Europe."

"I am," he said, clearly uncomfortable being hugged by anyone, but also happy to be in Wen's arms. "I mean, I was. Now I'm here."

Wen released him. "I'm glad."

"Nash Graham, my second favorite Astronaut," Spraggins said, giving him a slight bow.

"Second favorite," Chase echoed. "Who's your favorite?"

"Major Tom," Nash and Spraggins said simultaneously.

"Who's that?"

"He's every astronaut's favorite," Nash said. "But he may not be alive anymore. It's been eight years since anyone has heard anything from him."

"Oh, he's very much alive and well," Spraggins said. "I saw him less than two weeks ago."

The Astronaut looked impressed.

"Wait, how'd you get in the building," Wen asked the Astronaut, worried that if he could walk in, maybe anyone could.

"I gave him the code," Spraggins said.

"You knew he was coming?"

"I asked him to come."

Wen gave him a questioning look.

"We need all the help we can get," Spraggins said. "You think you know, that you understand what is happening, that fear is being used as a tool to control the masses, that the media is using propaganda and fake news, both in historical and modern contexts—and maybe you *do*. But the ramifications . . . that is where you are underestimating the consequences."

Chase leaned against a display case. "Social media has made it easier than ever to spread fear with fake news and dangerous rumors. Just look at COVID-19 and the vaccines. People are so afraid of the virus that they're willing to believe almost anything, no matter how absurd."

Spraggins shook his head. "All of that was nothing more than a test case. More is coming. As the writer H.P. Lovecraft once said, 'The oldest and strongest emotion of mankind is fear, and the oldest and strongest kind of fear is fear of the unknown.'"

Wen looked at him. "I'm thinking it's very bad, so how much worse is it?"

"The Remies are controlling what people believe, which changes how they act," the Astronaut said.

"Can't we educate them? Teach them critical thinking skills so they can better discern fact from fiction?"

"A famous journalist named Walter Lippmann once said, 'There can be no liberty for a community which lacks the means by which to detect lies,'" Spraggins said. "And he was correct. Here we are now."

Wen nodded. "But what about when those lies are perpetuated by those in power?"

"When a person is buried under so much propaganda, they begin to propagandize their friends, family, co-workers, even themselves," Spraggins said. "Mark Twain is often credited with the idea that, 'It's easier to fool people than to convince them that they have been fooled.'"

"People will do anything when scared enough," the Astronaut agreed. "Like children, just waiting for their parents to tell them it will be okay. Just do this or that."

"Why would they do this?" Wen asked. "What control do they get if everything is destroyed? Do they really want a world filled with chaos?"

"Yes," Spraggins said. "But who? Ask yourself who could stop that kind of chaos, and who would benefit from it? Only the military. And who controls the military?"

"The commander in chief," Wen said. "The president."

"And Snyder is most likely the next president."

"Fear," the Astronaut began, "is the problem. I have analyzed what Spraggins sent me. I have put it through SEER, along with inputs from all the latest news and social media posts. The Overwhelm could happen as soon as tomorrow. My independent analysis concurs."

"How do we stop it?" Wen asked.

"Only one way," Spraggins said. "As the philosopher

Aristotle once said, 'He who has overcome his fears will truly be free.'"

"Forgive me," Chase said, "but the words of dead journalists and dead philosophers will not help us."

"That's right," Wen agreed. "Tell me who to arrest, who to shoot."

"Fear is what fuels the Remies' power grabs," Spraggins said. "They all use it. Now it's out of their control. Soon it will be totally out of *anyone's* control. Look at what happened this morning. Your Terminators shot out the skylights of the subway station in public in broad daylight, yet there is no mention of a gun battle. All the witnesses to the events were arrested. If they don't agree that they didn't see what they thought they saw, they will disappear, or be labeled whack jobs. They'll be institutionalized or killed if all else fails, allegedly dying of natural causes or sad sudden accidents. I can give you lists of tens of thousands of people who have been killed in America for knowing too much, seeing something they shouldn't have. It's all done neatly, carefully."

"There are now fifty-one Remies, but the three most dangerous are Tane, Blanc, and Snyder," the Astronaut said. "Tane and Blanc's goal is to beat the other Remies for total control. They think they can do it with chaos and fear, but they don't understand about the fear index."

"If they did," Spraggins added, "they wouldn't care about the risks. They would use that, too. Their ambitions know no limits."

"What about Snyder?" Chase asked. "The flash drive contains his plans to take the White House in two months."

"Mayor Warren Snyder is not just a rich man," the Astronaut said, "he is a king Remie, and he plans to win the CapWar and cement all his power by becoming the first

Remie president. Imagine if the next president isn't a puppet like the last few. Imagine if he's the secret Remie. The richest, dirtiest, most powerful one of them all."

"Regardless," Spraggins said, "we are one or two big stories away from being unable to turn back. Two stories from the Remies going too far, pushing too hard, and unhinging this fragile society . . . two more fear-ridden stories, and the house of cards they have built, the one in which we all dwell, will fall and crush us all. The Overwhelm."

Chapter Thirty-Seven

NEW YORK CITY

Sunday - 8:47 pm - Eastern time

The energy was electric as New York City Mayor Warren Snyder took the stage at Yankee Stadium with only seventy-six days left until the election. The sun had set over the city, casting a warm orange glow over the bustling streets of New York, but inside the stadium, it was as bright as day, with more than fifty-thousand enthusiastic supporters packed into every seat, waving signs and cheering as they waited for their candidate to take the stage.

As the lights came up and the music began to blare, the crowd erupted. Snyder emerged from behind the curtain, his eyes scanning the sea of faces before him. He strode confidently onto the podium, a practiced look of destiny in his eyes as he gazed out at the crowd.

He began to speak, his voice ringing out over the stadium like a clarion call. "My friends, we have a fight on our hands. Only seventy-six days remain until the election, and the stakes couldn't be higher."

The crowd cheered, their voices echoing off the walls of the stadium. Snyder continued, his voice taking on a passionate tone.

"I know what you want. You want a leader who will fight for the little guy, who will stand up to the politicians and the big corporations. You want a president who will return America to the bountiful land of opportunity it was in the last century."

The crowd surged into a frenzy, their cheers and applause ringing out like a thunderclap. Snyder's eyes sparkled as he gazed at his fervent supporters. He knew he had them in the palm of his hand.

"And that's what I promise to do. I will fight for you. I will fight for the working people who have been forgotten by this broken system. I will fight for the small business owners who have been crushed by taxes and regulations. I will fight for the millions of Americans who have been left behind by the political elite."

The crowd was on its feet now, cheering and clapping and chanting Snyder's name. He raised his arms, basking in the adoration of the people, and in that moment, he felt truly unstoppable.

"So I ask you, my friends, to join me in this fight. Together, we can win this election and transform America into a glory land. But we must act now, with only seventy-six days left. The future of our country depends on it."

The crowd worked into a final burst of applause, and Snyder stepped back from the lectern.

"Nothing can stop us!"

Mayor Snyder climbed into the back of the limousine, taking a deep breath as he settled into his seat. His campaign manager, Kellerman, was already there, pouring over notes on his tablet.

"Great speech, Warren," Kellerman said, looking up from his tablet. "You really hit it out of the park tonight." He laughed. "Pun intended."

"Thanks," the Mayor replied. "But that's not important. What about Aarons?"

"We've taken care of it." Kellerman showed the Mayor a photo of Aarons, his deputy chief of staff, laying in a pool of blood on the floor of the closed City Hall subway station.

"That's horrid!"

"Yeah."

"But it's not going to come back on me, right?"

"Taken care of," Kellerman repeated.

"Good." The Mayor glanced out the window. His motorcade had grown since he'd won the nomination; Secret Service protection, his own security force, the NYPD, and State Police. "We need to talk about the election."

Kellerman nodded.

"We're ahead in the polls, but Blanc, Tane, Miner—you know the list—they can hit us with a surprise anytime, right?"

"We've got everything covered," Kellerman said. "Voter suppression, disinformation campaigns, you name it. And we're stepping it up going into the home stretch."

"Stop with the baseball analogies."

"Sure thing, coach," Kellerman said, tapping on his tablet. "We've got a team working on the ballot machines. We'll make sure the results are in our favor."

The Mayor glanced at the screen separating them from the driver, a man who'd been with him since the beginning, a man he trusted . . . except he really didn't trust anyone. "This is risky business."

"Nothing we can't handle," Kellerman replied with a grin. "We've got the best tech team on the job, and if anyone gets suspicious, we'll blame it on the Russians or the Chinese. We'll make sure it doesn't lead back to us."

The Mayor nodded slowly. "And what about the other candidate?" He never said his name. "Are we worried about him?"

Kellerman shook his head. "Not really. Tane and Blanc are working hard, but they have their hands full with Chase Malone."

"So do we, apparently."

"Not after this morning."

As the limousine continued down the street, the two men discussed the finer details of the multiple schemes in play, their voices low and conspiratorial. This was Snyder's moment, his chance to seize complete power and shape the future of the country, and nothing, not even the rules of democracy, would stand in his way.

Kellerman leaned back in his seat. "If all else fails, our October surprise will guarantee your win. Such damaging information about your opponent will make him unelectable."

The Mayor's eyes lit up. "Still planning to leak it to the media five days before the election, when it's too late for him to do anything about it?"

"If necessary. Hopefully we won't have to bother," Kellerman said. "Wouldn't want to do anything unethical." He laughed.

Snyder only grunted. "You have a safe outlet?"

"The usual. There's plenty of evidence that your opponent has been taking bribes from foreign governments for years. We have a dossier, bank statements, and recordings of conversations. It's all legit." He laughed again. "Well, at least it all *looks* legit, and we have many experts lined up who will assure viewers it *is* legit."

"And the media?" the Mayor asked.

"We'll leak it out across the media that we don't own first. Keep it above board. They'll do the rest. Then our outlets will pick it up. Before you know it, everyone in the country will know about it. It's airtight. Your opponent won't be able to get a job at a fast-food joint once this stuff gets out."

The rest of the ride was spent discussing the Remies and how Snyder would use his position as president to dominate them. As they pulled up to the Mayor's mansion, Kellerman turned to him.

"We've got this in the bag, Warren. You're going to be the next President of the United States."

Chapter Thirty-Eight

ATLANTA, GEORGIA

Sunday - 8:54 pm - Eastern time

Tane stared at a monitor of Snyder and his opponent, a man backed by Blanc and Tane. "Screw Snyder!"

"We have to go now," Blanc said.

"I don't want to be anywhere *near* DC tonight."

"I know, but there are people we must see."

"They can come here."

Blanc stood silently, waiting for Tane to calm down.

"Screw. Snyder," he repeated emphatically.

"We will."

"Will we? He's outplaying us on every front. *He's* going to be the president."

"So what?" Tane sighed. "It doesn't change his power."

"You're wrong."

"We've had presidents before."

"He's planning something. Everything is different since Flash-burn. This post-Trump world is a twisted version of where we've always played. Snyder figured that out first. He has first mover's advantage."

"We'll take it from him."

"I want him dead."

"I *know*."

Tane scowled at Blanc. The truth was, he wanted him dead too, and Blanc knew that. He decided to change the subject. "I just want to check the studio before we go."

Back inside the control room, they sat in movie-theatre style recliners. "It was too big to erase," Tane said about the bridge incident. "We should have gone with the terrorist story and made Snyder look weak."

"He would have spun it, turned himself into a hero, a modern Churchill."

"Oh, not that routine again. Why do they always compare them to Churchill? The man fought Hitler, ran a whole country, while his cities were bombed to pieces."

"I think the story that a production company was filming a movie on the bridge worked well. It's quite likely, plus it's fun. People love Hollywood."

"It's incredible people continue to believe this stuff."

"They believe what we tell them to believe." Another monitor caught his attention. "What's going on there?"

"I don't know."

Drone footage showed a smoldering warehouse on the waterfront.

"Southern California."

Tane frowned. "We don't have anything there currently."

"No," Blanc agreed, making a call.

While waiting for an explanation, they alternated between the fire, the bridge stories, and prelim on the stories that would cover the events scheduled for later in the evening, when a lot more Terminators, and perhaps Chase and Wen themselves, would die.

"Long day," Blanc said.

"Aren't they all?" Tane opened a cold club soda. "People always think they'd like to run the world. They never imagine how damned difficult it is to actually do it."

Blanc smiled, rubbing the stress from the back of his neck. "A full time, stress-filled job, but the pay is excellent."

Tane looked at him and smiled, then repeated his favorite mantra. "We are big tech, therefore we are the smartest. We are big pharma, therefore we are science. We are big media, therefore we are the truth. We are big government, therefore we know best."

Washington, DC
Sunday - 9:49 pm - Eastern time

For years, Chase and Wen had been cultivating contacts to help them bring down the Remies, but Hale, a renowned scientist, was at the top of their list. Finally, tonight, they would get the critical information they needed about an imminent false flag event planned by the Remies.

As was their habit, they approached the bar early for the ten pm meeting. The rainy night had Wen on edge.

"Who's that?" she asked, motioning to a figure in a long raincoat darting out the door. The man nearly knocked Wen over as he pushed past them.

"That's Hale!"

"What spooked him?" Wen said as they took off after him. Hale got a head start when they got trapped behind a Metro bus.

The two of them ran through the busy city streets, dodging cars and pedestrians as they tried to keep up with the fleeing scientist. The rain was coming down in sheets, making it difficult to see and hear. Wen wondered who had been inside the bar to make Hale run.

The marble buildings became a blur of lights and shadows as they pursued what was now a distant silhouette through the rain-soaked streets.

"We're losing him!" Chase shouted, frustration evident in his voice.

"We can't," Wen replied, believing Hale would be killed if they didn't get to him first.

"How is he so fast?"

"Fear!"

Their breaths came in ragged gasps as they pushed on. The buildings and streets were slick with rain. Chase slipped going around a corner and collided with a no parking sign. Wen jumped a large pothole puddle while trying to keep sight of Hale's rapidly disappearing figure.

Chase almost laughed at himself. After all he'd been through that day, a signpost had taken him down. Scrambling to his feet, Chase heard footsteps pounding the pavement behind him. He pulled out his Glock, but kept running after Hale.

"There he is!" Wen shouted from up ahead. He saw her duck into an alley.

At the end, he found Hale huddled against a wall, his eyes darting, looking for another way out, Wen trying to calm him.

"Please, you have to help me," Hale said, his voice shaking. "They're after me."

"*Who*?" Wen asked.

"I don't know," Hale replied, his eyes moving between

them. "But they're after the information I have. They'll kill me if they find me."

Wen looked at Chase.

"Someone is back there," Chase said.

"We can protect you," Wen said, taking a step toward the street. "But you need to tell us what you know."

Hale hesitated, his eyes still wild with fear. Confused, Hale watched Wen walking away.

"No one is going to hurt you," Chase said, moving him behind a stack of pallets.

Finally, Hale nodded and began to speak, his voice barely above a whisper. "I've been working on a project for the government," he said, his words tumbling out in a rush. "But I discovered something that could be catastrophic. I was going to take the information to my superiors, but I found out they were in on it. That's why I agreed to meet with you."

Three men appeared at the opening to the alley.

Chapter Thirty-Nine

Wen, waiting in the shadows, unleashed on the three men, shooting them all before any got off a single shot. She dragged their bodies across the wet pavement and left them piled in the dark alley.

"Come on," she shouted, "let's get out of here!"

The rain poured relentlessly. They found a parking garage up the street that was dry, and they took the elevator to an upper level. "Wen likes the high ground," Chase told Hale.

Hale wanted to talk now, afraid if something happened to him, no one would stop the event. Wen and Chase listened intently, learning the details about the potential terror strike. They asked questions and pressed for more information.

"This false flag," Hale said. "It's a dirty bomb."

"I have a vague idea," Chase said. "It's like a mini nuke?"

"A dirty bomb is a mix of conventional explosives and

radioactive material. The explosion spreads radiation, contaminating everything in the blast radius," Wen said, recalling her MSS training. "The long-term effects can be even more devastating. People will suffer from radiation sickness, cancer, and other health problems for years to come."

"Good summary," Hale said.

Wen walked towards the open wall of the parking garage, her eyes scanning down into the dark, deserted streets, trying to pick up any movement or signs of danger. The rain eased, noises rising from below, a low murmur that sounded like voices. She tensed, her hand instinctively reaching for her weapon. She turned back to Hale and Chase, who were deep in conversation. "I think I heard something," she hissed. "I'm going to check it out."

Chase nodded, his eyes narrowing as he gazed out into the night.

The murmur grew louder as she approached the stairwell, and she could just make out the sound of footsteps. She crouched, trying to remain as low as possible.

Wen spun around and saw two figures emerging from the shadows of the opening, their faces obscured by the darkness. Her hand still tight around her MP7, she was about to fire, but as they got closer, she realized it was just two homeless men, huddled together under a makeshift shelter of plastic sheets, coming in from the storm. She frowned, her hand slowly lowering from her weapon.

"False alarm," she called out to Hale and Chase, who had stood up and were now watching her with concern. "Just a couple of homeless guys."

Chase nodded, a look of relief crossing his face.

"We need to keep our focus," he said, his voice serious.

"Figure out how to find that bomb before it's too late." He turned back to Hale, who was now sitting on the floor with his head in his hands. "Where is it going to be deployed? Can you give us any information that might help?"

Hale looked up, his eyes tired and haunted. "Wen gave you the basics," he said, his voice slow. "The material used in a dirty bomb is typically highly radioactive isotopes that emit gamma rays and other high-energy radiation. This poison can travel long distances and penetrate through most barriers, making it extremely dangerous. The explosive blast from the bomb will spread the radioactive cloud over a large area, contaminating everything in its path."

"How does that help?"

"The immediate effects will depend on the size of the explosion and the type of radioactive material used," Hale said quietly. "It's a terrifying thought. The damage it could cause is beyond comprehension. They aren't going to want to do this in an important city."

"What's that mean?"

"Not DC or New York, not LA or Chicago. We're talking about St. Louis, or Portland, or Tempe, something west of the Mississippi."

"That doesn't exactly narrow it down."

"Give it to your AI, it'll figure it out. And there are two other questions you should ask."

"What?"

"Who are they going to blame it on?" Hale looked at them as if his next words were the most important. "And what kind of panic will ensue if word gets out?"

"People will be afraid to leave their homes, the economy will take a massive hit, and the government would have a hard time controlling the situation."

"They'll impose more restrictions, maybe even martial law," Wen said.

"Back to Fear again," Chase said. "Just like Spraggins warned."

Chapter Forty

WASHINGTON, DC

Sunday - 11:14 pm - Eastern time

With Hale safely tucked away in a high-end hotel protected by half a dozen Terminators, Chase and Wen checked into a cheaper place a few blocks away, deciding it would be too risky to be in the same building. They would only be there for a few hours anyway. Chase and Wen still had another event to attend that night.

"Long day," Wen said to Chase. "You should get a little sleep. We don't have to leave until one-twenty."

"I slept on the flight from New York."

"That was what, a thirty minute nap?"

"When I have to be somewhere at two am, and it's going on midnight . . ."

She sighed, shook her head, then pointed to the television. "No coverage of the three men I killed on the street earlier."

"But the bridge was just a Hollywood production," he

said, talking about the earlier headlines. "It did *feel* like an action movie."

"How are they getting away with saying two news choppers collided?" Wen asked. "With no injuries!"

"Nothing on our plane crash at all, and the subway was some gang related violence."

"The raid in the California mansion was another Hollywood production, filming on location."

"They cover everything," Chase said. "And it must be true, because I saw it on TV."

"What are they going to say about the three Rogues dying at O'Hare?" Wen asked as they showed images of planes taking off.

"This is a breaking news update," the anchor said. "Police suspect that a serial killer, dubbed the "frequent flyer killer," is on the loose. So far, there have been three victims at Chicago's O'Hare airport, one in Omaha, and one in Indianapolis. Just last week, three more suspected victims were found at three different airports across the country, including JFK in New York, LAX in Los Angeles, and DFW in Dallas. Experts at the FBI now believe the cases are all linked.

"According to eyewitnesses, the killer is a middle-aged Caucasian male, approximately six feet tall, with a slim build and short brown hair. He was wearing a blue sports jacket, and is known to carry a plastic hunting knife as his weapon of choice.

"Police are urging anyone who may have seen this man or has any information about his whereabouts to come forward immediately. They are warning the public to be extra vigilant when traveling alone, and to report any suspicious activity or behavior. However, they stress that flying is still safe.

"This is a developing story, and we will bring you more updates as they become available. Stay tuned to this network for the latest information on the frequent flyer killer."

"Can you believe these lies?" Chase said.

"They've completely changed it, too," Wen said.

"And I like how they assure the public it's *still safe to fly*," Chase mimicked.

"No one will believe that."

Inflight above Virginia
Monday - 10:13 am - Eastern time

The Surgeon appeared onscreen as Tane and Blanc sat on the corporate jet flying them to Washington. "What is it?" Tane asked, annoyed to be interrupted on the flight while he was trying to read Ernest Dempsey's book.

Blanc scowled at Tane. He was excited to hear about their latest efforts to destroy Chase Malone. Fortunately, the two men had slept before the flight. Neither liked sleeping on planes.

The Surgeon seemed even more gaunt than usual; something in how the magenta and blue light cast from all the computer monitors played on his nerdy face, or how the crazed mane of hair framed it.

"Wonderful news," he said, his Eastern European accent making it sound like *vondeeful*. "I have been successful in the replacements."

"What's that?" Tane asked, thinking the Surgeon said something about red placemats.

"The Killtrons," he replied, a little impatiently. "I have

created the new controllers to switch into the AI bots. It will be a circus for the Terminators, and not the good kind with clowns."

Tane looked at Blanc as if hoping for a translation. Blanc ignored him and asked the Surgeon about the timeline for using their new advantage.

"It is going to happen when they attack a Fed facility a few hours from now. Then we get in, and by the end of the day Monday, we'll have a party, I think."

"How effective?"

"Depends, depends." The Surgeon turned away from the camera and worked a keyboard, humming Wagner for a moment.

Tane rolled his eyes.

Finally, he returned. "I think we get at least one third of the Terminators. This could be three to four hundred. Depends, depends. Maybe we'll get lucky."

"But either way, we'll wind up with the Killtrons, correct?"

"Oh yes, that deed will be done. And trucks on the way will pick them up, put them on a plane, and bring them to me."

"It is a brilliant plan," Blanc said. "Implanting a Killtron while they attack us."

"Yes, yes, thank you. It will infect the other bots and reveal their whereabouts. All will be successful once we place the new controllers. Now, the circus tomorrow, and then we'll know just how big the party is."

Tane shook his head and went back to his book.

Blanc couldn't help but smile.

After the call ended. Blanc told Tane, "This will be the turning point. You shouldn't be so callous about it. After the

Surgeon's circus tomorrow, Chase Malone will be irreparably harmed."

"I am not callous. You mistake my impatience for indifference. This should have already been done. Chase Malone is wasting my time."

Chapter Forty-One

CHANTILLY, VIRGINIA

Monday - 1:57 am - Eastern time

What appeared to be an ordinary office park from the air, complete with a few dozen vehicles parked in the lots, seemed to be a securely fenced and gated federal government facility from the ground. What was thought to be an adjunct to a data processing unit of the Social Security Administration was actually one of the best kept secrets in the United States: a Federal Reserve storage facility that "didn't officially exist", known to the few who were aware of it simply as "The Vaults."

Chase and Wen had learned of its existence from the same informant who had told them of the seventh floor at the Fed headquarters in DC.

Diego, one of the few who'd survived the mansion raid with Weston, called Chase and let him know he was going in. At the same time strikes were occurring at Fed Banks in San Francisco, Philadelphia, New York, Cleveland, Chicago, Denver, Dallas, and Atlanta.

The muscled Mexican had been a cartel member since his teens, doing stuff he'd rather not recall, but had met Chase through Mars, and over the past couple of years, he'd become Chase's favorite Terminator. Diego also had the distinction, along with Weston, of being one of the big three that Blitz relied on most.

The idea was to coordinate the attacks on Federal Reserve facilities. Although the classified location in Chantilly was called *the vaults*, as Chase told Diego a few days earlier, "It doesn't hold money, it holds secrets—massive quantities of financial and economic data that, when released, will show a decades-long corruption scandal that will undermine the world economy and cause the complete collapse of the current fiat money system."

"What is it?" Diego had asked.

"Proof that the Remies, through the Fed, engineer the boom and bust cycles to gain control of more and more assets. They are stealing trillions!"

The warm night sky filled with distant thunder and lightning from a storm miles away. "No rain here yet," Diego mumbled, hoping it wouldn't come. He had studied the area, and knew it was completely protected by AI monitoring and a squad of forty-eight security personnel who were all former special ops soldiers.

A team of two hundred Terminators followed Diego through the dense forest surrounding the secret facility. The humid air hung thick with the smell of pine and earth. As they approached the perimeter fence, Diego signaled for the soldiers to slow down and get into position.

The fence was a formidable obstacle, surrounded by a

six-foot concrete wall and topped with razor wire. It was also electrified, making it impossible to cut through with conventional tools.

Diego gestured towards a nearby tree and his soldiers followed, the sound of their steps muffled by the soft earth. Diego motioned towards a soldier carrying a portable generator and gave the signal to power it up. A moment later, the fence was no longer electrified. Eight gaps had been blown at key locations.

Small groups funneled through the openings, moving silently towards the facility's entrance. The campus appeared deceptively ordinary, like any other modern office building, but they knew better. The high-security government facility, housing some of the world's most sensitive financial and economic data, would be a tough one to take.

Diego signaled for the Terminators to fan out, their movements quick and calculated. They moved with fluidity, taking up strategic positions.

Soon, someone was spotted, and guards began exchanging fire with Terminators.

Diego made it to the main building with an important Rogue named Harrison, who carried a portable satellite link. Since the amount of data onsite was way more than could be moved—somewhere between exabytes and zettabytes—his job was to hack the servers and feed it into the link. Diego had to keep him safe long enough to "drain the data."

By the time they hit the main server room, which was easily seven thousand square feet, filled with row after row of server racks, reports were coming in from outside that an ambush was underway. *It's the mansion all over again*, Diego thought. "Get the link up," he told Harrison. "We're out of time."

"Almost there." Harrison looked at the readings. "We're going to need a live link for seventeen minutes to get it all."

"That's a lot to ask."

Just then, the sound of gunfire erupted outside the server room, followed by screams and explosions. Diego drew his weapon and took cover behind a nearby server rack.

The Terminators in the corridor held off the guards and other armed personnel for six minutes before Diego had to venture out and clear the hall with machine-gun fire. The area was littered with bodies from both sides. Harrison huddled behind a server, his hands moving frantically over the keyboard as he worked to extract more data.

Diego could hear the clock ticking in his head as he fired round after round at the advancing security forces. Soon he was forced to retreat back into the server room, dodging and weaving between racks to avoid getting hit.

Chapter Forty-Two

A massive explosion violently shook the walls of the server room. Diego's ears were ringing as he stumbled to his feet, trying to assess the damage. Through chaos, smoke, and dust, he could barely make out Harrison's form.

"We have to go!" Diego yelled, grabbing the Rogue by the arm and pulling him towards the door. Diego downed five guards between them and an emergency door. The two of them sprinted down a hallway, dodging falling debris and avoiding gunfire as they made their way towards the main exit.

Harrison suddenly screamed and crashed to the ground. "I'm hit! Damn it, I'm hit!" Harrison held up a bloody hand after pressing it to his side.

"Can you walk?" Diego asked.

"I don't know."

"Try." Diego checked the time. "Is the link still connected?"

Harrison glanced at the box. "Yeah."

The man did surprisingly well, limping and jogging. Diego could hear the Terminators shouting commands and coordinating their retreat, but he knew that they were vastly outnumbered.

As they burst through the front doors of the facility, the entire area was swarming with security personnel and at least a hundred special ops soldiers. Harrison collapsed.

"I'm done," Harrison said, blood soaking his side.

"No you're not," Diego said, pulling him up at the same time he shot two soldiers, directing an evacuation plan into his comms.

With Harrison slung over his shoulder and the portable satellite link tucked under his arm, Diego charged towards the fence, firing his weapon wildly to clear a path.

Bullets whizzed past his head, but he kept moving, adrenaline pumping through his veins as he fought to keep them alive. A car exploded in a shower of sparks as they passed, and Diego barely had time to dive for cover before the entire area erupted in flames. He checked the time and knew the link needed six more minutes.

He could hear Harrison moaning in pain beside him, and knew he was badly injured. But he also knew that they had to keep moving, to find a way out of this hellhole and back to safety.

With the vibrations of explosions and the heat of the inferno at his back, Diego pulled himself up and ran towards the woods, determined to make it out alive.

Following his GPS, he made it to the car hidden in the underbrush, the young driver waiting for them fresh and ready. "Get us to the clinic," he told the driver, meaning a nearby warehouse with a waiting surgical team, then he noted the time. Forty-one seconds ticked down before they turned onto the main road near Dulles Airport. "The data is safe," he said to Harrison. "We got the bastards."

But Harrison was already dead.

Chapter Forty-Three

WASHINGTON, DC

Monday - 1:58 am - Eastern time

The Federal Reserve headquarters was as silent as the night sky. The rain fell only as a light mist, the bulk of the storm moving off to the west. Wen and her team of Terminators stood ready to breach the building and obtain the "origin" files that were locked away in a secret room somewhere under the mammoth H-shaped building.

"If it's true," Chase began as they waited for the signal to go, "those files could help us destroy the Remies once and for all."

The first wave of Terminators approached the walls, scaling them with ease, their black tactical gear blending seamlessly into the darkness. The fortress-like Federal Reserve Building, completed in 1937, had not been built to withstand real attacks. The Terminators broke windows at fourteen locations around the exterior. As they began entering, a barrage of gunfire blasted through the night air.

The Terminators were under attack from a unit of

Shadow Ops that had been waiting to stop them. "We're under fire, people! Move!" Wen yelled into her comms.

The Terminators moved quickly, using the cover of darkness to swarm the enemy. They fought their way through the Shadow Ops, initially taking out more than they lost. The two sides clashed in the hallways, exchanging fire and throwing explosives. Wen took cover behind a marble column, firing back at the enemy. Bullets ricocheted off the floor, spraying her face with chips of debris. She wiped the blood from her cheek with the back of her hand and kept firing.

Chase ran with the second wave of Terminators, but they quickly lost the advantage of invisibility when floodlights lit the area as if the sun had risen hours early.

The main offices of the Board of Governors, the public faces of the Fed, were inside the Marriner S. Eccles Federal Reserve Board Building. Although officially listed as six stories, Chase and Wen knew from an informant that there was a hidden subterranean seventh floor, only a fraction of the size of the upper levels. This "chamber" held historical documents and concealed histories. *This* was the prize.

Wen led her team through the building like a World War II general clearing a town. "Cover me!" Wen shouted, securing one of the two main marble stairwells leading up to the two-story boardroom where the Fed set monetary policies. But Wen didn't care about the boardroom, she wanted to gain access to the lowest level and join with Chase's group.

Chase barely made it into the other end of the building when more than seventy Terminators were lost in the fighting. "We're going to have more than we can handle in a matter of minutes," Chase told Wen through the comms. "Expect a military invasion. We have to abort."

"Not yet," she replied. "I'm here." Wen planted a high-tech plastic explosive on what they determined to be the weakest wall of the fabled secret room. "Clear!" she shouted, before detonating the charge. The room filled with the sound of gunfire and explosions from above as Wen's team battled to secure the upper floors.

As the conflict raged, Chase's team snaked their way through and helped defend the area as Wen and several others scoured the room, quickly gathering the incriminating documents, files, and digital records.

"Shadow Ops closing in," Chase reported through her earpiece. "We can't hold them much longer."

"We need to move, now!" Wen yelled as she grabbed the last files, shoved them in her pack, and ran towards the exit.

"Constitution Ave and C Streets are blocked," Chase warned.

"What about 20th?" Wen asked.

"I'm just getting that . . . 20th and 21st are filled with police and other armed hostiles."

"Roof!" Wen shouted. "It's our last chance."

Wen and her team made a break for the roof, fighting off enemy fire as they ran. Hand to hand combat broke out as they fought their way through the building. Wen took down several Shadow Ops soldiers with well-placed punches and kicks. Finally, they reached the roof and a waiting helicopter. Chase arrived at nearly the same time. The two of them and several Terminators boarded the chopper, leaving the rest to fight their way out below.

"It's a real war," Wen said, devastated to be abandoning her team, so many Terminators . . .

Chase nodded as he and Wen strapped themselves into the seats and felt the helicopter lurch as the pilot took evasive maneuvers to avoid the incoming bullets. Gunfire and flares punctuated the area as they engaged in a deadly aerial battle. The helicopter weaved through the night sky, dodging ordinances.

Wen manned a heavy machine gun and began firing at the Shadow Ops, taking out several of them. Chase, meanwhile, gathered the files they had just obtained, and consolidated them into one large canvas case.

Just as they thought they had escaped, a rocket slammed into the tail of the helicopter, sending it spiraling. The pilot fought to regain control, but it was too late. They crashed onto the rooftop of the Kennedy Center, the helicopter exploding into a ball of flames.

Chase and Wen stumbled out of the wreckage, bruised and battered, but alive. They looked up to see another chopper circling, their weapons raised and ready to fire.

They ran across the roof, slick from mist and rain and broke into the building. Soon, they burst out the ground level and dashed, dodging searchlights from the several choppers now in the air, and made it into the neighboring Watergate complex.

"Ironic," Chase said as they hid in the thick shrubs and caught their breath. "On so many levels."

Wen ignored his humor and called for evac. Six minutes later a car slowed on New Hampshire Avenue and they jumped in. The Terminator driving headed back to their hotel. "What's the report on the other raid?" Chase asked the driver.

"Worse than this one," he said grimly. "We've lost hundreds of people tonight."

Chase closed his eyes. "They were expecting us."

Chapter Forty-Four

WASHINGTON, DC

Monday - 3:39 am - Eastern time

The two men, Brock and Duncan, sat at a corner booth in a crowded all-night diner in Columbia Heights, a tough section of DC about fifteen minutes from the Federal Reserve Headquarters. Their voices were low as they argued over their recent failure to stop the Terminators from breaching one of the most secure facilities in the capital. Brock, a tall, broad-shouldered man in his mid-forties, with buzzed salt-and-pepper hair, appeared to be ex-military. Twenty-four years he'd given to Uncle Sam. "Wasted time," he said, now out in the lucrative guns-for-hire private sector.

The shorter and slimmer Duncan seemed the opposite. With a receding hairline and a nervous energy about him, he looked more like a slippery carnival worker. Duncan's habit of constantly glancing over his shoulder, as if he expected someone to be listening in, or trouble to arrive at any moment, drove Brock crazy.

The din of the busy diner provided cover for their tense conversation, though Brock still leaned in close to Duncan, his brown eyes fixed on the other man's face. "How could you have let this happen?" Brock hissed, his voice tight. "We were supposed to stop Malone from getting any information, and instead they walked out with *everything*."

Duncan shifted uncomfortably in his seat, his eyes darting around the room. "I know, I know, but we didn't have enough notice. I mean, they hit *the Fed*. That's crazy."

"Suicide," Brock agreed. "But they did it."

"This is on Khan, not us. The clients should have seen this coming, should have taken steps, and warned him. I mean, Brock, we weren't even in place. They were on the grounds before we got there. What did they expect?"

"They expected us to do our job." His voice grew a bit too loud.

"It's Khan's fault we got there too late." Duncan's gaze went to the window, then to a noisy table by the door, then finally back to Brock. "Khan should have been here himself."

"Excuses," Brock spat. "We were paid to do a job, and we failed. Now the information they took could ruin everything."

Waitresses bustled back and forth, delivering steaming plates of food to the crowded tables. The smell of bacon and coffee wafted past, making Duncan's stomach rumble.

"Besides," Brock continued, "if Khan was here, you and I might be at the bottom of the Potomac by now. Khan always finds a fall guy for his screw-ups."

"We annihilated most of their force, their so-called *Terminators*," Duncan said, craning his neck to see over and past Brock. "My guy at the cleaning outfit tells me more than two hundred of Malone's men are dead."

His eyes narrowed to slits. "How many of ours are in the morgue?"

"Around a hundred."

Brock shook his head. "Khan doesn't put up with this kind of stuff." Now it was his turn to check the room. "He'll find us and kill us, man."

The walls of the lively diner, filled with the sounds of clattering plates, sizzling grills, and chattering patrons, suddenly felt much too close.

"We can fix it," Duncan said, his mouth dry. He gulped from his hot coffee and coughed, fondling a pocket for his cigarettes.

"Only one way to do that," Brock said, his voice low and urgent. "We need to get that information back. If it gets out, it will expose the client." They both knew what they shouldn't know. Months earlier, Brock and Duncan had learned the identity of the client. "It's corruption at the highest levels—the financial schemes, the politicians, the whole damned system!"

"It could bring them down."

"It's not *going* down. It's too big to fail, man. Don't you see it? Look at what happened tonight. Three hundred dead in the nation's capital, and there's not one peep on the news about it. If they can cover that kind of incident up, they're untouchable."

Duncan nodded, his eyes downcast. "I know. Somehow we've got to get it back from Malone, kill him, kill anyone who's seen it."

"They're already underground," Brock said, frustration in his voice. "We go to Khan and tell him we'll do whatever it takes."

Duncan's gaze flickered to the door of the diner, where

a group of people had just entered. "I think Khan's coming to us."

Brock followed Duncan's gaze and nodded. "You're right. But we're cool. I know a couple of them. They aren't here to kill us. It's a crew. He's giving us another assignment."

"Another chance."

One of the men who'd just entered caught Brock's eyes and motioned for him to come outside.

"Yeah, but whatever it is, if we screw up, we're dead."

"Let's disappear," Duncan said. "While we still can."

"Too risky."

His eyes went wide. "Risky? We're swimmin' in risk, totally knee deep in it."

"Try your luck out there, then. See if you can escape the reach of Khan. I'm taking the second chance."

"You know at this point Khan's just going to set us up."

"Maybe." Brock signaled to the waitress for the check, his eyes never leaving the other man's face. "We'll continue this conversation elsewhere."

The two men stood up from the booth, their argument temporarily put on hold. But as they made their way through the busy diner and out onto the deserted street, the tension between them was palpable.

They found the four other men half a block down, standing around an SUV, a couple of them smoking cigarettes. Brock and Duncan exchanged intros with them.

"What's the job?" Brock asked.

"This guy, his wife, and two kids," a greasy man replied. "They want a murder/suicide. Or at least a single death."

"Who's the guy?" Duncan asked.

"Senator Wentworth."

"Wentworth?" Brock shook his head, thinking he'd seen a report that Wentworth was the most honest man in the US Senate. "Makes sense."

Chapter Forty-Five

MCLEAN, VIRGINIA

Monday - 4:54 am - Eastern time

As Brock hid behind a tree in the front yard of the senator's McLean home, he questioned everything he'd said and done in the previous twelve hours, and everything before that which had brought him to this point.

He checked his watch: 4:54 am. The greasy man had told him that Wentworth was always eager to be the first senator to arrive at the Capitol.

Brock could hear the sound of an approaching vehicle and guessed correctly that it was the Senator's driver. A minute later, a dark sedan eased through the automatic security gate. As the car came to a stop, Brock stepped out from behind the tree and pointed his gun at the driver.

"Don't make a sound, and step out of the car" he ordered, as the driver looked at him with wide eyes.

The driver obeyed, raising his hands in surrender and moving away from the vehicle. Brock motioned for him to lie down on the driveway, then quickly zip-tied his wrists behind his back, shoved a cloth gag in his mouth, and deposited him on the floor of the backseat.

Hearing a door shut, he turned and saw the Senator coming down the front steps of the house.

"Good morning, Senator," Brock said, his voice shaking slightly. "I have a message for you."

The senator froze, his eyes filling with fear as he saw the gun in Brock's hand. "What is it?" he asked, his voice trembling.

Brock didn't respond, but instead raised the gun and fired. The senator fell to the ground, his body convulsing in pain.

The sound of the gunshot echoed through the quiet suburban street. The senator's wife appeared in the doorway, her face contorting in horror as she saw her husband lying on the ground. "Oh my god!" she screamed, running towards him.

Suddenly, the sound of approaching footsteps rose from the quiet street. Brock knew he had to act fast. He spotted several security guards running towards him, their guns drawn.

As the sun began to rise, Brock made his escape, running through the now open gate. He noticed the greasy man watching from across the street. Brock gave him a nod, and the man nodded back, confirming that the job was done.

He made it back to his car and drove away, feeling as if he had just awoken from a nightmare. Forty minutes later, he was on 95 South near Fredericksburg, Virginia. When his cell rang, it was Khan.

"You did well," Khan said, his voice cold and calculating. "Now disappear for a while until the heat dies down. We'll be in touch soon."

Brock assured him he would keep heading south. "I've got a buddy in Florida."

"Good plan," Khan said. "Enjoy the sunshine."

After the call, he pulled into a rest area and leaned back in his seat, trying to make sense of it, to sort out the violence from the purpose, the fear from the truth. "Damn, damn, *damnit,*" he said, hitting the steering wheel, wondering how his life had gotten so out of control. He was counting on a lot of questionable people to do things they might not do.

His phone rang again. "Duncan," Brock said, answering it, "where are you?"

"Where are *you?*" Duncan replied, his voice agitated.

"Where I'm supposed to be."

"How do you know? They're shadowing me. I can't shake them."

"Who?"

"*Them!*"

"Didn't Khan give you another assignment?"

"Nah, nothing. I waited 'round after you jetted."

"I didn't jet, they made me—"

"Whatever. They're going to do me, man."

"Where are you?" Brock looked down the street. "I'll come get you."

"What? *No!*"

"Come on, Dunc, I'll get you. We'll work this out. We'll talk to Khan."

"Khan's blaming *me*. Handing me up to Tane. I'm the fall guy. Khan always has a fall guy."

"It's not you. It doesn't have to be. I'll come get you."

"Oh man, they're here—*No!*"

Brock heard the gunshot and knew Duncan was gone.

If it wasn't for the Senator hit, I'd be dead now, he thought. *But what if I'm just a patsy for Khan?*

Chapter Forty-Six

Brock sat in his car. The busy rest stop on 95 South was a good place to be invisible for a minute. His head was swirling as he tried to make sense of what had just happened. The Federal Reserve raid, the Senator, Duncan . . . he really did have to disappear.

He turned on the radio, looking for news of Wentworth.

An NPR bulletin was underway. "Breaking news out of Virginia this morning," the anchor reported. "We have just learned that Senator Lowell Wentworth has been assassinated. The popular US Senator from Massachusetts has been shot and killed outside his home in McLean, Virginia as he was leaving to head to the US Capitol. His driver and several security men were injured as well."

Brock's hands trembled as he realized the magnitude of what he had just done. He couldn't believe that he was caught up in the story he was listening to on the radio, and he wondered what would happen next.

The news report continued. "The FBI, US Capitol Police, and Virginia State Police are all involved in searching for the assailant. It is unclear at this time who is responsible for this heinous act, but authorities are urging anyone with information to come forward immediately."

In the studio, a reporter spoke to a neighbor who'd heard the gunshots. "Can you tell us what you saw and heard this morning?" the reporter asked.

"Well, I was up early and heard gunshots, but I didn't see what happened," the neighbor recounted, still in shock. "I live in a really good neighborhood, and we never have any trouble around here. It was terrifying to hear something like that. I wanted to run outside, but I didn't want to get shot. I'm so sorry about what happened to the senator. He was a really good man."

"This puts in jeopardy the Federal Reserve Audit Act," the reporter added, then went on to explain the special election process that would follow Senator Wentworth's death. "According to the Massachusetts Acts of 2004, a special election must be held within 145 days after a senate seat has been vacated for any reason. The rule eliminated the more typical form of transition in which a state's Governor names a replacement."

"Why was the law changed?" the anchor asked the reporter.

"It's an interesting bit of history. Back in 2004, then Senator John Kerry was running for President. At the time, the Massachusetts Governor was Republican Mitt Romney, meaning he could have replaced Democrat Kerry with a Republican. The special election ensures that the people of Massachusetts have a say in who represents them in the Senate."

Brock knew the news was now on every network across the country. *Probably even an international story*, he thought.

"More on this as events develop," the anchor said. "The

country is in shock as they learn about the assassination of one of their most beloved senators. The White House has issued a statement—"

Brock felt sick and shut off the radio.

What happens next? Am I about to get caught?

Sirens in the distance added to his panic. He'd told Khan he was heading to Florida. However, he had no intention of going to the sunshine state. Instead, Brock would get cleaned up at a hotel in the next town, make a few untraceable phone calls, change his appearance, and then head back to DC for some unfinished business.

Chapter Forty-Seven

WASHINGTON, DC

Monday - 5:59 am - Eastern time

Chase and Wen sat in the back of the Destino, their rolling command center. Blitz had arranged for the vehicle to be delivered overnight. The super rig looked like an ordinary eighteen-wheeler. However, it was anything but ordinary. Its name, Spanish for destiny, had been inspired by the inevitable showdown with the Remies. Exterior cameras monitored 360 degrees around and above the truck around the clock. The trailer was outfitted with state-of-the-art satellite communications, a supercomputer, multiple monitors, and a full broadcasting facility.

They watched the news of the Senator's death, not surprised. "I hope it was fast for him," Chase said.

"Such a nightmare for his family to deal with."

"All because the Remies knew he was going to vote for a full audit of the Fed."

"A full audit would mean the end of the Fed."

"That's why they ordered the hit."

She nodded, wondering how close the Vintons were. Wen glanced back at the Destino's full armory. It was loaded with weapons—machine guns including numerous H&K MP7s, MP5s, Thales EF88s, Tavor TAR21s, FN P90s, FN Scars, VHS-2 Hellions, Kalashnikov AK 12s, a dozen AT4 rocket launchers, grenades, a Vulcan mini-gun, a sizable assortment of pistols, including Faxon FX19 Hell Fire, Glock 19 and 21s, Beretta M9 A4 / M9 Centurion A4, Sig Sauer M17s, several sniper rifles such as the M110 SASS, Ruger Rim fire 22LR, Tikka T3X TAC AL 6.5 Creedmoor 24, a box of high-end tasers, various combat knives, and even some throwing stars. "We're ready for the next battle," she said.

"But not ready to finish the war," Chase said. "The Terminators are still a small force compared to everything else we're up against."

"That's why the Rogues will ultimately be the way we bring down the Remies."

The truck rolled through some slow traffic. A team of three operatives were onboard to drive the Destino in eight-hour rotations. Since the cab had two sleeping compartments, and the small, private bedroom in the trailer accommodated Chase and Wen, they could now drive twenty-four hours a day. The three drivers were also combat vets, which added to their protection.

"We may need to bail before we get there," Wen said. Two motorcycles were stowed in the rear. Inflatable combat-ready rafts and a few other escape tricks were onboard as well.

"That's why the Remies are going hard on the Rogues," Chase said.

"I wonder if those three would have died in one of the

O'Hare's parking lots if Mars hadn't sent them on the flights."

"No doubt," Chase said.

"So the Remies won that round."

"It's worse than that," Chase said. "They got the Fear Meter moving from all the fear that came out of it."

"Now we've got an airport serial killer on the loose, killing with undetectable polymer hunting knives, and everyone else is on the run. I don't know how they found Mars. The Astronaut is working on it, but it's probably like all the other times. We'll never know."

"Look at this," Chase said.

"Good morning, this is Eric Conway, bringing you breaking news about a developing story that has sent shockwaves throughout the world. An asteroid estimated to be half the size of the one that wiped out the dinosaurs sixty-five million years ago has been detected on a collision course with Earth. The asteroid is projected to hit our planet in approximately nine months.

"NASA and other scientific organizations have been working around the clock to track and analyze the asteroid since its discovery four days ago. According to Dr. Nelsman, a planetary scientist at NASA, the object is approximately three point nine miles in diameter, and moving at a speed of roughly four thousand miles per hour.

"In an exclusive interview with Dr. Nelsman, he stated, 'This is a dire situation. The impact of something this size would be catastrophic for life on Earth. The damage from the impact and subsequent earthquakes and tsunamis could be widespread and long-lasting.'

"The United Nations has called for an emergency meeting of world leaders to discuss a coordinated response to the threat posed by the asteroid. Meanwhile, private companies and international space agencies are working on plans to deflect or destroy the asteroid before it reaches Earth.

"Dr. Nelsman also said, 'There are a few potential options for deflecting this thing, including using a powerful spacecraft to collide with it, or using a nuclear explosion to alter its trajectory. However, each of these alternatives bring their own challenges and risks, so we need to weigh the options carefully.'

"It is important to note that the exact date and location of the impact is still uncertain. NASA and other scientific organizations are working to improve the accuracy of their projections, but as Dr. Nelsman stated, 'In a situation like this, there are always uncertainties and variables that can affect the outcome. We are doing everything we can to minimize the danger and prepare for the worst-case scenario.'"

Chase got Spraggins on the phone. "Is this *real?*"

"Space is very big. Objects appear all the time with little notice," Spraggins said. "However, I would bet your fortune that it is not."

"Then they're really messing with people."

"They're making a huge play. Imagine the fear they just introduced."

"What's the Meter doing?"

"Seven point eight."

"It's moved more than a full point!"

"And it will keep going. Each day, it will increase. They may have finally sent us to the tipping point."

"And you still think they don't know how much is at risk?"

"No, now I think they must know, and that makes everything even worse because then they aren't just greedy, they're crazy!"

Chapter Forty-Eight

WASHINGTON, DC

Monday - 7:53 am - Eastern time.

Tane and Blanc were grumpy, tired, and hungry. They were sitting around a small table on the rooftop terrace of Tane's Georgetown mansion, eating a late breakfast. They'd both rather be at Blanc's Great Falls, Virginia estate, but knew it would be better to be close to the action today. They might need to go to the White House, or need to run over to the FBI, or possibly to Langley, but it was too soon to tell. They might need to do a great many things.

"The past twenty-four hours have been terribly exhausting," Tane said. "Chase Malone couldn't have slept much."

"I don't care if he's slept."

"Yes, but it's nice that he hasn't."

"He's interfering with our plans, our business, and *my* sleep."

"Speak of the devil," Blanc said. "Khan is online."

"The Surgeon has found them," Khan reported across

the encrypted video link, his hardened face appearing on Tane's laptop.

Blanc shivered at the sight of Khan's cold gray eyes, happy he wasn't there in person.

"Chase and Wen?" Tane said hopefully.

"No. If we had that, they'd already be dead, but close. We know where their kid is, and the grandmother."

"We have their location for sure?"

"Affirmative."

"Do it," Tane said. "Kill them both immediately."

"And get video. Torture them," Blanc said. "Make it gruesome and painful. I want Chase Malone and that Chinese wench to squirm when they watch their loved ones dying brutal deaths."

Khan flitted his fingers as if playing a piano. "I can kill that boy and the old woman in a way that will make Chase and Wen vomit."

"All the better," Blanc said. "They've caused us so much difficulty, I'd like you to deliver the boy's head in a box."

"Easy enough," Khan said. "Give me a couple of hours to get my men in there and I'll make sure it's a blood bath."

Northern California
Monday - 8:47 am - Pacific time (11:47 pm Eastern)

Zu Mu turned the dark organic earth in her hands, working it in the ancient way her grandmother had taught her, and her grandmother's grandmother before her. Generations of Chinese women who had grown food for their families, and for their villages, remained alive in the old woman's fingers.

For years, she'd shown Tu how to plant and grow food,

the same as she had with her granddaughter, Wen, when she had been a girl. Zu Mu had taught them both much about herbs, natural healing, and staying healthy through Chinese medicine.

Tu loved gardening. It grounded his wandering intellect. He was no ordinary young teenager. His mind possessed special abilities, particularly in the fields of mathematics, science, physics, and logic, way beyond those of even the brightest men in those fields. She handed him some seeds.

"Why is it that the seeds you plant consistently do better than the ones I plant?" he asked. Tu always had questions. He never seemed to run out of them. Yet as he grew older, Zu Mu found he had more answers, while she asked more of the questions.

"How do you know yours do not do better than mine?" she asked.

"Because I memorize them all. Where you put in, where I do."

She smiled, not doubting him at all. Sad that his cells had been manipulated before his birth to give him all these advantages. A gift, yet a curse, since it had stolen any sense of normalcy from him. He had not had a typical childhood, although she'd tried hard to give him as much as she could of the ordinary and average.

It wasn't just his cells in mind that made him different, though. His adoptive parents, Chase and Wen, were both hunted and hunters in an international espionage war with intrigue and deadly consequences. Tu had many mental scars from having experienced a stream of dramatic episodes with them over the years, starting with when they'd rescued him from the experimental facility where he been held since his birth in China.

Zu Mu worried about the tall, lanky boy. The shadow

wars that Chase and Wen were involved in had expanded and become far more dangerous of late. *I am an old lady,* she thought. *What will happen when I am gone if Chase and Wen are killed? What will happen to our sweet Tu?*

Chase had provided numerous agents from the advanced security force known as Sepios to guard them around the clock, but that didn't mean they were safe. Even with all Chase's money, Zu Mu had learned that safety was perhaps the most difficult commodity to buy.

"This one," she said, giving him what she thought was the best of the seeds. Zu mu had learned long ago to notice the differences. "It isn't always size or even the healthy appearance of the seed," she told him for the hundredth time. "More often it's the grains and lines. They tell a story."

"I know. You always tell me this, but I still don't see the story."

"That's because you're only looking for patterns. Not everything is about patterns and numbers. You have to feel and look at the seed, and most important, you need to *wait* . . . it will always show you its story."

He studied the seed for a while. "I don't know," he said, "but maybe it tells me it wants to grow very tall and give many tomatoes."

Zu Mu laughed. "It will tell you more than that."

"Next time," he said. "Right now, it wants to go in the ground with its friends." He dropped it in the little hole.

"Which petal did you use?"

"Daylily."

She smiled. "That's right." Zu Mu had taught him the little-known ancient technique of including a single flower petal in with the seed. "It gives strength and a bit of sunlight to the seed when it is lonely in the cold, dark ground," she told him.

"I know," he said. "The trick is knowing which seed wants which petal."

"Yes, that is the magic."

"You know magic?"

She smiled again, but said nothing.

Zu Mu never heard the bullet.

Chapter Forty-Nine

Gunfire, a sound Tu knew too well, far better than anyone his age should ever know, shattered the idyllic setting. He could not identify the make of guns based on their sound like Wen could, but he knew they were submachine guns, and a lot of them. Tu also knew not to scream, not to panic. He'd been shot at before.

Moments prior, he'd been talking to Zu Mu, but had stopped planting to take a load to the compost bin. The four-sided structure, made of repurposed pine pallets loaded with organic cuttings, old food, and straw, had provided him with some cover from the onslaught. That chore had momentarily saved his life. From the bin, he also had a view.

He watched, terrified, as several of his security men dropped to the ground. A few of the attackers went down as well. Doing the quick math in his head, Tu already knew the good guys were going to lose this battle.

There are too many attackers. He asked himself the same

question Chase and Wen always wrestled with. *How did they find us?*

There was not much he could do to help. He peered around the side of the pallet, wondering where Zu Mu had taken cover.

He saw her laying on the ground face down.

She is smart, he told himself, pushing down the sudden spike of panic. *She's pretending to be dead so they will leave her alone. They will let her be since she is just an old lady.*

He knew why they were there. The Chinese MSS had been trying for years to erase proof of the existence of the scandalous and illegal program that had borne him, and he was the only remaining evidence. But these attackers were not Chinese, which meant they were here to kidnap or kill him as a way of getting to Chase and Wen. Leverage or revenge, but which one meant whether he would live or die today.

These men will kidnap me to force Chase and Wen to do something, or they will kill me in retaliation for something they have already done. It hadn't yet occurred to him that the Chinese might have hired an outfit of American bounty hunters.

The Sepios put up a good fight, but the struggle was not going to end well for Tu. One of the Sepios, a man named Frankie, who had always been one of Tu's favorites, ran toward the compost bin. Tu had formed friendships with all of them. He'd already seen Elaine and Aiden were dead, and he knew that it was Frankie coming to save him. Frankie and Tu had often played cards when Frankie was off duty, even a few times while he was on duty. Tu almost always won except when he pretended to lose. He tried not to count the cards, but he just couldn't help it.

"Tu, are you hit?" Frankie asked as he slid down next to the bin like a ballplayer going into home plate.

"No, I'm okay. What about you?" Tu responded breathlessly.

"Solid."

Tu could see a bullet wound on Frankie's left shoulder. *But he'll be okay.*

"I gotta tell you the truth," Frankie said. "This is a tough one. Not sure—"

"I hit my panic alarm," Tu said. The device he always carried meant reinforcements would be on the way soon, but probably not soon enough.

"Good man," Frankie said. "Help will be here any minute." He suddenly fired his weapon at a new line of attackers moving across the yard. Three of them stumbled, bleeding, dying on the ground.

Tu, both repulsed and impressed, watched the bullets rip open and expose the insides of one of the intruders. It was disgusting to see them gush blood, but he would happily watch it all day.

"I don't think anybody saw you run here," Frankie told Tu, ducking back down. "We've got to get the evac plan, you know?"

Tu nodded, but then realized since Frankie was on the other side of the bin, Frankie couldn't see him. "Yeah."

"It's no good going to the house, and no good to run for those trees. You'd never make either one."

"Then what do we do?" Tu asked, worried he was about to die.

"I've got one good idea," Frankie said. "Banana burial."

"What?"

"In the compost. It's dirty, it smells."

"Bury me in the compost . . . " Tu said, thinking it over. "And they'll never look there."

"Exactly."

Chapter Fifty

Tu immediately crawled into the compost bin and began shoveling at the food scraps and leaves, quickly making a small place to sit. He then frantically burrowed under more debris and pulled the pile on top of himself until he was completely concealed.

Frankie added more on top of him. "You'll be okay, just don't move."

"Right," Tu said.

"Make yourself a little opening for breathing. Don't know how long you'll be in there."

"Okay, I'm good," Tu said. "Go kill them all."

Though the smell of decaying food and waste made him gag, Tu managed to calm himself as he listened to Frankie jogging away. Worms crawled on his bare legs, but the sound of continuing gunfire worried him more. The weight of the dirt pressing against him made breathing difficult.

Better than a grave, he thought, shifting to peek between the slits of the pallet boards, watching the Sepios and attackers continue their battle. *Good, nobody's bothering Zu Mu. She's doing a good job of staying still.*

From his vantage point, Tu could just see one of her legs. The gap in the slats only allowed a narrow view of bits and pieces of the battle. Mostly, it was the constant sound of gunfire, shouts, and small explosions that gave him a gauge of the continuing danger. The action raged for another full seven minutes before, finally, an eerie silence took hold.

It could be just a lull in the fighting, or a trick to make me come out.

He fought that urge for what seemed like an hour, though probably lasted only four minutes. Tu began to stir, carefully at first, then all at once. He emerged from the dirt, but stayed inside the bin for another minute while he surveyed the area. Now able to see the entire field, he realized there was still a man alive. He also noticed a Sepio had died not far from the bin. It was a guy named Brian, who always shared his gum with Tu. Tu took Brian's weapon, recognizing it as Wen's favorite, an MP7. He crouched behind the bin and watched the attacker, then realized he was heading toward Zu Mu. Just then, another man appeared who Tu recognized as Frankie.

A quick exchange of gunfire left Frankie down and the attacker injured. The man tried to finish Frankie off, but his gun came up empty.

Tu knew this would be his only chance, and also that he shouldn't do it, but he took off, swallowing large amounts of fear.

The startled attacker spun, thinking another Sepio had shown up. Upon recognizing Tu, a smile crept over his face.

Tu stood less than seven feet away, aiming the MP7 at the man's chest, a distance Tu calculated was far enough that the man could not go for his weapon successfully, but close enough that Tu could not miss if he was forced to fire.

"Come on kid," the man began, maintaining eye contact with Tu. "You and I both know you aren't going to sho—"

Before he could finish, the man crumpled to the ground, his chest ripped open by several rounds fired at close range.

"Turns out you were wrong," Tu said.

Tu's eyes darted around to make sure there were no more enemies, then ran toward his grandmother.

"You can get up now, Zu Mu," he said. "You can wake up."

She didn't move.

"You can get up now. You can *get up now!*" he yelled, scared more would come any second, scared she might be dead. "They are all gone!" He jostled her. "You don't have to play dead anymore. It's safe now!" He looked around, confused. "Come on, please get up now. We need to go." His voice became more frantic. "*Please* get up." This time he turned her over, and he saw the blood. He cradled her head and heard her moan. "Yes, you are alive!"

"No," she said weakly. "I'm gone."

"No!"

"I love you," she breathed. "Always save the seeds." Her head dropped with her final breath.

"No . . . please come back," he sobbed, but knew she was gone.

Survival instinct took over. Tu had been drilled enough over the years that he knew seconds counted now. As he stood up, he realized Frankie was coughing.

"You're okay," Tu said, almost laughing with relief.

"Yeah, but I'm hurt pretty bad."

Tu could see the bloody wound on Frankie's abdomen.

Without hesitating, he pushed his hands onto Frankie's stomach to staunch the flow. He'd learned Chinese medicine from Zu Mu and combat first-aid and triage from Wen. He pressed and held until the blood stopped.

"Don't worry about me," Frankie said. "Go. Run. Get away from here."

"No. If I leave, you won't make it."

"I'm not going to make it anyway." He grimaced. "You know the evac routes, go!"

"No," Tu said, scared, but wanting to save somebody, even if it couldn't be his grandmother.

"I'm telling you." Frankie coughed. "I'm *ordering* you to get out of here. Everyone here was protecting you. Make their sacrifices count."

"No," Tu insisted. "You still owe me two dollars from our last poker game. I'm not leaving without payment."

"Take my wallet. You can have everything."

"No, we'll have to play a rematch."

"Take the money and run," he said, then sort of laughed, which turned into a bloody cough.

Finally Tu insisted he would leave if Frankie just stopped talking. "You need to save your strength." Tu didn't think he had much time left.

Frankie nodded.

A couple of minutes later, sitting there in a strained silence, grieving Zu mu, his hands soaked in blood, he heard a helicopter. He looked up, realizing he might yet die, and saw the Sepio logo on the bottom.

"Friendly," he said.

Seconds later, they were on the ground. A minute or two after that, he and Frankie were onboard. Medics had taken his place in tending to Frankie.

Chapter Fifty-One

WASHINGTON, DC

Monday - 12:20 pm - Eastern time.

Spraggins boarded the Destino. "Nice," he said, taking in the flashy command center. "It kind of looks like a bunker I have in Nevada."

Chase couldn't tell if it was a joke, but didn't doubt Spraggins had many advanced bunkers. "Thanks."

The three of them turned their attention to the monitors, expecting an update on the asteroid story, and instead were greeted with a breaking news bulletin about an entirely different story.

"We were asked not to run this story," the stuffy, Kendoll news anchor said gravely. "It is only after carefully weighing the public's right to know against the danger of inciting a panic and using our best journalistic integrity that we decided we *must* air this report."

The carefully quaffed blonde sitting at the slick silver desk next to him nodded thoughtfully. "That's right, Carl, and we want to remind all our viewers of the need to remain calm. There are many details we do not yet know, one of which is the exact location of this threat."

With that, they handed it over to a reporter standing in front of the Washington DC headquarters building of the Department of Homeland Security. The reporter, appearing serious and stressed, began spouting his narrative.

"Several senior intelligence officials have confirmed a credible threat exists that a radiological dispersal device, commonly known as a dirty bomb, will be detonated in a large American city within the next five days."

"Which city?" the anchor asked from the studio.

"Apparently they are still trying to obtain that information, or, as they say, *narrow the targets*. This is one of the primary reasons the administration asked our network and other news outlets to hold the story. They simply don't yet have enough information."

"Meaning they don't know where to evacuate."

"Correct, and the head of FEMA and DHS fear a mass-exodus of large urban areas will create chaos, something the terrorists are certainly seeking to cause. This is the reason we are told they did not want to publicize this threat, which they have been aware of since at least Saturday."

"Indeed. So tell us more about this weapon. What is it, what does it look like, where does it come from?"

"This is a radiological weapon, meaning it is *extremely* dangerous. Experts tell us these are created by combining radioactive materials and conventional explosives, with the intent to contaminate a large area. Make no mistake, the primary purpose of this dispersal device is against civilian populations."

"When you say a large area, just how large are we talking here?"

The reporter checked his notes. "It would depend on the size and type of the conventional explosives used, winds, and other factors, but the general danger zone would be a radius of up to several miles." The reporter stared into the camera, looking like a concerned parent. "Officials caution that we do not know where or when this will hit."

"However, they do consider this an *imminent* attack?"

"Sadly, they do, unless they can locate and stop the bombers."

"How likely is that? Do they have any leads?"

"As you can imagine, they are very tight-lipped, and have made no official statements. Privately, though, they are worried and frustrated."

"Of course. And where does something like this come from?"

"The conventional explosives are relatively easy to obtain. It's the nuclear spent fuel that is challenging."

"Joining us is John Thompson, a former member of the FBI's Counterterrorism Division."

"Thanks for having me."

"Let me read from the CDC website and then get your comment," the pretty anchor said. "'The main danger from a dirty bomb comes from the explosion, not the radiation. The explosion can cause serious injuries and property damage. People nearby could be injured by pieces of radioactive material from the bomb. Only people who are very close to the blast site would be exposed to enough radiation to cause immediate, serious illness. However, the radioactive dust and smoke can spread farther away, and could be dangerous to one's health if people breathe in the dust, eat contaminated food, or drink contaminated water. People injured by radioactive pieces or contaminated with radioactive dust will need medical attention.' So, when I see that, I wonder if the panic might be overblown? Clearly it's a bad situation, but we aren't talking about thousands of potential deaths, are we?"

"Well, let me first take issue with the CDC. Their bland explanation is meant to tamp down any kind of mass hysteria, and I certainly don't want to scare anyone, but terrorists have grown very sophisticated. There are numerous groups capable of this kind of attack. They will more than likely utilize a vehicle delivery approach, a truck-sized delivery, or they might use small aircraft, possibly larger planes. Depending on the population density and the time of day, we could see death tolls in the tens of thousands."

"That's considerable."

"There are scenarios where the numbers of dead could climb dramatically."

"Such as?"

"I believe an attack involving multiple vehicles, a ring of strategically placed bombs—and again, if they go at the right time and in a bigger city—casualties would easily exceed one hundred thousand."

"Frightening. And we are just getting word that apparently this is considered not just a credible threat, but the Department of Homeland Security believes that an attack on Wednesday is imminent."

Chapter Fifty-Two

Spraggins watched the screens inside the Destino, shaking his head.

"Is it real?" Chase asked. "Because we don't have proof, but our contact says it is."

"Does it matter?" Spraggins asked, pointing to a tablet linked to his global array of sampling and testing equipment. "The Fear Meter is running wild."

"And what happens if the crisis goes away? If the bombs never materialize, never blow?"

"The meter will drop, but not as low as before. When an event causes a rise, the spike occurs almost instantly. However, dips, or what I call *diminishments*, take much longer —weeks, months, years, maybe never."

Chase looked at the footage across several monitors, showing mobs already taking to the streets. "Then is one of the Remies making a play for more control?"

"Here's the thing. Whether they cooked up this scare, or a real terror group is out there about to bang down the door, the Remies or the government will always take advantage."

"Never let a crisis go to waste," Chase said. "Churchill said that."

"Did he? If he and Einstein, Mark Twain, and Lincoln said half the things attributed to them on the internet, they would not have had time to do much else other than talking."

"I thought he said it." Chase looked confused for a moment. "Anyway, it doesn't matter who said it, the point is that it is the Remies' creed."

"If the so-called *'expert'* is correct and a hundred thousand die, the government will implement new regulations, enact new laws, create new departments, commissions, and agencies, to ensure it will not happen again, and the people will support it. Fear makes people agreeable."

"The *just-keep-me-safe* mentality," Chase said.

"Correct again. And if this turns out to be a false alarm like Y2K, or Ebola, or the storm of the century, or murder hornets, or a thousand other forgotten headlines, the Fear Meter will slide in a series of *diminishments*, but a new scare will ratchet it up again before it recovers to where it was before the latest nonsense."

"Either way," Wen said. "We cannot let one, or a series of dirty bombs go off."

"It would be better for the Fear Meter if they did not."

"And better for all those who would perish in such an event," Wen said.

"True," Spraggins agreed with a shrug.

"Do you care about the victims at all?" Wen asked.

"Dear woman, I care about a great many things, but primarily I deal in fear, so inasmuch as those deaths—which have not yet occurred, and may never occur—affect the

Fear Meter, I am anxiously concerned. However, I freely admit that if all that potential loss of life somehow resulted in *diminishments*, I would celebrate them."

Wen, aghast, stormed to the other end of the truck to check the weapons locker.

"You're a cold man, Spraggins," Chase said.

"Not true, I am simply a practical one."

"But a *hundred thousand* dead . . . "

"I didn't kill them," Spraggins said, raising his voice so Wen would also hear. "No one has yet died, and let me be clear, if I relinquish my role in preventing the coming anarchy, who will take my place? I have spent decades studying this. There is no one else. I brought in the two of you to assist with the physical needs of this dilemma. That is my contribution to being sorry and worried about the suffering and dying of a minuscule portion of the remaining population. If I allow myself to be swallowed by the mourning, the fury—when I already dwell in an incredible absence of immutable existence—and become less effective, blinded to the imperceivable, paralyzed by the necessary extrication process of terror inflicted on the enervated plebeians sitting in the Colosseum waiting for their bread and circuses, then I assure you pandemonium will ensue. So please do not subjugate me to your morals and judgements when you have no idea the inner wrath I cope with every single minute of these sad days and tragic nights."

Chapter Fifty-Three

Chase took the call, assuming the Astronaut had news about how Tane and Blanc had been crushing them. He'd already called twice to give them profiles on the Surgeon and Khan, "The two agents of Satan running Tane and Blanc's side of the war." The Astronaut had moved to a secret location in the West Virginia mountains that belonged to a company controlled by Mars, impossible to trace. The two hundred and ninety acre apple orchard dated to the 1920s, but several buildings had been updated to handle the tech aspects of the Rogues. There were also three homes on the property, and even a commercial kitchen where some of the apples were converted to a variety of delicious treats.

"What's the update?" Chase asked, distracted, answering the call while staring at a news site covering the dirty bomb and asteroid stories, trying to glean any new information to determine the validity of the reports. There were also two new victims of the airport killer, which he knew to be fake news since the whole charade had begun to cover up Tane and Blanc's people killing his Rogues.

He'd been watching for hours. It was the dirty bomb story overshadowing even the earth-killing asteroid that fascinated him. Chaos ruled in urban centers across the country, with millions unsure if it was their city that would be targeted. Fleeing if they could, swarms of citizens expressed helpless outrage that they were not being protected. Violence had erupted in more than thirty metro areas as people fought to get out.

"He's safe," the Astronaut said, his voice jilted and stiff.

"Who's safe?" Chase asked, confused.

"Tu. He is alive."

"What do you mean?" Chase asked, suddenly scared, as he motioned for Wen to come and listen. "It's Tu," he said to her as she dropped her headphones and raced over.

"There was an attack in California, but he got out. He is alive."

"Is he hurt?" Wen asked.

"No, not him. But he is very scared and very sad."

"Sad?" Wen asked. "Is Zu Mu okay?"

"No. She is not."

"Tell me," Wen said. "*Tell me.*"

"She died. They killed her in her garden. Your grandmother is dead. It's not my fault."

"Oh, Zu Mu," Wen cried.

"It's not my fault," the Astronaut repeated. "I'm sorry you are sad."

Wen shook her head, crying. She held up a hand, trying to reassure the Astronaut that she didn't blame him, but couldn't find the words.

"Where's Tu?" Chase asked urgently.

"Wen is sad," the Astronaut said.

Chase, knowing how much Nash loved Wen and could not bear to see her upset, realized he would not get any more information about Tu or the attack without first calming him down. "She knows you had nothing to do with it, Nash. She just misses her grandmother. She was the last of her family."

"Not true. She has me and you and Tu still. We are all family."

"You're right. I just meant her family from China."

"Tu is from China."

"I know."

"I've been to China," the Astronaut said weakly.

"I'm okay," Wen said, her voice hoarse. "Where is Tu?"

"He is on his way here."

"Who has him?"

"Davis," he said, referring to one of the principle Sepios. "He flew in after the panic and got him out. He is escorting Tu to me personally. I talked to him."

"You talked to Davis or Tu?"

"Both. I talked to both. There are no injuries, but Tu . . ."

"What?" Wen asked, terrified anew. "What about Tu?"

"Tu had to kill a man."

Chapter Fifty-Four

WASHINGTON, DC

Monday - 5:12 pm - Eastern time.

Tane and Blanc watched the news from their Washington Studios.

"Good evening, and welcome to our breaking news coverage. We're tracking the still developing story that's causing chaos and panic throughout the country. As has been widely reported, our sources have confirmed that a dirty bomb is set to be detonated in an unknown location within the next two days. As a result, countless people are fleeing major US cities. Let's go to Mike Maskon, in the field, for the latest."

"Thanks, Carl. I'm here in downtown New York City, where the streets are packed with people trying to leave the city. Many are carrying their belongings on foot, while others are waiting in long lines for buses and trains. Traffic is gridlocked on all roads leading away from the city. It's the same story at JFK, Newark, and LaGuardia—all flights are full. It's chaos here, with some people visibly distressed, and others angry at the lack of information."

"Thanks, Mike, let's check with Lucy Ortega in Los Angeles."

"I'm reporting live from Los Angeles, where the situation is no different. The freeways are jam-packed, and people are abandoning their cars and running on foot to try and make it to safety. We've talked to several people who say they're leaving the city because they don't want to take any chances, while others are worried about the long-term health effects of a potential nuclear blast that—"

"Okay, it looks like we lost Lucy. We have additional breaking news just in. The Department of Homeland Security has just confirmed that the dirty bomb threat is credible, and that the government is working to identify the target city. The DHS is advising citizens to stay calm, but remain vigilant, and to report any suspicious activity to authorities. Back to Mike in New York."

"We've been talking to people on the ground, and many are expressing frustration and fear over the lack of information. They don't know which city is going to be targeted, and that's making it difficult for them to make informed decisions about where to go. I've talked to people who have left their jobs and their homes behind because they're not willing to take any chances, but there are also others who are staying put, hoping that the government will provide more information soon."

"Thank you for those updates. As the situation continues to unfold, we will stay on top of this story, and bring you the latest developments. In the meantime, we urge our viewers to stay safe and follow the advice of authorities. Thank you for joining us tonight."

Tane smiled. "The public will believe anything."

"It's a good production. Even I forget which stories are real and which are bogus," Blanc said, taking a swig of his drink.

"It's all about knowing how to manipulate the public. It's been so much easier since social media. Now we supplement the propaganda on our networks, and the public does the work of spreading it for us."

"A few million fake accounts help."

Tane nodded in agreement. "The fear and chaos created by the stories will continue to have a significant economic impact. It's always fun to have the side benefit of making a fortune by shorting stocks and manipulating the markets."

Blanc poured himself another drink. "Yeah, but screwing up Snyder's plans is the best."

Tane chuckled. "It's amazing how easy it is to manipulate people with fake news."

Blanc took a sip of his drink. "Don't worry, we're consolidating our grip. Censor anyone who questions our narratives. Keep them fighting among themselves."

"I have to say, Blanc, the asteroid story was a stroke of genius," Tane said.

Blanc smiled. "Thank you. It's all about knowing how to play on people's fears. Something so big that they can't do anything about it scares the hell out of them."

"On top of the dirty bomb, the serial killer—good god, they might find religion."

"Fear overload," Blanc said. "And the best part is, we're completely untraceable. We created fake experts and studies, and we spread the news through our networks, social media, and other outlets." He laughed.

"Next story is about Chase Malone. Let's finish him."

Chapter Fifty-Five

SAN FRANCISCO

Monday - 5:39 pm - Pacific Time (8:39 pm Eastern)

Dez, Chase's original business partner and still close friend, had never stopped working with the billionaire, but after an attack cost him the use of his legs, leaving him a paraplegic, on top of other threats, he went underground.

Desmond "Dez" Jefferson had once been one of the top minds in AI, and among only a handful of African American engineers in Silicon Valley. Six years older than Chase, Dez had been a grounding force in the younger inventor's life. The two of them had set out to change the world with the AI programs and apps they developed. However, their work shifted dramatically once they realized that corruption and greed mixed with advanced technologies was on the verge of destroying the fabric of society.

Now they weren't just trying to change the world, they were trying to *save* it.

Dez stood with the aid of what he called his million-dollar legs, an exoskeleton that he'd helped develop with some friends at Stanford. Bull, his girlfriend, paused her work at her computer to watch. She'd seen him stand and walk thousands of times, but still counted each one as a miracle after living with him in a wheelchair for so long.

Bull, a skinny, short-haired woman in her late twenties, had been a hacker since her teens. When Chase found her, she'd been chain-smoking and bloodshot eyed. Her love of the caffeine-infused beverage had earned her her nickname. Everybody in her line of work had one.

Dez and Bull were in a darkened penthouse suite, their faces illuminated only by the glow of multiple screens. The room, packed with high-tech equipment and elaborate computers, with massive monitors lining the walls, looked like a giant version of the back of the Destino. The air was thick with the hum of electricity.

Dez walked towards one of the machines, his exoskeleton making a whirring sound with each step. "Find anything yet?" he asked Bull, who was typing furiously on another computer.

"Just a bunch of cover-ups and conspiracies," Bull replied, taking a sip of her energy drink. "But nothing that ties everything together."

Dez nodded, grabbing a fresh orange slice and taking a bite. "Keep digging. We're close, I can feel it."

Bull nodded and went back to typing. Five minutes later, she let out a gasp. "Dez, come here. Look at this."

Dez quickly made his way over, the rest of the orange forgotten at his desk. He leaned over her shoulder, scanning the screen. "What is it?"

"The asteroid strike. It's all a fake."

Dez's eyes widened. "Are you *sure*?"

Bull pointed to a series of emails and documents on the

screen. "The Remies are behind it all. They've fabricated the whole thing to create panic and chaos."

Dez's mind raced. "But why? Why would they do that?"

Bull shot him a *that's a stupid question* look.

Dez took a deep breath. "We have to double check this. Make sure it's not just some elaborate hoax about a hoax. You know, like the story of it being a hoax is a hoax . . ."

She gave him another look and laughed.

They spent the next hour going over every detail, each piece of evidence, and the more they looked, the more certain they became. The asteroid strike was a fake.

As they sat back in their chairs, taking in the gravity of this discovery, the room fell silent.

"What are we going to do?" Bull finally asked.

Dez rubbed his chin, thinking. "We have to get this to Chase."

Bull nodded.

Dez stood up. "What we need to figure out is which Remie is pushing this."

Bull got up as well, grabbing her drink. "There's a back scan," she said.

"They can trace?" he asked, alarmed.

"Yeah."

"Then we're in real danger now."

She checked the window, looking for a helicopter. "The Remies can't let us live, knowing what we know."

"Can you cut the links, put up a mirror?" Dez asked. "Divert their scans?" They both had been attacked before by the powerful forces Chase was fighting. It was when Dez had lost his legs.

"Maybe." She looked at him. "But we have to get the information and evidence to Chase, just in case."

"In case they come for us?"

She nodded. "In case we're dead soon."

Chapter Fifty-Six

OUTSIDE RESTON, VIRGINIA

Monday - 3:27 am - Eastern time

Weston stood at the perimeter of the sprawling defense contractor headquarters, taking in the scene before him. The campus was vast, with imposing concrete buildings. At its center stood a black glass and steel high-rise, reflecting the lights of the surrounding structures like a mirror. At its top, the logo of the organization was emblazoned in golden letters, visible from miles away.

Weston's night vision glasses caught a few hotspots, but otherwise gave him a clear view. "Too clean," he muttered. He checked the main security gate, then scanned over to a far off building he knew housed the security command center. Cameras and other devices would be monitoring and supplementing information to thirty-six uniformed guards. He kept looking, searching for something else. Trouble, his gut told him, was lurking in the shadows.

The well-manicured grounds could have been a city park with its mature trees, several fountains, and large sculptures scattered across its eighteen acres. Outbuildings dotted the landscape, providing additional storage and facilities for the company's numerous employees.

"Where are you?" he asked no one, wondering where the evil he'd encountered at the mansion was hiding, but there was nothing apparent. Just his own people, or what he called *the approaching storm*, because that's what he and a couple hundred Terminators were about to create.

"Are we a go?" Sampson, a short, stocky subordinate, asked.

"I need all reports," Weston said, a little more cautious than normal.

"Last night's massacre at the mansion burned your margin?"

Weston scanned the sky above. "Something like that."

The stillness bothered him. His instincts told him to call it off, but he shouldn't even be there. He should have died last night with the others, but since he'd survived, he still shouldn't have been there. Still shell-shocked and wasted, he should have cashed out, but Chase needed him. There simply wasn't enough to go on, and yet he had to go.

"Final reports are in," Sampson said. "All ground points covered. Green lights on the bots. Clear on the overheads." He looked at Weston and waited, finally asking again, "So are we a go?"

Weston checked the glasses again, scanning the property of the second largest defense contractor in the United States, the headquarters secure and protected as one might expect by electronic surveillance and a fair amount of manpower, but not enough to compete with the two hundred forty men he'd brought. Before the mansion massacre, his force would have been less than half that, but they'd brought in more reinforcements beefing up their numbers to avoid another ambush.

He double checked the readings on the satellite link that acted as a critical asset in monitoring and protecting the facility in its partnership with the Department of Defense. The connection remained severed. The Rogues had taken on that assignment, to knock out the DoD interface, although the Astronaut had provided some of the codes. *Everything is clear and clean.* Weston knew it was time.

"What's wrong, Weston? You see something?" Sampson asked.

"No." He kept scanning.

"I think you're a little gun-shy after last night."

"You would be, too, if you'd been there."

"Yeah, I knew a bunch of the fallen. Lost some good friends."

"A lot of good men, gone," Weston agreed.

"We can't stay here all night. Got green lights, and it won't stay that way forever."

"I know, I just have a bad feeling. Something isn't quite right."

"I get it, man, but feelings don't really cut it in our business. Either abort this thing or take it, right?"

Weston nodded absently. He'd been around long enough to know that feelings could be a legitimate thing, and yet he also knew there was no way to stop an operation like this just on a hunch. "Okay," he finally said, still believing everything looked too good. "Let's get in there."

The mission was much more complicated than the mansion raid. It wasn't just about doing damage or a snatch and grab, this was about taking provable intel, equipment, prototypes, and every bit of history and computer drives they could find.

And, of course, they hoped to bring back all their own personnel this time.

The Terminators began marching through the property, cutting fences and circumventing the electronic surveillance. Even with the sat links severed, they utilized a new cloaking technology that would shield the operation from later reviews from normal satellite surveillance.

"We don't want to leave any useful record," Weston reminded Sampson. "Don't leave the footprint of the cloak. We want this blamed on the Chinese MSS. Brazen like a balloon over Montana."

"It's all cemented," Sampson said, pointing to his head.

Weston joined his men at the forward, pretending the nagging feelings were nothing, but as soon as he neared the surveillance shed, he realized his mistake.

Chapter Fifty-Seven

The Terminators suddenly became heavily engaged from a large maintenance shed that the pre-strike intel had told them only held vehicles.

"Swarm and regroup! Hit the trees!" Weston yelled.

Within minutes, at least eighty armored men streamed out of what they now believed to be a concrete bunker. Sampson cussed. "It's a full-fledged battle! Choppers, choppers!"

"We're taking heavy fire!" Weston called in to his commander, Blitz.

"Keep going," Blitz said. "We've already shown our hand, and we'll never have a chance like this again."

"Roger that," Weston said reluctantly.

"You've got Killtrons—use them!" Blitz said. "Just get the data and prototypes, then wreck the place."

After the mansion massacre, plans were altered, and in addition to the extra manpower, Weston had brought two autonomous AI military battle bots called Killtronics, or Killtrons. Weston was counting on the highly acrobatic killing machines with AI-assisted operating systems to make the difference.

As three attack helicopters buzzed his men, Weston gave the immediate order to deploy the advanced cyber warriors. The Killtrons locked in line-of-site with the airborne security force and almost effortlessly picked the two choppers out of the sky.

The crafts came spiraling down, ending in two fiery crash sites on the grounds of the facility. The Killtrons wasted no time leading and advancing the charge toward the main building, but it came at a high price as intense firefights broke out between the Terminators and the entrenched security forces.

The Terminators approached the building, their weapons at the ready. Weston still couldn't shake the feeling that something was off, but he pushed the thoughts aside and focused on getting inside.

Suddenly, another helicopter appeared on the horizon, its searchlight sweeping across the grounds.

"Incoming!" Weston shouted, signaling for his men to take cover. The helicopter hovered above the building, its door gunners ripping apart the Terminators below.

"Take it down!" he yelled, signaling for the Killtrons to open fire. The air was filled with the sound of gunfire and the roar of the helicopter's engines as it tried to evade the hail of bullets. The Killtrons connected with RPGs, and the helicopter exploded in a fiery ball, raining debris down on the grounds.

Weston took a deep breath, trying to steady his nerves. "That's another screw up," he muttered to himself. "Where the hell are they keeping their firepower?"

Just then, a larger and more heavily armed chopper rose from behind the trees.

"Killtrons!" Weston shouted, diving behind a nearby building. He peered out from behind the corner, watching as his men were decimated by the enemy's relentless barrage from the ground. Suddenly, a figure appeared at his side, and he turned to see Sampson.

"They're going to keep coming. We need to get inside, now!" Sampson yelled. "Mission moving. Let's leave one Killtron outside and take one in with us."

"Go," Weston said, then relayed the order. The pair took another dozen Terminators with them and followed the path cut by the Killtron. They sprinted for the building, dodging bullets and explosions as they went. Eventually making it to a heavily fortified and guarded side entrance, the Killtron wiped the opposition and forced the door. Once inside, armed with the building plans and schematics, Weston led the team to the lower research wing of the facility.

On the way, they encountered scores of private military ops. "This is a damned calamity!" Weston yelled, checking his wrist-tablet, which showed live views of the outside. "Get the other Killtron in here!" Then he contacted Blitz, who was monitoring the event. "Bring in air, now!"

"On the way," Blitz promised.

"They knew we were coming," Sampson yelled, though they both already knew that. Sampson, Weston, and a few others veered off into an adjoining corridor, leaving the Killtron and fifteen men to handle the main fight.

Coming to a highly secure inner core of the building, Weston checked the plans. "This is it."

More security turned on them.

"Take out the guards!" Weston shouted, aiming his submachine gun. Sampson nodded, already shooting, their bullets slamming into the guards and bringing them down one by one. Finally, the last guard fell, and they rushed inside, the sounds of battle echoing behind them.

They found themselves in a long hallway, the walls pocked with bullet holes and the floor littered with debris. Weston led the way, moving quickly and quietly down the corridor. Suddenly, they heard the sound of footsteps, and they froze, listening. The footsteps grew louder, and they could see the enemy rounding the corner up ahead.

"Get ready!" Weston shouted.

The enemy appeared. The two sides exchanged fire in a barrage of bullets. Weston and Sampson were outnumbered, but had better angles, and eventually the Killtrons punctured the line and cleaned out the security forces.

"We need to find the target and get out of here," Weston said, his voice tinged with urgency. "We don't know what else is waiting for us."

They moved deeper into the building. The clamoring noise of the continuing battle rang through the halls. "Listen . . . Additional ops getting closer!" Weston said.

"We have—"

The sound of glass shattering interrupted him. They looked up to see the windows being blown out of the building. More security swarmed in at them.

Firing wildly at everything that moved, Sampson shouted, "We're surrounded!"

Chapter Fifty-Eight

Weston saw Sampson go down and knew he was gone. He and a few men held off the onslaught until the second Killtron arrived after air support had cleared the grounds.

As Weston was about to escape with the prototypes, a fresh group of private military personnel confronted him. "Where do these bastards keep coming from?" he yelled. Later, he would learn from Killtron onboard cameras and AI analysis of the event that several cells of special ops units had been stationed throughout the building and grounds with delayed fuses, meaning they held their fire, remaining stealth until certain time and action requirements had been met.

"Blitz, they definitely knew!" Weston yelled. "How do they keep getting our mission plans?"

"We'll talk when you're safe," Blitz said over the phone.

"Blitz! Damn it, man! Damn it, we had two hundred forty go in, and we're coming out with twenty-three—*ninety percent gone*, man! Two nights in a row!"

"We're on pause until we find the source." However,

Blitz already believed he knew what was going on. The Remies had committed tens of billions to defend potential targets. Khan had a no-mercy policy, and a man called the Surgeon was developing plans and breaching Terminator data.

"We've taken massive hits once again—they *knew* we were coming!" Weston continued ranting. "How the hell did they know where we'd be? How did they *know*, man?"

"Maybe they didn't. Maybe they've got everywhere protected," Blitz said. "Let's talk about it in person. Get out safe."

"How could they *guess* to know where to put that much manpower in place?"

"Because they have all the money in the world."

"Yeah, but getting this many trained men?" he said, following the Killtron across the yard. "Only the Killtrons saved us. *Damnit.*"

"But you got the prototypes? You got the backup drives, the database, all their digital records?"

"Yeah, yeah, I got it, but I'm *telling* you." He looked back at the building, partially on fire, black glass shattered. The grounds were littered with scores of bodies, multiple craters, and three downed choppers, still burning between him and the structure. It looked like a different planet from the one he'd arrived at thirty minutes earlier. "Loaded."

The high caliber bullet went through his neck while he was mid-sentence with Blitz. He died on the way to the ground.

Already, Tane and Blanc's studios were creating the cover story. A gas line had ruptured and set the headquarters ablaze. No injuries were reported because those lies only got more complicated. Clean up crews would arrive in minutes to remove the dead and wounded. They would all be burned and deposited into a mass grave.

Blitz called the report in to Chase. "We lost more than two hundred, including Weston, but the Killtron got out with the data."

After the call, Chase stared in silence at the constant coverage displaying on six monitors, showing people in long traffic jams out of cities, walking, carrying belongings on their backs like refugees, extra wait times at airports because of the evacuations and the serial killer, riots in other congested areas as fury grew over the government withholding the dirty bomb threat for three full days prior to informing the public. "People are so easily controlled," he muttered.

"Yeah," Wen said quietly.

"It's getting harder and harder to know what the truth is."

"I know."

"The only way this ends is to change the game. If the Remies continue to make the rules, we'll eventually wind up in a dystopian society—monitored, censored, manipulated, controlled, propagandized, essentially enslaved."

"And then they'll come for the books."

Chapter Fifty-Nine

WASHINGTON DC

Monday - 8:27 am - Eastern time

Chase and Wen watched the news in the control center in the back of the Destino.

"Good morning, I'm Eric Conway, and we have some important updates on the asteroid that was reported to be on a collision course with Earth. It has now been discovered that the asteroid will miss Earth by a wide margin. Mistakes were made in earlier calculations, causing a false alarm and widespread panic."

Images showed a simulation of an asteroid in space, then cut to footage of relieved people celebrating.

"We're going live to a news conference with Dr. Nelsman, speaking to reporters."

"We apologize for any panic or distress caused by the earlier reports," Dr. Nelsman said. "We take our responsibility to communicate these types of threats very seriously, and we are constantly working to improve our systems and accuracy. In this case, mistakes were made in earlier calculations that led to the false alarm."

An image appeared onscreen, showing the trajectories of the asteroid changing.

"The asteroid will pass by our planet at a safe distance of approximately nineteen thousand miles. While, in astronomical terms this distance is a close brush with Earth, it's great enough to avoid endangering our blue *marble*."

"This is certainly a huge sigh of relief for everyone," another reporter said. "Can you tell us more about what caused the initial miscalculation?"

"Yes. It seems that there were some errors in the data that was used to track the trajectory. When these errors were corrected, it became clear that the asteroid would miss Earth. We are now conducting a thorough investigation to ensure that this type of mistake doesn't happen again in the future."

More images of people celebrating flashed across the screen. Spraggins phoned. "The Fear Meter is down to seven point four-three-three."

"I'm amused that they're spinning this as a calculation error," Chase said, "instead of it being a scam from the start."

"We forced their hand," Wen said.

"We still have to find the dirty bomb."

"And stop Snyder from winning the election."

"Snyder has his hands full with so many people fleeing New York, it's a prime target for the terror strike," Chase said. "And since his opponent is another corrupt politician handpicked by Tane and Blanc . . . "

"The lesser of two evils," Wen said.

"Exactly."

"So many cockroaches. It's hard to get them all."

"We may win the war against Tane and Blanc after the three raids tonight."

"If all goes well."

"And if we can get Snyder, too. Maybe expose the Remies' hold on the two political parties."

"More like one party claiming to be two."

"Then we might finally be able to get some real honest people as the nominees for president. Can you imagine?" Chase said, watching the images of spontaneous celebrations breaking out around the world and wondering if they were all real. *You never know what news is created these days.* "But everything we pursue from the deputy's flash drive seems to be a dead end."

"Because Snyder knows what we have," Wen said.

"We've drained a lot of resources and burned a lot of our credibility chasing down those leads."

"The deputy died getting us that drive. It has to hold the key to burying Snyder."

"Maybe it's not what's on the drive, because he can cover all that, maybe it's that he had one of his top aides killed and then concealed the fact that it even happened," Chase said. "We should be trying to pin the murder on him. No one will vote for a killer."

"What do the voters have to do with it?" Spraggins cut in. "You forget it's all manipulated. They use fear for everything. That's why I'm here, that's why I invented the Fear Meter, that's why I found you. We are all pawns in their game. We may have stopped the asteroid strike, we may find the dirty bomb, but there will always be another and another. The only way this ends is in ending them, exposing it, showing the people. Remember, we far outnumber them, but without understanding in what part they play, the masses will bring on the Overwhelm, or they could find understanding and bring on real change."

Chapter Sixty

WESTERN PENNSYLVANIA

Monday - 10:04 am - Eastern time

Blitz, a rugged blond military man, surveyed Chase's army at the Western Pennsylvania training center, a secret Terminator staging area, one of fourteen in the country. This one, now home to seven Killtrons, had suddenly become quite crowded since Blitz had brought the remaining seven hundred and twenty Terminators to the hidden base. The units had been moved in anticipation of hitting three Remie targets that night.

All the Terminators—mostly men but about ten percent women—were jammed into an empty aircraft hangar, waiting to receive orders and plans. Large screens behind Blitz showed maps, satellite images, expected defenses, and security. A slide presentation for each target would soon delve into the finer points of the operation.

Blitz walked across the platform with a handful of his top aides, including Diego. "Listen up. We're taking a deployment deviation," he announced. "Three ops tonight inside our radius." He checked his list, although the locations and details were already committed to memory. "We've got Philadelphia, Cleveland, and Northern Virginia." He wouldn't tell them anything specific because of the security risks. The Remies had spies everywhere. However, Blitz knew they were raiding two more Federal Reserve locations and a second defense contractor. "We're turning the tables on what the NSA collects and getting the data on those powerful people, those too-big corporations, the wild, corrupt institutions."

He continued to give the pre-deployment strategy for each op.

"All three missions will carry two Killtrons," he said, referring to the AI bots. He went on about how effective they were. "Killtrons have turned the fight in our favor, saving lives, just in the past twenty-four hours. These units give us an unprecedented advantage. One Killtron is easily worth five hundred men in the field."

The Terminators stood in the large aircraft hangar, divided into three groups. The respective leaders stood at the front with two Killtrons in each section. Blitz described there had been substantial losses and challenges faced in the earlier missions, but went light on details. He glanced at Diego, a veteran of two of the disastrous missions. He didn't want morale to suffer any more than it already had based on rumors.

"Tonight, we turn up the heat, and we will wreck them," Blitz said. "We know they know we're coming. They just don't know where we will strike, and they don't know how many locations will—"

His words were interrupted by the Killtrons attacking two of the three commanders. Diego never knew what hit him as the advanced bot blew his head apart.

Many of the Terminators initially thought it was a demonstration or training exercise, but Diego's violent and graphic death made it clear they were under attack.

Blitz began scrambling for control and yelling orders. Dozens of Terminators dove for cover and went for weapons. "What the hell, what the . . . " Blitz shouted as he manipulated the command app on his tablet, trying to reestablish control over the Killtrons.

He looked up to face what could have been a scene from a sci-fi horror film as all seven killing machines annihilated his forces. He quickly gave up on trying to regain control and went for the self-destruct override. "Damn, it doesn't work!" he yelled, ducking for cover himself as one of them opened fire at the platform.

"It's locked! They've locked us out!" his top lieutenant screamed. "Regular shut down won't work!"

The Killtrons continued ravaging the Terminators, killing Chase's soldiers with total impunity.

The Surgeon watched the massacre from the comfort of his office, viewed from dozens of angles via the multiple cameras in each Killtron, while singing a little song, "They march, they march, you can't stop them all, they march, they march, you can't stop them all." He pressed a button and sent the video to Tane, Blanc, Khan, and then looked back at the screen. "I think Chase Malone should like to see this as well."

Within minutes, his phone rang. He looked at the number—Tane and Blanc.

"How did you do this?" Tane asked.

"In case you've forgotten, I am brilliant," the Surgeon

said. "I've turned his killer bots into weapons for me." He laughed. "A little malfunction. Do you hear all the screams of men, and especially those of the women? It sounds like . . . like music."

"It's like shooting fish in a barrel," Tane said.

"I must admit, I never dreamed that fool in charge would put all the Terminators into one place," the Surgeon mused.

Watching the live feed, Tane and Blanc were almost repulsed by the absolute carnage. Several were fighting back, including Blitz, but he knew better than most that the Killtrons were virtually indestructible.

"What's going to happen?" Blanc asked.

The question momentarily confused the Surgeon. "What's going to happen?" he repeated, as if the question might make more sense after he'd heard it in his own voice. "What's going to happen is every last member of Chase Malone's pathetic army is going to die in the next eight or nine minutes." He paused and looked back at the massacre. "Enjoy the show!"

Chapter Sixty-One

Blitz had seen action on five continents, dozens of countries, hundreds of hot zones, but he'd never been in the stew like this. Cussing every other word, his mind jerked and stuttered between instinct and experience, attempting to find a way to stop the AI from wiping them out completely.

"The Killtrons are too smart," his lieutenant shouted an instant before dying. Blitz continued trying every workaround to get into their enhanced computerized brains. Nothing happened. He directed several explosives at the bots. Nothing happened.

From underneath the speaking platform, he called the Astronaut.

"I'll try," Nash said. "But hit them with an EMP mini."

The Astronaut patched the feed through to the Destino.

"Blitz, take whoever you can and get out of there!" Chase said.

The Surgeon laughed as microphones on several of the Killtrons picked up the order. "I'm so glad you joined us," the Surgeon announced through a speaker on the Killtron closest to Blitz. "Chase Malone. It's like watching the Super Bowl and the Olympics all in one, isn't it? Except everyone gets to die in this one."

"Who is this?" Chase demanded.

"You can call me the Surgeon, and I'm operating on your paper army today. They're all going to die. Your private army is over. *You* are over."

"I can't get access," the Astronaut said on a line only Chase could hear.

"Very impressive," Tane said to the Surgeon. "Can you track Malone through his communications somehow?"

"That's exactly what we're doing right now," the Surgeon replied after muting his voice to the Killtron. The Surgeon would thank Khan later for this great victory. He'd had a team at the defense contractor's headquarters who'd gained physical access to one of the Killtrons and had installed the virus that ultimately infected all seven of the killing machines.

"What can we move there?" Wen said.

"Looking at resources," Chase replied, "but virtually everything is in Pennsylvania!"

"Chase? *Chase?*" the Surgeon called. "Are you there, Chase?"

"I'm here, you bastard."

"Is that any way to talk to a friend?" the Surgeon said in a mocking tone. "I've just saved you a fortune by cutting your payroll by seventy-five percent—oh, make that seventy-nine, eighty-one percent. And look at them go. I think in a few more minutes we'll have put an end to your military payroll completely."

Blitz had managed to get out of the hangar with two other men. Now, they burst back through the small side door and launched a mini-EMP. One of the Killtrons immediately seized up, tumbling over.

"That's impressive," the Surgeon said, "but not nearly enough range."

One of the men who'd been with Blitz was ripped apart by machine-gun fire. He'd been holding another EMP. Blitz detonated it remotely and a second Killtron fell, but that was all the EMPs they'd had on site.

"I must insist that you refrain from further damaging my property," the Surgeon began.

"Nothing is yours!" Chase barked.

"Oh, they most certainly are mine. I have trucks on the way to pick them up. I am hoping to have them in place to kill whatever ragtag team you can put together for your next silly exhibition into one of my employers' properties."

"Your employers are not going to get away with this!" Chase yelled.

"Look at the show," the Surgeon said, laughing. "There are only forty or fifty left alive and they will be dead in a minute. Oh, did you see that? There goes your friend Blitz."

A Killtron camera zoomed in on the bullet-riddled body of the Terminator's leader. Chase coughed as if he'd been kicked in the stomach. "I'm going to see you in that same position," Chase growled. "I promise you that. And not just you, but Tane and Blanc, too!"

"Chase, that's tough talk for a little man who just lost his army," Blanc said. "I think you should go take your paltry billion dollars—or whatever you have left—and go hide somewhere. If you don't, we're going to take everything from you. Everything and everyone."

"Almost got it," the Astronaut said. "I have a workaround. I think I can fry their circuits."

"A little late," Chase gritted out.

"At least we can prevent the technology from getting into the Remies' hands," Wen said.

"Chase, get off the line, now!" the Astronaut said. "They're tracking your location. Move, now! *Move!*"

The Astronaut actually cut Chase off the link before he could do it himself, then sent a self-destruct signal to the five Killtrons still standing. The instructions caused the bots to overwrite their programming, combined with a diagnostic run and patch update that would essentially fry their chips and memories.

Chase looked at Wen. "What now?"

"We destroy them."

"How?"

He glanced back to the now blank screen "Blitz is dead. We've got no army left to strike with. *They took out our entire army.* Now they have Killtrons, and we've got nothing but death."

Chapter Sixty-Two

WASHINGTON DC

Monday - 11:48 am - Eastern time.

The exodus from the major cities continued. The breakdown of order at airports grew worse.

"The news is so slick," Chase said. "They've gotten so good at pushing our buttons. Spraggins is right, the media knows just how to enrage us, upset us, make us sad, and most of all, how to scare us."

A Terminator who had missed a flight to the training center arrived and discovered the carnage. He immediately contacted Mars, whom he'd worked with on several prior missions. However, minutes before Mars reached Chase, a video featuring the brutal highlights of the attack transmitted to the Killtrons' reception center link on the Destino. The incoming reel tripped an alarm, something that had to be manually set.

"Unbelievable!" Chase said as the images spilled onto a screen. He switched it to a larger monitor, but regretted it almost instantly, realizing the horror only got worse with each passing frame.

"The Surgeon actually had this complete version of the massacre produced with a musical score," Wen said, joining him.

Chase shook his head, his ability to concentrate and think now temporarily wrecked.

Wen picked up the call from Mars and put him on speaker. "I'm sorry to say I have tragic news," he said. "The Pennsylvania training center was wiped out. Total annihilation. All the Terminators are dead. The Killtrons are missing."

"We know," Wen replied. "We're watching the footage now."

"They *filmed* it?" Mars asked.

"Somehow they turned the Killtrons on them," Wen said. "The cameras in the bots captured the entire slaughter. Chase, you should probably stop watching."

Without taking his eyes off the screen, he replied through gritted teeth, "I owe it to the people to watch every second of this, to watch it over and over, to memorize it, to get sick on it, so that I never forget it, never forget them."

"I still think you should stop," Wen said gently.

"Then I'm going to find who's responsible for this, and hunt them down, and kill every last one of them."

The images of the Killtrons dominating the battle seemed unreal, like something from a scary sci-fi movie. It was unrelenting.

"Do you see?" Chase yelled to no one in particular. "These bots are killing people I know, ripping them apart, cutting them down with their installed automatic guns . . .

Do you see the blood, the chunks of *actual* flesh, of these courageous men and women fighting the machines, screaming, clawing, crying!" Chase did feel nauseous, smothered by the misery, the cruelty of it. "The cold mechanical monsters that *I* helped create . . . just devastating some of the best trained soldiers in the world . . . *our* soldiers . . . Could you imagine being in the middle of that, knowing you were up against AI whose single purpose was ending your life as quickly and efficiently as possible?"

"No," Mars said across the line, unable to see the awful scene playing out on the Destino's monitors, but picturing a nightmare. "I cannot."

"And it's as if they've been programmed for sadistic practices, like they *want* to be cruel, like they *need* to be!" As Chase watched, his outrage mounted. "The Surgeon has taught the Killtrons to be malicious, to mutilate. It's a requirement in their new base command. Why would they do that?"

"To send us a message," Wen said. "Tane and Blanc wanted us to know they're not taking prisoners. Every response to our raids has been harsher than normal."

"Look at this!" Chase pointed to the screen.

The Surgeon's face came on. "Chase Malone, Wen Sung, this little film has no doubt found its way to you," he said in his clipped accent. "I hope you enjoyed it. I certainly did. Loved seeing so many of those dangerous rebels you employ suffer and perish. I like that word, *perish*."

He paused, and several particularly brutal scenes played out, including Blitz dying.

"Yes, it was a good day. And you will have a date with us very soon. Perhaps tomorrow, if we can trace you through this feed. I suspect you may be too smart for that, though.

Possibly using a mobile set up, or at least a sophisticated multi-hop. Regardless, we will locate and terminate you. It is only a matter of time—a very, very short time. Count on it."

Chapter Sixty-Three

WASHINGTON DC

Monday - 12:53 pm - Eastern time

Still heavy hearted from the massacre, Chase and Wen wandered down the narrow streets in a section of DC famous for its murals, waiting to meet Spraggins.

Wen was worried about Chase. She'd never seen him so despondent, so enraged. She'd been trained not to let brutality get to her, but Chase had not. He'd seen a lot of terrible stuff over the years they'd been running, but nothing like the massacre of nearly eight hundred people he'd known in a span of minutes.

She tried to change the subject, giving him an update on Snyder. "Bull hacked into the voting machines manufacturers and found nothing."

"They're covering it up, keeping it off servers. They may even have separate companies or subcontractors handling the manipulation."

"I know, but running that down is taking time."

Chase stared at a large mural covering the side of a

building. A wild, abstract nature scene stretched up several stories high. "Bribery, blackmail, voter intimidation, smear campaigns—all of it's being investigated by our teams, including the Astronaut, but we're hitting zeros."

"We'll crack it," Wen said.

"If we don't stop the Remies from introducing more fear," Chase said. "it's going to lead to the end of the world."

"'The end of the world is a concept as outlandish as living forever.' A good line from *1Q84*, by Haruki Murakami," a man from the shadows said. "Although, you are only a normal brilliant, a genius level IQ. Not insane enough to take all that intelligence and drive it to its full potential."

"What?" Chase said, the large mural that had held his attention moments earlier seeming to take on a sinister appearance now.

Wen turned her gun in the direction of the voice. "Come out—"

"With your hands up," the man finished for her. "Wen, you're always so predictable. It's truly astounding you've lived so long. Then again, the average shadow person who has been pursuing you all these years is, well, just average."

The man walked out of the alley, hands held palms out next to his face. "Surprise."

"Franco Madden!" Chase said.

"Yes. You're surprised. Judging by your silly expression, I'd say you are actually quite stunned."

"Because you're dead."

"Apparently not."

"But Tess killed you!"

"Did she? I don't recall it that way."

"What do you want?" Wen said, waving her gun as if she might use it to actually kill him this time.

"I have a proposition I'd like to discuss, but it would be a far more pleasant conversation if I could put my hands down."

"I don't think so," she snapped.

"Why? Do you believe I might harm you?"

"You've tried to kill us so many times I couldn't possibly count them all."

"Yes, that's true, and while I would like to see you both dead—"

"See what I mean?"

"Silly Wen, there's a wonderful sentiment on this very subject in the odd little novel *Welcome to Night Vale*, by Joseph Fink and Jeffrey Cranor, that I believe you should think a lot about. 'Death is only the end if you assume the story is about you.' This has always been about so much more than you and pretty boy Chase."

"Not making a good case for putting your hands down," Chase said. "However, you're wrong about us. We really don't think we're very important."

"Oh, that is very funny," Franco said. "So funny, in fact, that later, I'm going to write your words down, and whenever I'm feeling low, I'll read them and laugh hysterically."

"Is that another quote from a book?"

"No." He smiled, a strange, amused thing. "I do think life would be easier for all of us if everyone just read more books."

"What is your proposition?" Wen asked impatiently.

"It is long and involved, but it begins with the death of a man who calls himself the Surgeon."

"We would like that very much," Wen said.

"Excellent. I can give you the details, and you can kill him for me."

"How do we know this isn't some elaborate trap you're setting for us?" Chase said.

"I could have killed you by now, and I might in the future, but this is something different. I need the Surgeon surgically removed. Plus, I promised Spraggins I would not harm you today."

Later, they asked Spraggins why he'd obviously arranged the meeting with a man who wanted to kill them.

"Franco and I go way back," Spraggins said. "Don't be so surprised. As long as he doesn't *want* to kill you, he's quite an interesting guy."

"But he *wants* us dead," Chase said.

"Yes, well, if he *does* want to kill you then he can be kind of a jerk."

Chapter Sixty-Four

WASHINGTON DC

Monday - 2:08 pm - Eastern time

Chase looked at his phone and then turned to Wen with a surprised expression. "I think it's Tess."

Tess Federgreen, the former head of the ultra-secret Corporate Intelligence Security Section—or CISS—had been a friend and sometimes adversary to Chase and Wen ever since Wen had first escaped China and the MSS, but mostly a friend.

"First Franco and now Tess?"

Tess had led CISS, arguably the least known and most powerful clandestine agency in the world since its inception as a joint operation of the CIA, NSA, and FBI, with an unusual mandate to prevent war between corporations. However, she had been forced out when she'd tried to stop the high-level corruption extending into all areas of the government.

"What makes you believe it's her?" Wen asked.

"Because the caller ID says it's from Flint Jones."

"Your former head of security? He's been dead for years."

"Yeah, but he and Tess were a couple." When superiors in the intelligence community, with the blessing of the White House, ordered her death, Tess had slipped into the night, lost to the whispers and dark realms where secrets and lies remained steeped in a heavy fog. Numerous teams had been sent to find her, to kill her. They were unsuccessful.

However, Tess wasn't just hiding. She covertly maintained control over several elite IT-Squads within CISS. She'd been preparing for years, knowing the End Game with the Remies was coming. Tess had large quantities of sophisticated weapons and technology hidden away. She'd traded favors and built loyalties over her lengthy career, leaving her with a black book of trustworthy contacts in most parts of the government and the world.

She'd carefully chosen a series of safe houses in Mexico and Central America in order to remain close to the United States because she said, "That's where the fight is." Chase and Wen had not heard a word from her for two years.

He hit speaker and accepted the call. "Hello?"

"First you attack Miner's home, then you raid the Federal Reserve headquarters—*the Fed's headquarters*—the same night you hit the Vaults in Chantilly, a site not even supposed to exist. *That* was all bad enough, but then you went after one of the largest defense contractors in the world. Chase, you already had too many enemies . . . "

"Hi Tess. What's your point?"

"You're going too fast."

He wanted to ask how she knew about all their strikes,

but it was Tess. Even in exile, she could uncover secrets better than anyone. "Do you know what we're dealing with?"

"Same stuff, just a different day."

"Well, yeah, sort of, but this time it's the end of everything. The fear is about to reach—"

"The Overwhelm," Tess finished. "Spraggins found you, I see."

"You know about him?"

"How close is the number on the Meter?"

"Eight. We're over eight, and with the dirty bomb, the airport killer—"

"The killer isn't real."

"What about the bomb?"

"Can't say for sure, but it looks like an authentic crisis. That doesn't mean the Remies aren't exploiting it."

"A MADE event."

"Exactly, but we might shave a few points off. A story will break in about half an hour showing the airport killer has been caught."

"Great, but can you help find the bomb?"

Chase wanted to ask where she was, but knew she'd never answer. He knew Tess had been hiding in Mexico—that much he'd learned from the Astronaut, who was only speculating—but she'd been living in a border town, and had a powerful drug cartel contact. He could picture Tess south of the border with her collection of cowboy boots and love of the dusty corners of the American southwest. She'd have ways to sneak across the border, maybe hit a two-stepping dance hall. With her fiery eyes the color of wet jade, and whatever color her long hair was this week, she could always find a partner.

A text message came in from Tess while they were talking, it told him not to mention it, just to say yes if he'd received, read, and understood it.

"Yes," he said. He'd tell about this secret communication later.

"Good," Tess replied, as if it was nothing. "I'm working on the bomb. It could be so many people if it's real, so many more if it's not."

"Causing major disruptions."

"Isn't that what they always want? Whoever it is."

"Yeah."

"But the reason I'm calling is that you have to slow down," Tess warned. "You're going to miss something, and that will get you killed."

"No way I'm slowing down," Chase said. "They've already killed Wen's grandmother and gone after Tu. They've wiped out my army, they're going after my family—everything."

"You won't survive if you're being fueled by revenge, not logic."

"I'm being driven by fear," Chase blurted. "I'm afraid they're going to swallow up everything, that they'll take whatever shreds of freedom we have left, that they will butcher the truth so that we won't be able to recognize it anymore, even when we're in the middle of it. Even when we know, we *won't* know. I'm afraid they'll get that final piece, whatever it is, and the fifty-two Remies will own the world."

"They already have."

"No . . . I can't believe that," Chase said.

"The rape is complete."

Chase said nothing for several moments. "We have a chance, at least until the Fear Meter tips over eight-two-nine."

"You can try," Tess said flatly. "If anyone can do it, it would be you and Wen, but I'm preparing for what must come next."

"What could possibly be next?"

"Revolution."

Chapter Sixty-Five
WASHINGTON DC

Monday - 2:32 pm - Eastern time

Before Tess ended the call with Chase and Wen, Chase asked her about Franco. "You recall telling me several years back that Franco Madden was dead?"

"Maybe."

"I asked if you had questioned him about the Killcore program, about the connections to Mossad and other intelligence agencies, including the CIA."

"Sounds vaguely familiar."

"I handed him to you, left him there for you to pick up. What happened?"

"Had to release him."

"Why?"

"He knew the right people."

"What people? Remies?"

"Franco seemed like a common player," Tess explained. "Easy to underestimate with his *head of security for a major corporation* job title, but haven't you learned by now it's often those odd, quirky types that work the gaps? The Astronaut, Spraggins, Franco—I know you could list many more."

"So?"

"Franco might help you out."

"I can't trust him."

"No, of course not."

"What's his angle? Who is he working for? What's his objective in all this?"

"I'm not sure. With Franco, we may never know."

"We're at the same place we were when you lied about his death and that his knowledge of the Killcore program went with him. I told you that day that if you live long enough, eventually you learn everything."

"Then live a little longer."

"You didn't tell Tess *why* Franco contacted you," Wen said afterwards. "Do you think she knew?"

"No. She probably assumes it has to do with the Killcore program. It's where quite a bit of the technology came for the Killtrons."

"You haven't asked him, either."

"No. After we take care of the Surgeon."

"Then Franco may want to kill us again."

"I don't think so."

"Why?"

"Something in what Tess said. I think we're on the same side now."

"My enemy's enemy is my friend."

Chase nodded.

Chase and Wen spent the ensuing hours in close contact with Spraggins, monitoring the constantly moving Fear Meter as it bounced with each news story of civil unrest, and then fell again as a natural settling that followed every spike.

Bull called in about things on their end. After successfully debunking the asteroid, she and Dez were focused heavily on the dirty bomb, but thus far it was proving to be a legitimate story.

Bull had also chartered a series of private jets to fly them from Washington to Miami. For security purposes, they would switch planes twice to cover their tracks.

Spraggins joined them later in the day once the Fear Meter hit eight-point-one-two. "It could tip at any time."

"And there will really be no turning back?" Chase asked.

"Haven't I explained this well enough? The difficulty in getting back from where we are *now* is extreme. The possibility of getting back once we pass eight-two-nine is *none*."

"Didn't we get a big subtraction from the collapse of the asteroid story?"

"Not as much as we would have if we weren't drowning in the dirty bomb."

"The Airport killer was just arrested," Wen said.

"There!" Chase said, wondering why it had taken several hours longer than Tess had predicted.

Spraggins fiddled with the controls. "That bought us a little time."

"How much?"

"Can't say for sure. At least an hour, but based on the trajectory of the initial results, I'd say we'll be down to eight-zero-five by this evening—unless something else pops."

"That's it?" Wen asked, disappointed. "It won't even drop below eight?" She had told Chase earlier that this was perhaps the most nerve-racking situation they'd ever dealt with, since anything at any moment could tip them past the point of no return and send the world spinning into anarchy. The stress of having so little control and not even knowing when the ticking clock could explode on them was terrible.

"We have some contacts," Chase said. "Let's put out a story across the internet that since the Asteroid was fake news and there's evidence that the Airport killer is a fraud, the dirty bomb could very well be bogus."

"Will that work?" Wen asked.

"Anything to cast some doubt on the finality of these stories," Spraggins said. "But that might only buy us hours."

"How do we get more?"

"Stop the five."

"Five?"

"There may be fifty-two Remies, but only five earn the title *Fear Master*. Tane and Blanc, Doorset, Miner, and Snyder are the five Fear Masters. They have to be locked up to stop this madness."

Chapter Sixty-Six

SAN FRANCISCO

Monday - 9:52 pm - Pacific time (Tuesday, 12:52 am Eastern)

Dez and Bull were enjoying the view of the San Francisco Bay from their twenty-million-dollar, multi-level penthouse, a towering monument of modern architecture with sleek glass walls and steel beams that reached up sixty feet. Their lavish home sat perched on the top four floors of a new four-hundred-foot tower. As well as the bay, the place offered a stunning panorama of the city skyline.

After the financial meltdowns and all the threats against Chase and Wen, Dez had created the sanctuary that included AI-enabled security systems and a full-time staff of private security guards made up of sixteen former special ops agents. "It's supposed to be impenetrable," he told Chase more than once, but they knew nothing could ever be totally safe.

However, when a loud explosion shook the building,

followed immediately by sounds of shattering glass and frantic shouting, whatever illusion of safety had existed immediately fell apart.

They'd been thrown to the ground by the shockwave. Bull quickly got to her feet and helped Dez up. She ran to the window. "Oh my god! There's a group of armed men descending from a helicopter!"

"What?"

"It's hovering over the roof. Why didn't the AI deploy the laser pulses?" She grabbed her sleek, black, customized laptop and began furiously typing, her eyes fixed on the screen. "We're being hacked!" she shouted. "The firewalls are down!"

"Are they in the security system?" Dez asked. The faint hum of his exoskeleton legs was drowned out by machine-gun fire on a lower floor. He gave a voice command and the screens of the security monitors flickered on, and then went dead. "They've cut the power to the penthouse!"

"Here," she handed him her laptop, "you can see the last positions of our people and the attackers."

"Where are you going?"

"We have to get in touch with Chase," she shouted.

A series of dim backup lights illuminated automatically, along with multiple blinking red warning bulbs.

Dez typed into the laptop, sending the images to his security chief, then grabbed his phone and tried calling him. No signal.

"I can't get a call out!" Bull yelled. "They're jamming everything!"

"I know. I can't reach Preston, either," he snapped, attempting every way to get the chief of security to respond to his urgent requests.

Bull nodded and reclaimed her laptop. "Here." She gave him his, which was also a powerful, specially built computer with satellite access. She frantically typed away, trying to bypass the jamming signal. As she worked, the sound of gunfire and explosions grew louder. "Keep trying to get through to Chase," she said. "See if you can do a work around on the network."

"If I can access Heaven . . . "

"I'm into the AI security program. The drones are charged and don't need power."

"Launch them."

"Already done," she said as ten small drones equipped with micro-tasers left their stations on the lower level.

The luxury penthouse became an apocalyptic wasteland. The attackers unleashed a violent onslaught of bullets, whizzing past their heads. "We need to get to safety!" Dez yelled over more booming explosions as their security team fought back.

Bull nodded, her eyes darting frantically around the room as she searched for an escape route, still attempting to hack back into the security system to release the AI weapons defense. "I can't get in. They're *blocking* us," she yelled, furious. "*How* are they doing it?"

"We need to move. They're getting closer," Dez said urgently, motioning towards the steps.

Bull nodded, and they made a dash for the open staircase.

"Do you smell that?" Dez asked, coughing as smoke overtook the area. At the same time, he pulled a pistol from a drawer.

As they descended the stairs, the couple could now see their security personnel engaged in brutal gun battles with the intruders, who were armed with AK-47s, limit-explosive devices, and body armor. The guards fought hard, but they were outnumbered and outgunned.

"That fire is spreading," Bull said, pointing to the lower level. "We have to get out of the building."

"Too dangerous," Dez shouted. "Let's get into the panic-room. It has an oxygen system."

"No good if the building burns around it."

"I'm sure the fire department and police are already on the way. This is visible for miles."

A masked man appeared below the stairs. Without hesitating, Dez, having the advantage of being directly above him, shot the man at close range in the face.

Startled, Bull jumped. In the near darkness, she hadn't seen the approaching figure. "Good shot, babe!"

After ducking and weaving their way through the now unrecognizable landscape of the ravaged third floor, they finally reached the panic room, a massive steel vault designed to withstand the most extreme attacks. Bull tried to call Chase again, but the strong jamming signal still blocked it.

"We're completely cut off from the outside world."

"We're going to make it through this," Dez said, his voice strong and confident. "There's enough food, water, and supplies to last us for days."

"Days . . . the fire isn't going to take that long to bring down the building."

"We can hold out until the police arrive."

Bull nodded, her eyes fixed on the laptop. "I won't stop until I find a way back into the system," she said determinedly.

The sounds of explosions and gunfire still filled the once

grand penthouse, but they were safe for now. However, the once-impressive structure was now a shell of its former self, with broken glass and debris littering the floors, fires raging, and an ongoing battle as the surviving three members of their team fought to hold off another wave of attackers.

Chapter Sixty-Seven

SAN FRANCISCO

Monday - 10:09 pm - Pacific time (Tuesday. 1:09 am Eastern)

Dez and Bull, now cornered in the safe room, continued to work their laptops, trying to thwart the vicious attack. Bull maneuvered the taser drones into position and managed to disable eight men before the micro aircrafts were destroyed.

The action allowed the final three security guards to kill those eight, plus another six, but it wasn't enough. They were soon buried by the never-ending onslaught.

As Dez and Bull watched the CCTV feed on their laptops, they saw Khan's imposing figure loom into view, a deadly aura emanating from his very being.

"We're screwed," Bull said. "That's Khan out there."

They both knew of the brutal killer employed by Tane and Blanc. He'd ordered the hit on Zu Mu and Tu. The massive resistance the Terminators had encountered at the Federal Reserve, the defense contractor, and other recent raids had his fingerprints all over them. Chase had asked

Bull to try to find anything they could on Khan. She hadn't come up with much more than a photo. That, plus the trail of death and destruction in his wake, not unlike his namesake, told them all they needed to know about their situation.

"If he's here, we're dead."

"He can't get in," Dez said as they huddled closer together in the confined space.

"This guy will blow the whole building apart to get to us. He's like a torture expert."

"We've got the pistol and," he opened a drawer, "this uzi, with plenty of ammo."

She nodded. "Okay, okay. Maybe I can get the AI up."

"And the police are coming," Dez said. "I've just seen the report."

Suddenly, the power went out, leaving them in complete darkness. A few moments later, they heard a faint beeping sound, indicating that the failsafe third backup generator had kicked in.

"Something's not right," Bull said, noticing that the CCTV feed on their laptops was now displayed blurry and distorted.

"What's that sound?" Dez asked, pulling himself up out of the hard chair.

Bull's fingers danced on the keys of her laptop, hoping she could locate the source of the camera hack and restore the images, their only view to the outer world. "Damn it!" she yelled. "Khan's infiltrated all the systems. He's trying to bypass the locks." She pointed to the vault door.

"No way," Dez said. "The locks are too sophisticated. The codes are randomized and ever-changing. Without the key-code template—"

"Damnit! He has the blueprints of the penthouse and the schematics of the whole AI security system."

"No! How?"

"And the door. I can see the hack. He's using a synchronizer-randomizer."

"Even so, it'd take twenty-four hours or more for the right sequence to select."

"Try two minutes."

"*What?*"

Bull put the laptop down, stood up, and aimed the Uzi at the door.

Dez tried the electronic keypad, desperate to contact the police, anyone. "It's fried!" He turned the pistol toward the door.

"I love you, Dez."

"Me, too." He stared into her eyes. The only light, coming from the blue hue of the two laptops, gave her a soft, angelic glow. "We're going to be talking about this night for years. Don't worry."

"Yeah, a great story for our kids."

Just then, lock cylinders inside the heavy door clicked, released by some electronic series of numbers that should never have been known.

Khan, the ruthless killer, had found a way in.

They were trapped. They had fought their way through countless obstacles to get to the safety of the room, but now it seemed like it was all for nothing.

Two men clad in bulletproof armor, including heavy face shields, entered with steel clubs and quickly disabled and disarmed the pair.

"Why didn't they kill us?" Bull yelled to Dez, but before he could answer, Khan walked in.

The vicious man stared down at them, the room now lit with powerful light bricks. "They didn't kill you because that's my job."

Chapter Sixty-Eight

Khan stood tall in the center of the room, his gray eyes flickering over Dez and Bull, calculating his next move. His hand was wrapped around the hilt of a gleaming knife. The Nesmuk tattoo on his wrist seemed to pulse with his heartbeat.

Bull took a step forward, her eyes fixed on the knife in Khan's hand. She knew that if they didn't act fast, they would both be dead. "You're not getting out of here alive," she growled, her fists clenched at her sides.

He laughed. "That's amusing."

One of the men grabbed her roughly, shoving Bull against the wall and securing her wrists with zip ties. It felt like the man had broken her arm.

Dez knew it was useless to fight, but he tried anyway, lunging toward Khan. One of the men used a taser device to disable his exoskeleton legs and Dez fell backwards.

"You two don't get it, do you?" Khan said, his voice low and dangerous. "I *always* get what I want. And what I want right now is for you both to suffer."

Bull cussed at him, unleashing a long stream of profanity, knowing that if she didn't remain angry, she might cry, and that was not how she wanted to die.

"I hope you don't mind putting these cameras on. It would be a big help."

"No!" Dez snapped.

"Help what?" Bull asked angrily, trying to imagine what possible use a camera could have.

"I'm glad you asked. The cameras will record your deaths from your point of view. We're going to send the footage to Chase. The men I work for want him to see the people closest to him die. You understand, don't you? A kind of psychological warfare."

"Forget it!" Bull said.

The men put the cameras on them anyway, and then led them out of the safe room, pushing and shoving Bull and dragging Dez. Finally, Bull kicked and bit enough that one of the men slung her small, slender body over his shoulders as if she were a sack of grain.

Soon they were on the balcony, four hundred feet above the busy street below.

"I wish I had more time, but since you fouled up my plans by calling the police, although I enjoy killing law enforcement, that would be a whole other episode, and I'm quite busy as of late. Although my schedule will be opening up a bit now that Chase Malone's pretend army has been eradicated. Yes, that's correct, I see the terror in your eyes. No one is coming to save you. Regardless, I must keep to a schedule, can't be sloppy."

"Go to hell," Dez spat.

"Yes, that is quite likely, but not tonight. You, on the other hand, are going to learn a great deal about how the universe works, which religion got it right and all that fun stuff. But, I am a gentlemen, so, ladies first." He carefully raised his knife, and in almost slow motion, he pushed it toward Bull's chest. "This is for the camera. We'll speed it up in post-production. Please do your best to look scared. Terrified might be overdoing it, but you decide."

Then, all at once, with a cold, calculated movement, he plunged his knife into Bull's chest. She collapsed to the ground, her eyes wide with shock and pain.

"One quick twist and it's done," he said, then turned to Dez. "I've done this before—many times, actually. I assure you she felt a great deal of agony, but only for a brief time." He wiped the bloody blade clean on Dez's shirt.

Dez gasped and stuttered, unable to find words, choking on a wretched scream. His face contorted into something unrecognizable as shock overtook his senses.

"What do you think of that?" Khan asked. "Your girlfriend is dead. Look at the death on her face. She makes a good victim. Pretty, but by no means beautiful. I think Chase will be disgusted by her brutal death. Wouldn't you love to see his expression when he watches this?"

"You . . . you *animal*!"

"Great ad-libbing, that will definitely make it into the final cut. Thanks for your dedication to the project. I wish you had time for a goodbye kiss. That might add to the drama, but be a little too romantic. Let's just get to your big scene, shall we? It's the finale."

"Chase will avenge me!"

"Excellent! You're a real natural. I'd love it if you would scream, 'Chase, avenge me, avenge me!' kind of like you're giving him the assignment. Deathbed promise and all that. Drama, real drama."

Dez shook his head.

"Okay, we'll work with what we have." Khan smiled.

"Anyway, on to it." He nodded, and the two men picked Dez up, one holding his metal legs, the other his arms. "Now, Dez, remember, the camera is rolling. You're going to scream for me," Khan whispered, a cruel smile on his lips. "And then I'm going to watch you die."

Dez just scowled. Then he realized *how* he would die as the men lifted him up and held him over the rail. He could feel the wind against his face, and suddenly shivered and felt very cold.

"Oh, sorry, didn't mean to confuse you. I'm really not the best director. You don't have to scream *now*, just scream on the way *down*. I assume it will be automatic. Everyone always screams as they fall from the top of a building."

Dez glared back at him.

"Okay, here we go. On the count of three. One . . . Two . . . two and a half . . . Two and three quarters . . . I'm just prolonging it to make you suffer more. You understand my little counting-trick to torture, don't you? Okay, seriously here we go. Three!"

The men tossed Dez off the roof. Dez didn't utter a single sound as he fell to his death.

Chapter Sixty-Nine
WASHINGTON DC

Tuesday - 9:08 pm - Eastern time.

Another film came in via the Killtrons' reception center link on the Destino. Chase and Wen stared in horrified silence as they watched Khan personally murder two of their oldest and closest friends. Neither of them cried. Witnessing the brutal, cold callousness of Khan transformed any sad emotions into something else, something more akin to rage, something like vengeance, but what it actually was was a temporary abandonment of hope.

At the end, when Dez didn't scream. Chase let out an anguished moan, as if his heart were torn in half, as if all the good had vanished from the world. His hands were trembling, so he balled them into fists. "We have to find Khan."

"We won't have to," Wen said. "He'll find us."

"How do you know?"

"Because that's his job." She turned back to the screen. "Just look at him. Pure efficient evil. He'll find us soon."

"I hope so."

"We have to be ready."

"I'm ready."

"Remember what Tess said. Don't let yourself be fueled by revenge instead of logic."

"Screw logic!" Chase barked, pointing to the screen. "You saw what I just saw. Khan is the antithesis of logic. Hell, this guy is the antithesis of anything good. Khan is the antichrist."

"Maybe, but don't let him consume your soul."

"See that timestamp? Ten-oh-nine pm," Chase said, pointing to the paused footage, frozen in the moment when they tossed Dez off the roof. "That's exactly when we're going to storm Blanc's home."

The Astronaut called to let them know that he and Tu were on their way to Denmark, which really meant France. They'd decided that as much as Tu needed to see them in person, it was too risky in this climate. As soon as they arrived in France, a video chat would have to do. They did allow a brief conversation where Tu told them of none of his bravery and instead talked about how much he missed Zu Mu, about how she'd told him to protect the seeds, how he still had them. Chase and Wen told him how much they loved him, how proud they were of him, and that they would talk to him again soon. It was one of the hardest things they'd ever done, to not go to him immediately.

The Astronaut confirmed the information Franco had given them. The Surgeon's offices and Blanc's favorite mansion were both in Miami. Chase and Wen would be there in a matter of hours, weapons delivered and building plans sourced.

"More trouble with Snyder," the Astronaut told them. He had been tracking several of the key pieces of evidence from the Deputy Chief of Staff's drive. "Snyder must be aware of the entire contents you received. They're already covering things up."

"What about the leaks we sent to our solid media contacts?" Chase asked.

"Those attempts failed. The journalists and bloggers were unable to verify. We have suffered credibility issues now."

"And the law enforcement?"

"The few people we have a reputation with pursued what we gave them and came up with nothing."

"What's going on?"

"We have wasted considerable resources, exorbitant amounts of time, and lost the faith and trust of our valued allies."

"Yeah," Chase said. "And with all that evidence, *something* should have happened."

"It seems suspicious."

"Maybe they already control everything, even the people we think are on our side."

"Perhaps the elites have so much control that even we are compromised without knowing it," the Astronaut said.

The thought gave Chase a headache. "Spraggins calls Tane, Blanc, Miner, Doorset, and Snyder the 'fear masters'. They've been increasing the global fear levels in order to institute total control. What if they've already won?"

Chapter Seventy

ATLANTA, GEORGIA

Tuesday - 1:10 pm - Eastern time

The Hartsfield-Jackson Atlanta International Airport was teeming with people, each rushing to their destinations, the low drone of announcements creating a background noise to the chaos. The travelers moved in tangles, some quickly, some a more confused meandering, toward their gates. Chase and Wen scanned the crowds for any signs of trouble as they exited the terminal and walked across the tarmac toward the private jet that would take them to Florida. The hot, humid air hit them like a smothering blanket. Just as they reached the jet, they noticed a group of heavily armed men and women moving toward them.

"We're under attack!" Wen snapped.

Inside the plane, they quickly grabbed guns from the supply that had been preloaded and delivered from the grocery agencies. The assorted weapons were meant for use in their meeting with the Surgeon later in the day.

"Get in the air!" Chase yelled to the pilot, but before he

could even start the engine, bullets shattered the windshield and filled the cockpit, killing both crew members.

On the tarmac, the sound of gunshots added to the complex mingle of taxiing planes, starting engines, airport equipment, and vehicles, sending screaming workers running for cover.

"Get out, get out!" Wen yelled, spotting a man about to shoot an RPG at the plane.

They hit the concrete hard and scrambled away seconds before the plane blew up. The force of the blast knocked them off their feet. They recovered and ran for shelter.

The humid air, thick with the smell of jet fuel and the constant hum of engines, coupled with the burning plane, sounds of gunfire, and distant sirens, gave the tarmac around them the feel of a disaster scene. Debris and smoke obscuring their vision, they stuck close to a line of airport vehicles.

As the air cleared, they spotted a towering figure with a muscular build among the attackers, his cropped brown hair and trimmed beard matted with sweat. "That's Khan!" Wen shouted. The Nesmuk knife tattoo on the underside of his wrist was visible even from a distance.

Khan's men had fanned out, each taking up positions.

Chase and Wen, badly outnumbered, exchanged a quick glance, their unspoken communication colored in the tension of the moment.

"We need to split up, take them from different angles," Wen said.

Chase nodded. "You go left, I'll take the right."

She pulled out another two magazines and gave them to him.

"You take the bag of tricks," he said, reaching in and pulling out two grenades.

With that, they moved in opposite directions. As they drew closer to their targets, Wen ducked behind a line of luggage trucks, peering out as she exchanged shots with Khan's men. She could hear the sound of Chase's gun from the other side of the tarmac, and knew he was facing the same intensity of resistance, but they did not have comms in. Wen began setting off small explosions, which tipped Chase off to her plan.

Fires erupted in fuel storage areas.

Wen moved like a panther, appearing and disappearing, the blasts acting as diversions and eliminating groups of Khan's men. The sounds of sirens in the distance and the thick black smoke added to the chaos as ancillary explosions occurred on their own.

Wen, moving in quickly from the left, took out men as she went searching for her ultimate target. She could see Khan a few feet away, his face contorted in fury. She fired at him, the bullet grazing his arm, but he refused to go down.

Khan bellowed in rage, firing back with even more intensity. "You're nothing!" he shouted, unloading the Uzi at her as if he were a gangster with a tommygun.

As Khan ducked behind a catering truck, Chase appeared on top of a maintenance vehicle.

Khan's cold gray eyes fixed on Chase. A sneer twisted his lips as he raised his Uzi and fired. "Find the weakness in your enemies, and your enemy's weakness will defeat them!" he yelled.

Chase fell from the roof.

Chapter Seventy-One

Wen tackled Khan, sending him crashing to the ground. Khan's Uzi clattered out of his hand, and he struggled to reach for his knife. Wen pinned him down, but Khan was much stronger, and managed to flip her over. Straddling her, he pulled out his knife. "You look like your grandmother. She was ugly when she was about to die, just like you. I wasn't there, but I saw the video. You would have loved it." Ready to plunge his knife into her chest, he raised it high. "My chest cam will record this, so look scared. I'm hoping to show it to that little boy of yours before I kill him. He won't escape next time."

By slipping at the exact moment Khan had fired his Uzi, Chase had avoided being killed. Later, he would say he felt hands push him, hands he instinctively believed had been those of his dead best friend, Dez. Chase climbed up the exterior of the movable corridor connecting a terminal gate to an aircraft to get a better view. He spotted Khan about to kill Wen. Chase didn't have time to aim, or get a better angle, or to think at all. While running on top of the jetway, he squeezed the trigger.

To be sure his bullets didn't accidentally hit Wen, he aimed high. Two bullets entered Khan's upper back. He fell limply onto Wen, his knife dropping onto the pavement next to her head. The weight of him surprised her as she wrestled to get out from under his body.

"Oh, princess, I'm not dead yet!" Khan barked while he elbowed her in the face. Getting to his feet, the big man kicked her several times in the head. Although he wanted to find his knife and finish her off, or at least drag her away with him to be a hostage, he saw Chase jumping off the jetway, heading toward him.

"Live to fight another day," he muttered, knowing his three bullet wounds would be weakening him by the second. He darted off under the plane.

Woozy, Wen recovered Khan's Uzi and stumbled after him. She cut through a maintenance area and got close enough to take a shot.

Running across the runway, Khan stumbled backward as at least one bullet hit him in the leg. Khan cried out in pain, but kept going, running and limping, disappearing in front of a plane.

Chase pursued across the tarmac, firing bursts at Khan, but he managed to evade Chase's bullets this time and climbed up the wing of a passenger jet that was preparing for takeoff. Chase had no choice but to follow, knowing that Khan would be able to escape if he got clear of the runways.

As Chase reached the top of the wing, he saw Khan standing at the edge, looking down at the tarmac. Chase raised his gun and pointed it at Khan.

"You're finished, Khan," Chase yelled over the loud engine.

Khan looked at Chase with wild eyes. "You think you've won? You have no idea what's coming," Khan said, his voice laced with hatred.

"I'll enjoy seeing you in prison."

Khan lunged at him, but his injuries slowed his strike and Chase fired two shots. Khan tried to duck and fell backward off the airliner. "That's for Dez and Bull, you bastard," Chase yelled, believing one of his shots had connected. He ran to the edge of the wing and looked down at Khan, now desperately trying to grab onto anything to stop his slide towards the jet engine.

"Help!" Khan shouted, just as his feet got sucked into the turbine. He let out a bloodcurdling scream as his legs disappeared into the spinning blades, rotating at 20,000 times per second, pushing 1.2 million tons of air through the engine at the same time. The thin blades cut his feet and legs into millions of tiny pieces.

Chase could only watch in horror as the powerful thrust sucked Khan in further, slicing the rest of him apart. Khan squealed and shrieked. The deafening sound of the engine meant no one could hear his last gasp of life.

The powerful turning pulled the rest of him in, and the remaining puree of Khan filtered into the engine's combustion chamber, which cooked him at temperatures exceeding 1,100 degrees Fahrenheit. Chase covered his nose as the smell of burning flesh filled the air.

Before being ejected out the back of the engine, one more set of blades minced anything remaining of Khan and sent the liquified waste of the cruel man out as part of the hot gases and exhaust blowing at a velocity above 600 mph.

"Wished we'd filmed that," Chase muttered, jumping down off the wing. The airport was thrown further into chaos as fire, rescue, and security rushed to the scene.

Wen joined Chase on the tarmac, his gun still in hand.

"Hard way to go," she said, making a disgusted face.

"Too good for Khan," Chase said. "Delivered to hell in a cup."

Chapter Seventy-Two

WASHINGTON DC

Tuesday - 2:29 pm - Eastern time

The TV news anchor sat nervously in the bright studio of the network's Washington bureau, her hair and makeup touched up seconds before going live. "Good afternoon, I'm Rachel King, and we're coming to you with an exclusive story. According to our sources, Massachusetts Senator Lowell Wentworth, who was believed to have been assassinated just yesterday outside his home, has cast the deciding vote on a controversial piece of legislation."

The camera panned to the on-air reporter waiting in front of the US Capitol, the imposing building looming behind as he began his report. "That's right, Rachel," he said, his voice hushed. "I'm Peter West, coming to you live from the steps of the United States Capitol, where we've just witnessed an incredible event. As you know, Senator Wentworth was believed to have been assassinated yesterday. The news of his sudden, violent murder sent shockwaves through the country, and no one knew who was behind it."

Rachel's brow furrowed in confusion. "But now it seems that the Senator's death was all part of a secret security measure? That, in fact, Senator Wentworth was actually alive and well all along, and that his death was faked in order to protect him from numerous threats?"

The reporter nodded gravely. "That's right, Rachel. And the reason for this elaborate ruse? To allow Senator Wentworth to cast the deciding vote on a controversial piece of legislation that would mandate regular and complete audits of all Federal Reserve operations. The vote for this bill is a long time coming. It was originally scheduled to occur this Friday, but was moved up to this morning as part of the extreme measures taken to assure the safety of Wentworth and other senators."

"And what exactly will this legislation do?"

"The bill will bring much-needed transparency and accountability to the Federal Reserve, which has long been criticized for its opaque financial dealings."

Rachel shuffled some papers in front of her, as if looking for an answer to the strange story, and repeated, "So the Senator was *faking* his own death all so that he could make this vote?"

"That's right, and it's a vote that could have huge ramifications for the country's financial system. Now that this bill has passed the Senate, if it is signed by the president, something he has indicated he *will* do prior to election day, it would mean much greater transparency and accountability for the Federal Reserve, something that many people believe is sorely needed."

"Where were these threats originating from?"

"That's unclear. However, it is well known that this bill

has been vehemently opposed by the Fed, and many wealthy bankers and billionaires, who do not want the Fed subject to these kinds of audits. Critics say that is because they are hiding details of market manipulations and the siphoning off of trillions of dollars in taxpayer money over the prior two decades."

"Amazing." She shook her head. "But what about the laws and senate procedures? Wasn't faking his own death illegal?"

The reporter checked his notes. "Actually, no, Rachel. It's actually not illegal so long as no financial claims are made, such as insurance or other death benefits. In fact, there are no senate rules against such a tactic."

Rachel nodded slowly, her mind spinning with questions. "Well, there you have it, folks," she said finally. "An incredible turn of events, and one that is sure to have everyone talking. For now, we'll have to wait and see what happens next. One thing is for sure, this is a story that we'll be following closely in the days and weeks to come."

Chase and Wen caught the news of the successful senate vote in the Miami International Airport. "Khan is dead, and the vote is secure," Wen said, smiling.

"Neither affects the Fear Meter directly, but I'll take it," Chase said. "Big blows against the Remie empire."

"He's *alive*!?" Tane barked. "Wentworth *faked* his death? What trickery!"

The aide looked at both Blanc and Tane, trying to

decide who was angrier. "Apparently Chase Malone had a plant inside Khan's organization. Someone named Duncan."

"Have Duncan killed," Blanc ordered. "And get Khan on the phone."

"I've been trying," the aide said. "He hasn't been responding."

"I bet he hasn't," Tane said, scowling.

"Can we get the president to delay signing? Leave it for the next administration? Snyder will never sign this garbage, and our man will shred it if we somehow beat the Mayor."

"Doubtful, but we'll look at it."

"Then the current president may need a scandal."

"No time for that," Tane said

Tane and Blanc shared a glance.

Blanc lowered his voice, as if it were necessary. "Then the president may have to die."

Chapter Seventy-Three

NEW YORK, NEW YORK

Tuesday - 4:29 pm - Eastern time

The grand ballroom of the Plaza Hotel, located in the heart of Manhattan, was filled to capacity with reporters and journalists from all around the world. The place buzzed with anticipation as they waited for Mayor Warren Snyder to arrive.

As soon as the Mayor entered the room, the reporters fell silent. He made his way to the podium, his face stern and serious. The room was filled with tension as the Mayor began his address.

Snyder stood by the NYPD Police Chief, several other police officers and city officials flanking him on either side. "Ladies and gentlemen, I come to you today with some very important news. As you all know, for the past few days our country has been gripped by a grave threat after federal officials received intelligence that a group of terrorists had planted a dirty bomb somewhere in the United States.

However, we did not know which city was the target. Today, hours ago, we discovered the city."

There was a collective gasp from the reporters, followed by a moment of silence as they waited for the Mayor to continue.

"Today, I am pleased to announce that an elite unit of the NYPD has apprehended the ring of terrorists who planted the dirty bomb in Manhattan. They have been neutralized, and the bomb has been safely defused."

The room erupted in applause and cheers as the reporters let out sighs of relief. The Mayor continued his speech, answering questions from the reporters and giving details about the operation and the exact location.

The mood in the room lightened. There was a palpable sense of relief as the Mayor spoke. "People had been fleeing in huge numbers from virtually every city in the country, and the panic and riots had caused chaos across the nation. But now that we've captured the terrorists and the bomb has been neutralized, things can return to normal."

As the press conference ended, the reporters swarmed around the Mayor, asking questions and trying to get a statement. He answered them all patiently, reassuring them that the situation was under control.

In the corner of the room, a young woman with a press badge pinned to her blouse stood watching the scene unfold. She had been sent by another Remie, and already knew what the Mayor would be saying. She was there for a different reason: she needed to know *everything* about the man she would one day have an affair with, a plan that she hoped would end in his death.

Miami, Florida
Tuesday - 4:48 pm - Eastern time

Chase called Spraggins.

"The Fear Meter is down to seven-seven-seven," Spraggins reported.

"Sounds like our lucky day," Chase said.

"Yes, the Overwhelm is delayed for now" Spraggins said, his tone one of relief mixed with concern. "The dirty bomb had ratcheted up the Meter, but it's fallen back nicely."

"You could be happier," Wen said.

"Perhaps, but we know they are already planning the next MADE event."

"So are we," Chase said. "We're still trying to get a location on Tane, but we have appointments with the Surgeon and Blanc later this evening."

"Are they expecting you?"

"No, that would take all the fun out of it."

Spraggins watched the Fear Meter bounce still lower as the media reports replayed clips from Snyder's speech. "Blanc and Tane are one thing, but the next president of the United States is going to be Warren Snyder, and that may be the scariest thing ever."

"A wolf in sheep's clothing," Chase said. "He's on our list."

"You're going to need a new army, and a much bigger one this time."

"Or a secret weapon."

"You have one?"

"Working on it."

New York, New York
Tuesday - 6:27 pm - Eastern time

In the grandiose, multi-floor penthouse overlooking Central Park, Snyder, who had never resided in the traditional Mayor's residence at Gracie Mansion, huddled with his campaign manager.

"You're a national hero," Kellerman said.

Snyder sipped a drink and stared out over the Park. "Not a bad day's work."

"You were already leading. Now you're so far ahead in the polls, I predict you'll win the presidency by the largest landslide in history."

"Let's not make it too large," Snyder said, turning around, a large grin on his face.

Another man walked in.

"Aarons, good to see you looking a lot better than you did in your crime scene photos," Kellerman said.

"Yes," Snyder added. "Last time I saw you, you were lying dead in a pool of blood."

"To quote Mark Twain," the deputy chief of staff said, "'The reports of my death have been greatly exaggerated.'"

"Unlike Senator Wentworth, there were no reports of your death," Kellerman said. "Funny that Chase Malone used the same tactic against Tane and Blanc that we used against him."

"He might have figured it out if he wasn't so busy chasing down all the phony leads about me," Snyder said. "Busy enough to miss the real stuff, like the fact that we were behind the bomb."

"Perhaps we're the ones who missed the trick," the deputy said. "We should have recognized that Wentworth's death was as fake as mine."

"In our defense," Kellerman said, "Tane and Blanc *wanted* Wentworth dead. We knew they'd ordered the hit, so . . ."

The deputy nodded. "But the Fed audit will be a problem for us, too."

"We'll deal with that once I'm inaugurated."

"We can't just repeal the law," the deputy said.

"Then we will just need a good old fashioned banking crisis."

"That may not be enough."

"We'll throw in a pandemic or a war if we have to—the point is when *I'm* in charge, things will go as they need to go. Everything is about to change. Even Tane and Blanc won't like it, but the beauty is everything they've been doing for the past twenty years has set up the perfect storm."

"Perfect for you," Kellerman said.

Snyder raised his glass in the air. "I'm a damned hurricane, and the world isn't even remotely prepared for what's about to come."

Chapter Seventy-Four

MIAMI, FLORIDA

Tuesday - 8:53 pm - Eastern time

Chase and Wen, dressed in tactical gear, stood in a dark corner of the parking garage adjoining the building that housed the Surgeon's operations. They'd reviewed and memorized the blueprints of the building, and they were adequately armed. There were multiple plans and contingencies in place, but in the end they understood that this was a secure Remie facility, and once they went in, they might not come back out.

"Everything Franco gave us seems to check out," Chase said, testing their comms. "But why do I still not trust him?"

"Because he tried to kill us so many times," Wen said.

"Yeah, there's that."

"The Astronaut verified this. We go get the Surgeon, that, that . . . "

"Psycho," Chase finished, "and reunite him with Khan in hell."

"Yes. Let's do it."

The advanced technology facility stood at ten stories. However, the nerve center, where the Surgeon operated, was a long, narrow room occupying the upper two levels, known as *910*.

Wen pointed to the room on her wrist pad. "That's the target."

Just before nine pm, when few workers remained, Chase and Wen initiated the assault. Donning gas masks, they began at the ground level and worked their way up floor by floor, utilizing knock-out gas to take out the isolated stragglers and occasional security personnel. They minimized casualties, and were able to quickly ascend the tower.

However, when they burst into 910, their tactics changed.

The room, more like a broad hallway, resembled the bridge of a futuristic spaceship. Its lighting was cold and muted, almost all the illumination coming from the countless monitors and advanced computer equipment lining the walls. Twelve technicians busily worked at what was nearing the end of their ten-hour shift. Another group would show up at midnight.

They killed most of the small team, who they considered accessories to the murders of Zu Mu, Dez, Bull, Blitz, Weston, Diego, and more than one thousand Terminators. They left three alive to question.

"Where is he?" Chase asked one of the men.

"Who?" the man asked.

Wen shot him in the leg. "Wrong answer."

He fell to the floor, reeling in pain.

"Where is he?" Chase asked again.

"You're going to kill me anyway."

"That's right," Wen said, shooting him in the chest. She turned to the next man. "Where?"

The man pointed to a door at the end of the room. "He's in there, his workroom, calls it his 'operating room'. Been in here since we got here at two."

"Long day," Chase said.

The man nodded, then explained how there were rotating ten hour shifts for those working in 910.

"Seems hunting us down is a twenty-four-seven gig," Chase said.

The man nodded meekly, even though Chase had been talking to Wen.

While Wen moved deliberately toward the door, Chase quickly duct taped the two men together back-to-back, then secured their wrists and legs.

Almost at that same instant, a six-member crisis team appeared from the stairwell, tossing flash bombs.

"Where'd they come from?" Chase said into his comms, diving to the floor, thinking of Franco, wondering if this was the set-up, the final trap. "They weren't on the prelim!"

Wen didn't answer Chase. Instead, she answered the crisis team by hurling a specialty explosive that killed two instantly, and badly injured a third. It also ignited a small fire.

The other three men shot back. A stray bullet caught one of the unlucky prisoners in the head.

Chase opened up with his submachine gun, but soon they were retreating deeper into the room. Wen sent another explosive their way, this one bigger. Chase saw it go and jumped behind a pony wall concealing racks of computers. The windows shattered as the device left a smoldering crater in the floor, taking out part of the exterior wall.

"Police, fire, and rescue will be coming," Chase said into his comms. They knew from the blueprints that there was no exit from that side of the building. If the Surgeon was really in his operating room, he was not going to escape.

"Let's finish this then," Wen replied, already marching toward the door to the mysterious section of 910.

"No one left to shoot at us?" Chase asked, already knowing the answer. Wind whipping in from the wrecked wall fanned the flames. He wondered if they would become trapped by the fire, but part of him didn't care. He wanted to get the Surgeon.

"Not now, but, you know, we're not exactly stealth anymore."

Chase and Wen rushed into the operating room, guns drawn, ready for a firefight, ready to take down the Surgeon for good, but what they saw stunned them.

Chapter Seventy-Five

The operating room was dimly lit, with sparks flying and machinery whirring all around them. As they approached, they saw the Surgeon hunched over a console, working feverishly on one of the stolen Killtrons.

The Surgeon spun around as he heard the door slam open, a maniacal glint in his cobalt blue eyes. His hair was a wild mess, as if it hadn't been tended to in weeks. The Surgeon's gaunt face looked even more menacing under the flickering light of the fires outside.

"Ah, Chase and Wen. How nice of you to finally join me," he said in his accented English, hardly glancing up from his project. "I was beginning to think you didn't have the courage to face me yourselves."

Chase and Wen didn't flinch at his taunts as they surveyed the strange room, searching for additional signs of trouble. They'd already seen the source of his bravado. The seven Killtrons, stolen from the Terminator's Pennsylvania training center, lay on the room's workbenches in various states of service.

Chase wanted to kill the cold, dangerous man on the spot, but he also wanted answers. They slowly approached, guns still aimed at him. The operating room opened to the top floor, and Wen eyed the area for drones, but nothing but smoke could be seen.

"You people are angering me with this destruction," the Surgeon said, then cussed at them. "You will regret this mistake of yours."

"He's trying to stall for time until he gets that Killtron working," Chase said. "He's planning to use it against us."

"You have no idea what I am doing. You are not as smart as I expected, and that is something I have suspected." He frowned. "Please excuse my accidental rhyme, I was not trying to entertain you."

"You are anything but entertaining," Chase said as they moved closer. "You have been responsible for the deaths of countless innocent people—people I *cared* about."

"You care about nothing but yourself," the Surgeon sneered, his eyes narrowing. "It takes one to know one. In any regard, I have no regrets. I do what needs to be done. People must die. It is progress. The world cannot be easily molded without sacrifice, without trimming the herd. Evolution is wildly inefficient."

"Who decides who to trim?"

"I think you know that already."

"Enough talk," Wen said, inching her MP7 closer to the Surgeon, looking toward Chase. They had not decided what they would do if the Surgeon wasn't armed or fighting back. "Move your hands away from the Killtron."

"You two are upper echelon. Although annoying to me, you are still well above average. You see it, the waste that the masses consume and create. There must be a plan. This cannot be allowed to continue in a random manner. What disastrous outcomes could we expect, would we *deserve*, if we allowed it to run without proper guidance?" He shivered, as if this thought were unbearable. "Can you imagine? The disgusting people in charge of their own lives?"

"Stand up!" Wen demanded.

"Your army was counterproductive, your friends were annoying, your family in the way, you—"

"Shut up and get up!" Chase snapped.

Suddenly the Killtron that the Surgeon was working on came to life. Its advanced AI immediately recognized a threat as its complex weapons system came online.

The first person the powerful Killtron saw was the Surgeon, and in a partially malfunctioning state, it grabbed his hands to stop him from typing more commands that could harm the bot. Then, without warning, it ripped two of the man's fingers off.

The Surgeon shrieked in raging agony, which seemed to startle the Killtron, which reacted by pulling two fingers from his other hand.

Chase and Wen watched in macabre fascination as the machine quickly pulled the Surgeon's remaining fingers off one by one.

The Surgeon's blood-covered arms flailed wildly. He screamed obscenities as the staggering levels of pain left him on the verge of passing out. Finally, he began spouting voice commands to shut down the bot.

The Killtron took that as a new threat, and immediately ripped out the Surgeon's larynx, silencing him forever.

Yet somehow, still barely alive, he fell into the bot, his bloody fingerless nubs contacting broken and shorted wires inside the Killtron's exposed power center. A magnified pulsating surge instantly electrocuted the Surgeon.

Chase and Wen looked at each other, stunned.

"That was extremely unpleasant," Chase said. "In a slightly pleasant way."

Wen looked at the gruesome sight of the Surgeon's bloody, smoldering body. "Poetic justice."

The sprinkler system triggered as smoke, fire, and spraying water combined to make a toxic, dangerous fog.

"Time to go," Chase said. "Don't want to miss our next appointment."

"Wish we could take him," Wen said, pointing to the Killtron as it blinked out, a victim of the water and electrical jolt.

"Hopefully we won't need him." Chase glanced back at the Surgeon as they made their way to the stairs. "Anyway, I don't want anything between me and Blanc. Let's take him alive. I want him to rot in prison for his crimes."

Chapter Seventy-Six

MIAMI, FLORIDA

Tuesday - 10:09 pm - Eastern time

The warm tropical night air was suddenly shattered by the sound of gunfire through the vast ocean-front mansion. Timothy Blanc's eyes snapped open as he jolted awake to a thundering explosion. He sprang out of bed and rushed over to the massive monitors that dominated the walls of a control center adjoining his bedroom. The screens flickered to life, revealing a swarm of armed attackers storming the perimeter of the ninety million dollar, sixty room monstrosity he called "his primary residence."

Blanc's heart raced as he watched his private security force, the Vintons, already engaging in a brutal firefight against the invaders. Blanc had been expecting them, but never believed they'd have the nerve to *actually* show up.

The attackers were heavily armed and relentless, and he knew who they were.

"Filthy Terminators!" he yelled, not knowing that all the Terminators had been lost in the Pennsylvania massacre, that Chase had no army left, and had hired mercenaries from Sepio Security Agency to help to apprehend Blanc.

Blanc didn't just employ the Vinton private military company, he *owned* them. His normal forty-person detail consisted of the most highly trained and well-equipped force in the entire firm. He'd recently more than doubled their size. The eighty-six fierce men and women held their ground. However, the Vintons were supplemented by AI-enhanced weapons built in key locations across the property, including interior stations.

Blanc watched for what felt like an eternity as the battle raged on. Explosions rocked the mansion, gunfire and screams providing a frightening soundtrack. "How dare you challenge my authority, my power, my control over the world!"

But even as the Vintons fought on, it soon became clear that the attackers were gaining ground. They'd breached the outer defenses, and now were streaming into the mansion itself, pushing ever closer to Blanc's sanctum.

Then he caught a glimpse of something in the monitors that truly boiled his blood, and yet delighted him at the same time: two figures sneaking their way through his expansive wine cellar—though, they didn't quite match their file photos.

Obviously using some kind of AI visual enhancement, he thought. *But that is definitely Chase Malone and that Chinese viper Wen Sung.*

Blanc phoned Tane. Through gritted teeth, he told his Remie partner, "The maggots are here!" His clenched fists pounded a keyboard as he said it, momentarily darkening one section of the screen. "They are invading my home," he barked. "*My home!*"

"Do you have enough Vintons?"

"I am *not* going to be defeated. My enemies will never triumph. They have come to my castle, but they will not leave!"

With a fierce determination in his eyes, Blanc strode towards his armory, ready to join the fray and take down any attacker who dared cross his path. "I'm a hunter."

"These aren't elk and deer," Tane warned. "Chase and Wen have killed hundreds of the toughest fighters we've—"

"This is *my* home," he repeated.

"No one has survived a battle with these two. Let the Vintons—"

"The Vintons can have them, but if these parasites, the damned do-gooders, get past them, do not doubt that I will emerge victorious."

Chase accidentally knocked over a rack of priceless wine, the dusty bottles smashing on the Italian marbled floor.

"You probably just cost Blanc fifty thousand dollars," Wen said.

"I plan to cost him a lot more than that," Chase responded. "Quite a wine cellar." He glanced down a row, lit by their headlamps. "There must be three or four thousand bottles in here. How can anyone need this much?"

"Shame more of it's about to get spilled." Wen checked

her wrist, streaming images from some of the Sepios's chest cams. "It's brutal up there."

"If we don't cut the cable before his AI gets activated, it's going to get beyond brutal."

"Back here." Wen led him behind a thick, exposed brick and concrete wall. "Go-three."

Chase slipped on ear protection, counted to three, then detonated the explosives they'd just planted. After the cloud of dust and debris dissipated, they ran back through the wine cellar, now reeking of alcohol and covered with broken glass.

"We're in," Wen said. They picked through the rubble and made their way into the back of a mechanical space filled with wiring, conduit, cables and other electrical equipment. "There must be a thousand wires in here . . . which one?"

"As you know, I'm a top engineer, and an expert in this area," Chase said in an announcer's voice.

"So which one kills the AI?" she asked again.

"Stand back," Chase said, raising his submachine gun.

"You don't know!" She pushed his gun down, not wanting to get hit by ricochets.

"Cut them all," Chase said. "Blanc knows we're here and we're out of time."

Wen tossed an explosive device into the tight space. "We've got twenty seconds."

The pair ran back through the wine cellar, down a long hall, past a twenty-four-seat theatre, an indoor shooting range, and finally reached a wide staircase. They were halfway up to the next level when they heard the explosion and the house went dark.

Chapter Seventy-Seven

Emergency lights came on, but only enough to safely exit the building. Blanc charged through the mansion. His private security force and advanced AI weapons had been decimating the attackers. "Somehow Malone's goons have beaten back my Vintons," he told Tane in the phone as he moved through the mostly darkened mansion. "Now both sides have dwindled to not enough."

"Get to your safe room," Tane warned.

"As we learned in San Francisco, safe rooms are never safe. I'll get out." Although sounding defiant, Blanc had lost his gun in a skirmish on another flight of stairs with a Sepio. He'd managed to get past the man, but had come out empty handed when he fled. "I'm almost there."

Tane figured out where Blanc was heading. "Are Chase and Wen still alive?"

"Of course, but I don't know where they are. Just before I lost cameras, they were down in the lower levels." He panted as he climbed the final steps. "Who do these pieces of trash think they are?"

But as he reached the roof of his stronghold and a waiting helicopter, he came face to face with his greatest adversaries, Chase and Wen, who had already restrained the chopper pilot. The area, lit with the battery-powered emergency landing lights, provided an eerie backdrop to the scene.

For a moment, the three of them stood in silence, eyeing each other with contempt and fury.

"You've manipulated the world into an awful, fear-driven, corrupt place," Chase spat, his eyes blazing with anger. "Your greed and elitism have destroyed so many lives. Now you'll answer for your crimes." He held up a pair of cold steel handcuffs.

Blanc sneered and cussed at them, his face contorted with rage. "You're nothing but dirt," he growled. "It doesn't matter what you think. I'm too rich and money is power. I'll walk away from anything you throw at me."

Chase and Wen exchanged a knowing glance, then suddenly, without warning, Chase raised his gun and fired.

Blanc stumbled backwards, gripping his side as blood seeped through his fingers. He stared at Chase with a look of shock and disbelief, then collapsed to the ground, gasping, his phone falling from his hand.

"Don't worry, you'll live," Wen told him.

Chase snatched the phone and pushed it into a pocket before helping lift the billionaire into the helicopter. While Chase rode in the back with Blanc, Wen took the controls and the chopper lifted in the air. A few minutes later, well out over the ocean, Chase yelled in Blanc's ear, "How's that gunshot wound?"

"I demand that you take me to a hospital."

Chase laughed as Wen flew higher.

"You remember my friend, Dez?" Chase shouted right next to his ear. "Khan tossed him off a roof."

"No!" Blanc yelled, realizing what Chase was about to do. "Please, I can give you billions of dollars! A hundred billion—just fly me to the hospital!"

"Money may mean everything to you," Chase shouted, "but I'm not like you. I'm human."

Chase pushed Blanc to the open side of the helicopter.

"No! No, please, you can't do this! No!"

"Don't worry, the water's warm." Chase shoved him out, but Blanc manage to get ahold of the side of the opening, his hands gripping the metal, his legs dangling.

"Pull me in, pull me in!" Blanc screamed. "Two hundred billion!"

Chase moved over. "Should have given me your best offer first. I might have taken it."

"Please!"

"No one saved Dez, or Bull, or Zu Mu, or Shelby, or Blitz, or Weston, or any of the tens of thousands of others." Chase stomped on Blanc's boney fingers. Blanc screamed and fell.

Chase looked out and was amazed to see Blanc's arm curled around one of the skids. "This guy just won't die," Chase said to Wen through the headset.

She sent the chopper climbing higher, then banked until Blanc could hold on no longer. He slipped and plunged, screaming the entire way, more than a mile down toward the ocean.

When they landed thirty minutes later, Chase used Blanc's cell phone to call Tane. "Blanc?" Tane asked.

"No, it's me, Chase."

"What do you want?"

"The Surgeon is dead, Khan is dead, and Blanc is dead," Chase said. "Be afraid, be very afraid, because we're coming for you next."

Epilogue

Three months later...

Warren Snyder won the general election in November by a landslide and was now the President-Elect of the United States. Early announcements by his transition team had Kellerman serving as the White House Chief of Staff.

Unfortunately, Aarons, the mayor's deputy chief of staff, died of a brain aneurysm in the days following the election.

"He was a wonderful asset to my team, and will be greatly missed," the President-Elect said at his funeral.

As it turned out, the alleged masterminds of the dirty bomb strikes were not apprehended the day the NYPD stopped the attack. However, the pair were identified based on their fingerprints being on the bomb, and other numerous eyewitness accounts, including fourteen separate surveillance cameras. A worldwide manhunt was underway for the two fugitives: Chase Malone and Wen Sung.

Fortunately, the secret Tess had imparted to Chase via the covert text message during their previous call had been an ultra-secure safe house located in the *Chihuahuan* desert in northern Mexico, and specifically a mysterious region there known as the *Zona del Silencio*, or the Zone of Silence, where, for unknown reasons, radio signals were blocked, compasses spun out of control, and other electronics failed.

They'd been laying low there for most of the time since their charges were brought against them. Finally, things had cooled enough that they risked an important outing.

Mars and Tess waited in a small, gritty border town on the Mexican side. All four of them had fresh applications of vIDs on their faces, even though there wasn't a surveillance camera for fifty miles.

Sipping *cervezas*, gathered around a large plastic table in a makeshift outdoor diner behind a dusty former gas station, they discussed the situation in hushed tones, even though there were no other patrons and the server spoke no English.

"What do you want to do?" Mars asked.

"Kill them all," Chase said. "Grimes was right, the only way to stop this is to execute every last Remie. We start with Snyder, then take out Tane, and go on down the list until every last one is gone."

"You want to assassinate the President of the United States?" Mars asked.

"Yes," Chase said, "but I'd prefer to kill him prior to the inauguration."

Mars looked at Wen and then at Tess. "What do you two think?"

"What are we waiting for?" Wen said.

"And you?" Mars asked.

"We can't stop at the Remies," Tess said. "Everyone who enables them, anyone who has perpetrated their corruptive grip on the world must go too."

"Wow," Mars said. "That's a lot of people."

Chase looked at each of them carefully. "Then we'd better get started."

Chapter 15

Mara began to walk towards it. "No," Max began, "we must..."

"Where are we taking her?" Max said.

"Podsnap?" Mara asked.

"We can't stop at the Bunny's," Des said. "Everyone who watches them, anyone who has prepared their compulsive trip on the world must go too."

"Wait," Max said. "Here's a bit of paper."

Chase looked at each, in their zest lobby. "I say," with a heavy search.

Next in the Chase Malone Thriller series

vinci-books.com/chasing-lost

Sometimes, to find the way out, you have to lose yourself first.

Chase Malone is at his lowest—stripped of his wealth, separated from his partner Wen, and watching the world's final chance at survival fade.

Turn the page for a free preview…

Chasing Lost: Chapter One

Chase Malone stood in the Chihuahua Desert of northern Mexico. A burnt-out car, whose color could no longer be easily determined, sat a few feet away. His mouth dry, he eyed the wreck suspiciously, even though he'd seen it for weeks before leaving the forgotten and derelict outpost where he and his girlfriend Wen had been hiding.

Now that he'd returned without her, without much of anything, he wondered if danger was lurking inside its battered steel shell.

Chase glanced toward the old adobe house nearby. It didn't look to be in much better shape than the car. Taking a deep breath of the dry, dusty air, he gripped his pistol and headed toward the door. Not too long ago, living in a place like this would have been out of the question for the brilliant tech engineer.

That was before they'd taken everything from him—his billion-dollar fortune, his family, his friends, and now Wen.

"What if she's not here?" he muttered, pushing open the heavy wooden door.

He'd been asking the same question every moment of his journey after arriving back in Mexico, sneaking across the border in a remote region near the Texas coast. Really, he'd been asking it ever since he'd lost her in Miami. Chase had been haunted by the notion that she might not be waiting for him here.

"The moment of truth," he whispered, stepping across the worn concrete threshold.

But he already knew. She would have heard him coming a mile away. Wen, a former Chinese MSS operative, one of the best in the world, would not have allowed anyone to sneak up on her. Ever.

She hadn't made it back.

A new thought occurred to him.

Maybe . . . if she is here, she's injured.

That was possible—it might even be the best case.

Wen could be dead.

He let that thought crawl around his weary mind for a few seconds, wondering if he could endure such a reality, then shook it off. Wen wasn't the only one who could be here. Shadow agents, mercenaries, US government operatives, corporate guns, a roster of trouble looking for him could be waiting.

Pay attention.

Even prior to Chase and Wen being blamed for planting a city-killing dirty bomb in New York, more groups were hunting them than he could keep track of. After so many years on the run, every sound was suspicious, each shadow potentially deadly. Wen had taught him to automatically see the escapes first, the advantages and angles of the fight second, and to assess the enemy third. "Know your opponent in every situation," she often said.

He knew this place, knew every run-down inch of it.

The old structure may have been a thriving hacienda a hundred years earlier, or maybe not. It seemed filled with ghosts, but none were Wen's. It also appeared empty of any assassins.

He stumbled through the crumbling rooms, knowing someone could be coming because someone was *always* coming. Making his way to the far corner of the interior courtyard, he stopped at a pile of used and wasted building materials, where he quickly moved the stones aside, revealing a small hole in the wall. He crawled through the narrow passage, feeling the rough edges and jagged rocks scrape against his skin.

Finally, he found the hidden doorway in the tight space, expertly disguised to look like a stone wall. On the other side, an inches-wide, essentially invisible cavity created a hollow alley that now connected what once were separate walls. At the end was a hatch one could only find if they knew exactly which floorboards to lift. Chase pulled them up, revealing what seemed to be a pit. He descended several broken steps better described as a carved ladder of sorts, the only light coming from his small flashlight. Musty and damp, he felt cobwebs catch in his brown hair. At the bottom of the stairs waited a room barely big enough to stand in, dark and lonely.

She was not there.

A distant noise caught his ear. He froze. Listening. Hardly breathing.

It could be her. Or it could be a killer.

After a full minute, he decided it was likely a kit fox. They were always coming around. Might even have been a Mexican wolf. He and Wen had seen a few a couple weeks back. Still, he moved slowly, steps deliberate and soft until he reached a footlocker, which was the only thing in the room other than a folding chair and a tiny table. There were also some faded Spanish words on the wall, scrawled long ago by some unknown inhabitant of the old hacienda.

Ángel de la Guarda, mi dulce compañía, no me desampares, ni de noche ni de día, porque sin ti, yo me perdería.

Wen had translated them for him: *Guardian angel, my sweet friend, do not abandon me by night nor by day, because without you, I would lose myself.*

Chase had taken to reciting it occasionally. *Every bit of help is welcome . . .*

After dialing in the combination and pulling off the padlock, Chase breathed a sigh of relief as he saw the contents were just as he'd left them: Eighteen passports from various countries and identification papers—half his, half Wen's; several burner phones, useless here, but he'd need them later; a small amount of cash—Mexican pesos and US dollars; a couple of submachine guns and extra ammunition. Then he checked the most important items, two sophisticated custom laptops, chargers, some communications equipment, and external drives.

He took a deep breath and allowed himself a moment to savor the knowledge that he was still in control of his fate.

Then he noticed something he *hadn't* left there—a slim leather-bound journal, smaller than a pack of cigarettes. It belonged to Wen. He opened the book and saw it was filled with notes, contacts, and locations, but they were written in a code that only Wen could decipher.

"If she is alive, this may be the only way I can track her down," he whispered, tucking the journal under his arm, and shoving the other items in a pack. "*If* she is alive," he repeated.

Chasing Lost: Chapter Two

Back outside, shielded by the decaying walls of the hacienda, Chase walked around the courtyard, his footsteps noisy on the hard-packed dirt. He checked the sky, but saw nothing. He knew if they were up there, he'd never be able to see them, but the instinct to look was a hard habit to kick.

"If anyone is watching me, I'd already be dead," he whispered.

Something stirred. He pulled the pistol from his belt and aimed into the darkness. A sleek gray cat bolted from behind an old pile of wood.

"El gato!" he snapped, putting the gun away. The cat had come with the place. On their first day, Wen had caught it and carefully inspected it to make sure it was real and not equipped with cameras or other monitoring devices. Chase watched as Gato slipped into the shadows. "Catch a mouse or something."

The cat ignored him and disappeared.

His thoughts were jumbled and chaotic, like the rocks and brush that surrounded the hacienda. He couldn't believe how quickly his life had fallen apart. One moment he was a billionaire, the next he was penniless. Although the shift had started years earlier, after he and Wen had decided to challenge the corrupt and greedy forces using technologies for nefarious purposes, things had worsened dramatically in recent months. His business partner and long-time friend had been murdered, the entire army he'd recruited and built to take on the wealthiest and most corrupt group known as Remies, had been destroyed. Then, after being falsely accused of a crime they did not commit, he and Wen were left running for their freedom, for their lives.

"And now Wen is gone," he said to the warm breeze. The sun, beginning to set, cast an orange glow across the bleak, endless landscape. But they hadn't come there for the scenery. The area, known as the Zona del Silencio, was an unusual and mysterious place with an electromagnetic anomaly that had fascinated scientists and paranormal enthusiasts for years. Chase had always been a skeptic, but he couldn't deny the strange energy the place had.

The Zone, which was fifty kilometers across, sat inside the Mapim Biosphere Reserve, a vast expanse with few inhabitants. The Reserve occupied a small area of the 200,000-square-mile Chihuahuan Desert, the largest in North America. It stretched across six Mexican states and parts of Texas and New Mexico, making it bigger than the entire state of California. Located between two huge and often forsaken mountain ranges, the eastern and western Sierra Madre, most of the region consisted of harsh terrain interspersed with jagged mountain outcrops.

Tess Federgreen, the former head of CISS, the most secret and powerful branch of the US intelligence community, had clued him into the zone as somewhere he could hide. It's where she'd first gone when the powers-that-be decided she'd become a liability.

"It's a fantastic place," she'd said. "Radio Signals fail, compasses spin out of control. The stones have strange properties."

"Why?"

"No one knows," she'd said. "But an unusual number of meteorites have crashed there. They still do. It's kind of the Mexican version of the Bermuda Triangle."

"Come on, you don't believe this stuff."

"I've been there. They can't find you in that place."

"Yeah, but . . . "

"There are some logical explanations. One theory claims the disruptions are, at least in part, due to subterranean deposits of magnetite. Of course, with the many documented meteorite strikes and the associated space debris . . . "

Chase stopped thinking about Tess, although he wished he knew where she was right now. He could sure use her help. If anyone could locate Wen, it would be Tess. He scanned the courtyard again. Maybe she would show up here. Maybe she'd arrive with Wen riding in a truck loaded with weapons and cash.

How long can I wait? How long until someone finds me?

On their way to the Zona del Silencio, Chase and Wen had researched the area beyond what Tess had shared. They discovered that the region's wider reputation grew to exceed casual curiosity after an Athena rocket launched from a US air force base in Utah crashed in the middle of the Zone. Allegedly, the rocket had been part of a scientific mission to study upper atmosphere conditions, and was designed to come down at White Sands, New Mexico. Some unknown occurrence instead sent the Athena dramatically off course. No one knew why. In the early morning hours, the rocket came down in the darkness of the desert, and the legend of the Zone instantly intensified. Suddenly, the area received international media attention.

Chase gazed out at the wasteland, wondering what really caused the blackout. He couldn't get a cell signal, no internet, or even satellite connectivity inside the Zona del Silencio, exactly as Tess had told them. In the digital age, it made for the perfect hideout.

He thought about the strangeness of the Athena crash, how it got even more bizarre when Wernher Von Braun, the renowned Nazi rocket scientist, so instrumental in helping the US build their space program, was sent to the Zone by the US government to investigate. Von Braun personally flew in reconnaissance flights to verify the crash site. They brought in three hundred local Mexican workers to construct a sixteen-kilometer rail spur from the impact crater. For four weeks, Von Braun supervised an American team as they excavated the site around the clock. The military built a runway in the desert and sent in temporary dormitories, medical facilities, kitchens, showers, bathrooms, and, most important, labs staffed by groups of scientists. The runways moved materials directly to Houston while the rail line facilitated in hauling away tons of debris.

Chase left the courtyard and walked into the darkening desert. "What were they doing there? What was on that rocket, what was in the soil, what magic happens here?"

Chasing Lost: Chapter Three

Chase glanced around, scanning the horizon for any signs of danger. He knew he couldn't let his guard down, not even for a moment. He thought about Wen and tried to recall every detail of those final minutes before she had vanished in Miami. Having no idea where she was or if she was even still alive, concentration was difficult.

Chase thought back to how it began. They were in Miami's Little Havana to meet with a man who they believed could prove their innocence against the charges that he and Wen had planted the dirty bomb in New York City months earlier. Clearing their names might not end their problems or even allow them to stop hiding and running, but getting off the top ten most wanted lists around the world would make things much easier for them. "It's worth risking the trip," Chase had pushed a reluctant Wen.

He recalled the scent of fried plantains and a cacophony of Latin music on that hot, sticky evening as they checked the area along Calle Ocho fifteen minutes before the meeting. But it was the roosters that haunted him. Along the historic district there were five-foot tall rooster sculptures painted in wild colors and patterns. He'd noticed them, but hadn't given them much thought until the attack.

Two gun-wielding men dressed as tourists emerged from behind one of the roosters. He spotted them a second before Wen did, which was unusual, but she got her MP7 submachine gun out of the duffle before him as they both dove for cover behind a passing car. Wen began shooting even before the men could. Chase pointed to Domino Park, which seemed their best bet for concealment, but it turned out to be more like a courtyard filled with locals playing dominos. The older men, smoking cigars, turned furious as Chase and Wen barged through their refuge and destroyed one game by using the table as a springboard.

The angry men could still be heard protesting and yelling profanities in Spanish as Chase and Wen exited *El Parque del Dominó* via a couple of palm trees and dropped onto 15th Avenue. Its patterned surface, created with colorful pavers interrupted by a path of giant dominoes, left them too exposed, so they darted back across Calle Ocho. However, now at least a dozen shadow operatives clad in black tactical gear had joined the initial assault. The men streamed toward them from both ends of the street. Wen pulled out another MP7 and tossed it to Chase.

Bullets ripped through the Azucar Ice Cream Company neon sign above their heads, tearing up the giant five-scoop multi-colored ice cream cone. More shots splintered the carved wooden Indian standing sentry in front of the Little Havana Cigar Factory as they ran by, shattered glass filling the sidewalk.

The after-work crowds, tourists, and Friday night partiers scattered around them with panicked screams. Chase and Wen continued returning fire as they raced past bars and more cigar shops. The scents from Cuban bakeries, still pumping out warm treats, surrounded them as they zigzagged through the crowded sidewalks, breaths coming in short gasps.

"Too many of them!" Wen shouted, ducking through an alley.

They emerged on another street bathed in neon lights. The streetlamps were beginning to come on, illuminating the vibrant colors of the buildings, creating a dazzling backdrop for the battle. Chase and Wen leaped over crates of vegetables, ducked under awnings, and dodged around more pedestrians. "We should be dead by now," Chase choked out breathlessly while they rounded a corner.

The operatives were relentless, their footsteps a steady thud behind them. Chase and Wen veered off into another alleyway, hoping to lose their pursuers. The walls were covered in colorful murals depicting Cuban life, but their focus never left the looming figures of their attackers as they entered the narrow passage.

"This will test the theory," Chase said.

"What theory?"

"I think they want us alive."

"Let's *not* test that."

Chase grabbed Wen's hand and pulled her up onto a nearby dumpster. They scrambled up the fire escape of the building next to them, their breaths ragged as they climbed higher and higher.

The operatives fired up at them, bullets pinging off the painted steel rails and steps. "They *seem* intent on killing us," Wen argued, their black forms visible in the shadows below.

"Are they really that bad at shooting, though?" Chase asked as they reached the rooftop and paused for a moment, scanning the skyline for their next move. A maze of buildings and openings stretched out before them, the neon lights casting a kaleidoscope of colors across the scene.

"You know how hard it is to shoot while running."

"Yeah, it's not like the movies, but—"

Suddenly, a gunshot rang out, and a bullet whizzed past Chase's ear, narrowly missing him. They ducked behind a large air conditioning unit as the attackers began firing at them from a building just below.

Chase wheeled his gun around. It barked loudly as he shot back at the shadowy figures. Wen fired off several rounds, causing the operatives to leap for cover. Taking advantage of the momentary distraction, Chase and Wen took off running, jumping across rooftops and scrambling over ledges. Soon they dropped down onto a busy street and darted through traffic, leaping over the hoods of cars, barely avoiding collisions with each passing vehicle.

They just couldn't shake the relentless pursuit, the operatives never far behind. Chase and Wen broke into a deserted building, their chests heaving with exhaustion. They took a moment to catch their breath, their sweat-soaked clothes sticking to their skin.

"Looks like an old restaurant," Chase said. "A big one."

"Let's find the backdoor."

They made it to the far end of the room before the operatives burst in, guns at the ready. Chase and Wen flipped over tables and dropped behind overturned chairs. The gunfire was deafening in the confined space, bullets ricocheting off walls, tearing into the furnishings. Chase and Wen exchanged a desperate look, knowing that they were outnumbered and outgunned.

Grab your copy…
vinci-books.com/chasing-lost

About the Author

USA TODAY Bestselling Author Brandt Legg uses his unusual real life experiences to create page-turning novels. He's traveled with CIA agents, dined with senators and congressmen, mingled with astronauts, chatted with governors and presidential candidates, had a private conversation with a Secretary of Defense he still doesn't like to talk about, hung out with Oscar and Grammy winners, had drinks at the State Department, been pursued by tabloid reporters, and spent a birthday at the White House by invitation from the President of the United States.

At age eight, Legg's father died suddenly, plunging his family into poverty. Two years later, while suffering from crippling migraines, he started in business, and turned a hobby into a multi-million-dollar empire. National media dubbed him the "Teen Tycoon," and by the mid-eighties, Legg was one of the top young entrepreneurs in America, appearing as high as number twenty-four on the list (when Steve Jobs was #1, Bill Gates #4, and Michael Dell #6). Legg still jokes that he should have gone into computers.

By his twenties, after years of buying and selling businesses, leveraging, and risk-taking, the high-flying Legg became ensnarled in the financial whirlwind of the junk bond eighties. The stock market crashed and a firestorm of trouble came down. The Teen Tycoon racked up more than a million dollars in legal fees, was betrayed by those closest to him, lost his entire fortune, and ended up serving time for financial improprieties.

After a year, Legg emerged from federal prison, chastened and wiser, and began anew. More than twenty-five years later, he's now using all that hard-earned firsthand knowledge of conspiracies, corruption and high finance to weave his tales. Legg's books pulse with authenticity.

His series have excited nearly a million readers around the world. Although he refused an offer to make a television movie about his life as a teenage millionaire, his autobiography is in the works. There has also been interest from Hollywood to turn his thrillers into films. With any luck, one day you'll see your favorite characters on screen.

He lives in the Pacific Northwest, with his wife and son, writing full time, in several genres, containing the common themes of adventure, conspiracy, and thrillers. Of all his pursuits, being an author and crafting plots for novels is his favorite.

Acknowledgments

Chasing Fear had long been planned to be a set up for *Chasing Lost*, which I expect may be the final book in this series. For that reason, this one tended to be a bit darker, populated with a few more corrupt and rough characters. I do believe those who have been reading Chase and Wen's adventures since *Chasing Rain* will especially enjoy it. This was written entirely in Mexico, however during the main story no scenes take place in that country. I have a feeling at least some of the characters might find their way south in *Chasing Lost*. Stay tuned.

So many people do so many things to help out during the course of a book, the list below highlights a special group who bear the brunt of the action.

Ro, for being so good with a machete, I'm so grateful for all the coconut water, and for taking care of me in the exhausting churn and the blissful moments, for sharing the adventure, for inspiring me again and again.

My mom, Barbara Blair, for being the most enthusiastic and positive cheerleader I've ever had, and for always wanting to read more.

Joan Osborne for making me feel far smarter than I probably am, which is a direct reflection of her intellect.

Gil Forbes for providing strong and forceful corrections of concepts in the most generous way.

Jack Llartin, a wonderful copy editor, who has for years

made me look better, a man with a talent for tightening an entire story with well placed keystrokes.

To my mysterious new cover designer for this dramatic cover, which led to an audacious opening.

And, finally, to Teakki, for sharing clever ideas, posing smart questions, and for knowing these stories better than anyone, and especially for patiently waiting to beat me at chess until I finished writing each day.

Most of all, to all of my readers, the ones that have read everything I've published, and the ones who have just finished their first Booker thriller or Chasing adventure. You make it possible for me to live this dream, to create these worlds, to live with these characters and tell these stories. Thank you for the time you've shared with me via my books. Please drop me an email any time. Responding to reader emails is one of my favorite parts of the day!

I'd like to give extra thanks to some special readers and/or members of my street team for their support, kindness, reviews (I love reviews), suggestions, and encouragement.

(If I left anyone out, I apologize. Please forgive me, and let me know. I can fix it!)

Please don't let the fact that there are so many of you do anything to diminish your importance to me. This ever-expanding group is the fuel to my creative fire.

In alphabetical order (by first name):

Adam Tanner, Alec Redwine, Amber Hunt, Anne Kaplan, Bette Lou Thompson, Bill Borchert, Billie Harkey, Blake Dowling, Bob Browder, Bob Dumas, Brian C. Coffey, Brian Schnizlein, Cara Johnson, Carl Howard, Carol M, Cathie Harrison, Cheryl Olson, Chet Keough, Chis Bond, Chris Tomlinson, Christine Moritz, Christopher Bowling, Chuck Gonzalez, Cid Chase, Claudia Wells, Consuelo

Ashworth, Debra Harper, Dennis Lowe, Derek Redmond, Diane Smith, Diane Whitehead, Donna Slaton, Doug Wise, Douglas Dersch, Douglas Meek, Elaine Dill, Ernest Manpino, Ernest Pino, Frank Fusco, Frank Murphy, Fred Bowditch, Gary Human, Gene Leach, Gene Legg, Gerry Adler, Gil Forbes, Gillian Charlton, Glenda Dykstra, Glenn Legge, Ingo Michehl, Irene Witoski, Jacky Dallaire, Jan Dallas, Janice Gildea, Jean Sink, Joan Osborne, Jody Huneycutt, John McDonald, John Nicholson, John Nunley, John Oliver, John Wood, Judith Anderson, Judy Hammer, Julie Price, Justin Lear, Karen Mack, Karen Markovitz, Kat Heyer, Katherine Atwood, Kathleen Robbins, Kathy Creecy, Kathy Troc, Ken Clute, Ken Friedman, Kevin Burton, Kyle Dahlem, LA Dumas, Leslie Royce, Linda Loparco, Linda Petty, Liz Miller, Marcel Roy, Marie Maritz, Mark Perlmutter, Martha Heckel, Martin Gunnell, Melanie C. Hansen, Michael Ferrel, Michael Picco, Mick Flanigan, Mike Brannick, Mike Lauland, Mitzi McAllister, Nancy Lamanna, Nigel Revill, Normand Girard, Pam Gilbert, Patricia Ruby, Paul Gyorke, Peggy Gulli, Randy Howerter, Raymond Aston, Rick Ferris, Rick Woodring, Rob Weaver, Rob Zorger, Robert Smith, Robyn Shanti, Ron Babcock, S. Michael Smith, S.W. Kelly Myers, Sally Vedder, Sam Rhoades, Samantha Jackson, Sandie Parrish, Sandra Zuiderhoek, Satish Bhatti, Sharon Moffatt, Stephane Peltier, Sue Steel, Susan McGuyer, Susan Moore, Susan Norlund, Susan Powell, Terry Myers, Tom Strauss, Tony Sommer, Tricia Turner, Vicki Gordon, Virginia Beck, Vivienne Du Bourdieu.

Many authors I've met along the way have impacted my craft and career as well. This is far from a complete list, but each one included has made a difference to me:

Robert Gatewood, Mike Sager, Craig Martelle, Michael

Anderle, Mark Dawson, Nick Thacker, Ernest Dempsey, John Grisham, A. Kelly Pruitt, Eric J. Gates, Dale DeVino, Phil M. Williams, Jennifer Theriot, Haris Orkin, Brian Meeks, Jennifer Theriot, Michelle McCarty, Zoe Saadia, and to the memory of Mollie Gregory, Judith Lucci, and Matthew Mather.

There are so many friends of mine who are creatives as well. Many of them are from Taos, where parts of this story are set. Their work inspires my work (and my life):

Tony Schueller, David Manzanares, Geraint Smith, Michael Hearne, Don Richmond, Lenny Foster, Jared Rowe, Jimmy Stadler, Scott Thomas, Carol Morgan-Eagle, Deonne Kahler, Bart Anderson, Jill Fuller, Ernest James, Jenny Bird, Angelika Maria Koch, Brad Hockmeyer, Verne Verona, Brooke Tatum, Markus Kolber, Terrie Bennett, and many others!

Speaking of reviewers, the prolific readers and top Amazon reviewers who have been of great support to my work deserve extra recognition. Thank you so much, and special gratitude, to the remarkable Grady Harp, and to whoever the reviewer "Serenity" is!

There is a goal among some authors to turn readers into fans, fans into super fans, and super fans into friends. I am fortunate to have been able to achieve that goal on numerous occasions.

Thank you.